TUMBLING OVER THE

Tight End

A BEAUMONT LEGACY NOVEL

VAI DENTON

Tumbling Over the Tight End

Copyright © 2025 by Vai Denton

Editing: Rachel Bunner (@rachels.top.edits)

Proofreading: Chelsey Brand (@theimperfictionist) and Laura Hartley

Cover design: Cindy Ras (@cindyras_draws)

ISBN: 979-8-9904429-4-8 (paperback)

ASIN: B0DKB6KZTL (ebook)

First Edition: April 2025

10 9 8 7 6 5 4 3 2 1

Author's Note

*T*umbling Over the Tight End is the third book in the *Beaumont Legacy* series. It is recommended that you read this book after enjoying *Gridlocked on the Gridiron* and *Love on the Line*, the first and second books in the series. Otherwise, there may be some spoilers. That said, this book can be read as a standalone and will have no cliffhangers.

Your mental health is incredibly important to me, so please take the following content warnings into consideration before continuing: death of a parent (off page, prior to the start of the book), verbally abusive parent (prior to start of book), estrangement from a family member, alcohol use and brief instance of driving while under the influence (not an MC), explicit sexual content, on-page mention of pregnancy complications leading to death, on-page real world medical encounters between the FMC and her patients (contact me if further detail is required).

To those who have spent their whole lives working toward a future they didn't really want—I hope you've found something you love.

And to me—my reminder that taking a break is better than burning out.

Chapter One

Keala

Much like the White Rabbit, Keala was very late for a very important date. Only, the date was evening practice with the San Jose Sentinels cheerleaders, and unlike the White Rabbit, Keala cared too much about what other people thought of her *not* to say hello and goodbye. She stopped and said plenty of them as she swiped her team badge, rushed through security, and ran past custodians.

She hadn't *wanted* to be late to rehearsal. She'd been on track to finish her shift at Westfield Methodist Hospital with enough time to get made up and ready for practice...until that last patient had vomited all over her.

And that hadn't even been the first time that *shift* that she'd been the victim of a vomiting accident.

But now she was approaching twelve minutes late, rushing through the tunnel of the training facility to the field the professional cheer team used for rehearsals, poms in hand. She'd fixed her makeup in the evening traffic, so that was one less thing Angelica, their coach, could be upset with her about. Still, if the look on Angelica's face—like she'd been sucking on a sour candy—told Keala anything, it was that her makeup couldn't *make up* for being tardy.

Again.

Angelica already wasn't her biggest fan. Her need to exert control over the girls with her no-fraternization rule couldn't be enforced with Keala because her cousin played on the football team, and that seemed to irk her. But being late for two practices in a row the week of their first home game of the preseason certainly wasn't doing Keala any favors—a thought that paralyzed her when she sat with it for too long.

"Sorry, sorry, I'm so sorry," Keala panted as she ran past Angelica to where the girls were still stretching and getting out their resistance bands. Her angry eyes bored into Keala as she set her poms on the fake grass, dropping to the ground to stretch out her legs. After a long day in the emergency department, Keala's muscles needed it.

Bright green turf was made brighter by the lights built into the hangar-like ceiling above the training field. More often than not, the Sirens—the Sentinels' cheerleading team—used the same practice fields as the Sentinels players, though they were always gone by the time the Sirens' practices started. It was a standard football field, a goalpost at each end zone, and surrounded by four concrete walls.

"Is she still looking?" Keala asked Zoe, her line captain and friend. Keala had only moved to San Jose this summer at her parents' behest, and while she was excited to do her final year of cheering with the team she'd grown up supporting, it had been scary to start fresh somewhere new. The very first day of tryouts, Zoe had seen how nervous Keala had been despite her extensive dance training and four years with the Virginia Vipers. With Zoe's encouraging words, a fast and strong friendship had bloomed.

Zoe shook her head. Sweat beaded along her light brown skin, the red sports bra they wore for Wednesday practice darkened from her typical pre-practice warm-up. A permanent smile was etched on her friend's face. "No, but you're lucky Cora likes you and talks Angelica down," she answered, referring to the team choreographer who'd become a mentor to Keala over the last couple of months.

"I know. I need to change my shifts so I don't have to work on practice days." They'd been practicing Friday, Saturday, and Sunday, but with the season beginning, practices had shifted to Tuesday through Thursday.

Len, one of Keala's teammates, cocked her head to the side, her long brown hair curtaining her pale face. "Did something happen at the hospital today?"

"Nothing out of the ordinary. Just had a last-minute throw up situation I had to deal with."

"Isn't that outside of your job description? Cleaning up throw up?"

Keala huffed a laugh. "Not when the throw up is on me."

"Oh, sweetie, nooooo." Zoe leaned over and draped an arm around Keala's shoulders.

"You don't have to deal with that as a school counselor?" Keala wondered.

Zoe pulled her resistance band over her knees. "Nah, not really. They typically don't sit close enough for it to end that way." Her friend squinted, looking Keala up and down. "You're pale, Kay. Did you eat anything today?"

Keala thought about the protein smoothie she'd had for breakfast and the carrots she'd snacked on throughout the day. It had been an odd combination with her trusty Pedialyte and coffee, but she'd been running around so much that food hadn't crossed her mind.

As if reading her thoughts, Zoe pointed to her bag. "Energy gel and water. Now. You need pep in your step or Angelica's going to have your head."

Keala knew better than to ignore her captain, so she did as instructed, swallowing the grape-flavored gel and taking a swig from her water bottle. Len stretched quietly beside her before they both began the workout Angelica called to the group of women. Four groups cycled through exercises alongside the four line captains, and when Angelica was satisfied that they were warm and ready to go, she nodded for Cora to get the music started for the first number.

As a group, the thirty-six women lined up in the tunnel like they would before the game on Saturday and danced toward midfield. Keala gave it her all, though she felt exhaustion creeping through her, sinking into her bones. With poms waving, music flowing through her veins, and a smile on her face, Keala executed every move she'd been practicing since tryouts. Every free minute of her day, or just when she was alone at the hospital, she rehearsed, making sure she was perfect.

Chaine to Calypso jump, roll to stand, pop arms to a low V, turn to walk to the back.

"Bigger smile, Eleanor," Angelica called to poor Len.

Pivot back to the front, pop left leg in front, left arm to broken T close to chest, right arm up and rounded above head.

"More energy Kay-ah-luh!" Angelica yelled a few seconds later, her annoyance bleeding into the three syllables. Despite her disagreeable manner, there was something to be said for her effort to properly pronounce a name that confounded many.

Keala tried to be more energetic. She didn't know if Angelica had called her out because of her strange hatred for her, as usual, or if she simply looked as drained as she felt. She'd gotten back from practice yesterday after midnight because she had stayed for a choreography session, then she'd been up at six for her shift.

She had been on her feet for twelve hours straight three days in a row, and her energy reserves were dangerously low. Her ankles were swollen, her calves itchy from wearing compression socks. She desperately wanted a hot shower before crawling into bed and attempting to turn off her brain.

But dance was the part of her life she loved more than anything. Angelica's snide comments about her waist, her energy, her smile...all of that was worth it to be here, dancing with the women she'd gotten close to over the last couple of months for the team she'd grown up wishing she could cheer for. So she threw herself into the movements, smiling wide and forcing herself to expunge the last of her energy, poms and hair flying as she moved.

Right pom push across front of chest to left, left pom push across front of chest to right.

By the time Angelica felt they were perfect, it had been nearly two hours and it was past ten.

As they packed up their equipment, Cora yelled, "Captains and Keala, choreo again tomorrow after practice." She pushed a strand of straight blonde hair behind her ear, and when all five had acknowledged the sentiment, she smiled the megawatt smile she'd worn since her own cheer days and waved good-bye. Brooklyn, the assistant choreographer, who'd been on her phone most of practice, trailed after her.

"KayKay!" Nova, one of the third-years in another group, jogged over. "Do you remember the week you handled socials?"

Keala dreaded where this was going. "Yes!"

"So far, you've done the best for our engagement, so a few of us were wondering if you'd handle socials for the next couple of weeks."

Keala hated herself as she agreed. "I can do that."

Handling it for the next couple of weeks meant she would spend hours every week for the rest of the season—because it was never *just* two weeks—figuring out trends, videos, and other content to make ahead of practices and games, showing up early to film them, and engaging with comments on the platforms.

When Nova walked away, Zoe grimaced. "Yikes."

Keala shrugged, grabbing her things and heading out of the tunnel with Zoe and Len. "It's no biggie. I only work three or four shifts a week, so I'll have time."

Mentally, Keala watched the last bit of her free time on off days slip through her fingers like a balloon disappearing into the ether.

Chapter Two

Keala

Her cousin's spacious apartment had every light imaginable on when Keala walked in later that evening, placing her keys on one of the wooden hooks she'd hung on the wall in his foyer. Ikaika, a Sentinels fullback, lived only a couple of minutes away from the Sentinels facilities, which Keala was grateful for after long days of work and practice.

"Hi!" she called. The apartment was one of two on the top floor, and from the foyer, she couldn't see into the kitchen. To her right was a long wall with three large arches cut out of it leading to the living room. The TV was on and his gaming console was out of the TV stand, which told her he was home. Past the living room, the curtains on the three sets of massive doors leading to the balcony were shut.

Ikaika appeared a few feet in front of her in the doorway of the kitchen, a large sandwich in hand and his shoulder-length, curly black hair held out of his face with a thick headband. His golden skin was deeper than her own due to his being full Hawaiian to her half, though she was sure she would have caught up to him if she'd spent as much time in the sun as he did.

Chowder, his orange tabby, rubbed against his legs, glaring Keala's way like she'd disturbed *her* dinnertime too.

"Hi," Ikaika said over a bite of the sandwich, waving for her to follow him into the kitchen. They'd barely said hello to each other in the last couple of months that she'd been living in his apartment, let alone had conversations of substance, as much as they both would've liked to.

When Keala wasn't at work or cheer practice, she was at Zoe's practicing some more, and since they hadn't been in season until last week, Ikaika had been out a lot when she'd gotten back from work or practice. Now, with camp ending and preseason in full swing, he'd been home the last couple of evenings.

Keala dropped her bags in the hallway to her left beside the staircase that led down to Ikaika's suite, too tired to walk farther down the hall to her room. Joining her cousin in the kitchen, she marveled at the tall wooden cabinets and beautiful dark granite countertops on the island and the rest of the counterspace, like she always did.

One day, when she'd paid off all her student loans, she was going to find a little place with a kitchen just like this one. Not because she was a particularly good chef, but because it was stunning.

Ikaika pulled her in for a side hug, an arm around her shoulders as he led her to the dining table in the room beside the kitchen. "I brought back a turkey sandwich for you from the facility. There were a ton of extras, and I know you had a long day. Plus, I wanted you to have a reason to talk to me for the first time in what feels like months."

She leaned into him. "You don't have to give me food to convince me to hang out with you. I moved here to be closer to you. But you're the best. Thank you."

He truly was. Ikaika hadn't been using the second bed or bathroom, but still, allowing her into his space was a testament to how sweet he was.

She and Ikaika had grown up together from the time they were eight and nine—though his teasing that she was his baby cousin sometimes made her feel younger. When her family had moved from San Jose to Dallas, his parents had sent him to live with them because of his love for football. They'd felt he would have a better chance at getting somewhere if he was being coached by the football-crazed people in Texas.

Despite her having a younger and older brother, Keala and Ikaika had become closer than siblings, and she considered him a best friend more than a cousin. She was so happy to be living with him again, especially after they'd gone their separate ways for college.

College without him had been a shock, and they'd both been so busy that their relationship had faded a bit into the background. They'd texted a couple of times a month, called once every couple of months—mainly when something important happened in their lives and they'd needed support or advice. It hadn't improved much after college, when they'd both gotten busy with their careers. But now that they were living together, it was like no time had passed; their relationship was as strong as before.

"I think you're ignoring the small but very relevant piece of information that your parents also moved here and convinced you to come back to be closer to them. But we can go with what you said."

True enough. Keala had left her job and her final year with the Vipers because her parents had retired in San Jose and wanted her there. It had always been her dream to be a Siren, but with her schooling in Virginia and the fact that San Jose was the hardest team to make it onto, she hadn't thought it had been in the cards. When she'd tried out for the team in May and made it, she'd decided it was too good an opportunity to pass up and agreed to make the move. It had been a huge adjustment, and there were days lined with regret, but she appreciated not having to pay rent and being closer to everyone in her family.

She smiled at Ikaika and sat, unwrapping the sandwich. He was half done with his, Chowder in his lap, gazing lovingly up at him.

"How was practice?" he asked, feeding the cat a small piece of turkey.

Keala made a face. "The usual. Angelica was her typical bright self. And I was late again."

"You have to switch your shifts, Keeks." She'd told him in passing this morning about being late yesterday and needing to alter her work schedule.

"I know, but I didn't think it would be an issue, even when I heard our practice days were shifting. Now that I clearly can't do both I'll talk to my boss, but it'll probably still take a couple of weeks before it changes."

Ikaika hummed. "At least the season opener isn't until mid-September. So you've got almost a month."

Keala rolled her eyes. "You know that doesn't matter. Apparently, Angelica plans to treat the final two preseason games like they're regular season." The Sirens only danced at the ten home games each year, and according to her friends, Angelica took all of them *very* seriously, preseason or not.

"She needs to pull the stick out of her ass."

Keala chewed thoughtfully. It was the most she'd eaten all day, and her stomach begged her to inhale it as quickly as her six-one, 250-pound cousin was.

"Agreed. But I only have to deal with it for one season." It was standard for cheerleaders in the league to complete five years. While she'd hoped that they might allow her to stay on longer with the Sirens since it was a new team to her, Angelica had made it clear she would only be able to join the team for her final year.

"They might have a choreo spot open for you sometime next year, and then you can stop pretending you like healthcare." Keala tensed and looked around, then remembered they were alone. He laughed. "Relax, your parents aren't here. Though I suspect they'll be expecting you to go over there tomorrow."

Since her move, she'd been at her parents' house a minimum of once a week, often helping her mom with silly things like house décor, most especially when she didn't have the time to be there. "Yeah. Planning to eat breakfast with them. But if I did stay on as, like, an assistant choreographer, I'd still have to work at the hospital. There's no way I'd make enough to stop."

Ikaika balled up the paper that had held his sandwich, petting Chowder. "You could take a full-time coaching job at SJSU or something. You should look around."

"Right. Like Mom and Dad would be okay with that. Especially with Akoni breathing down my neck constantly." Her brother was five years younger and yet had always found a way to best her academically. If Keala had brought home a 98, he'd bring home a 100 in that same class years later, and once they'd gotten older, he'd only been four years below her because he'd skipped a grade. He had graduated from college at twenty-one, and now, at twenty-two, he'd started his second gap year working at a hospital while he applied to medical school.

"Yeah, but Akoni's a genius."

"Gee, thanks."

"I just mean stop comparing yourself to him. He's built different."

It was probably true, but Keala lived in the middle of the road between her two brothers. And the last thing she wanted to do was slide any closer to her older brother, her parents' greatest disappointment.

"I'll think about it."

Keala knew she wouldn't. Ikaika probably did too.

Chapter Three

Landon

Landon tossed the used condom into the little trash can tucked into the back of his bathroom closet. Even after a year of hooking up with Raegan, he didn't trust her enough to stop ensuring it was properly discarded. It's what he did with everyone to make sure there were no little Beaumonts running around.

At least none of his.

He frowned when he returned to his bedroom and she was still under his sheets, auburn hair spilling across his pillow and the belt that had restrained her wrists wrapped around her fist.

Despite the shadows, he thought her eyes lit up as he came to stand at the foot of the bed.

Landon didn't know what to say. Sure, he liked Raegan for many reasons, not the least of which was that he felt comfortable exploring the things he couldn't with a one-night stand. Being with her was easy. When he called, she came running, ready and willing to do anything and everything.

He also liked her because she usually knew when it was time to get going. Landon wasn't exactly a cuddly, let's-fall-asleep-together person. He liked his space, especially before an early practice.

Plus, allowing anything more introduced the possibility of one-sided feelings from the women he slept with, and he couldn't think of anything worse.

"I was thinking..."

Damn. Everything he had liked about her went out the window. *I was thinking* was always a recipe for disaster. Now he was going to have to find someone new, and that would be a hassle, especially with preseason in full swing.

Landon shook his head, and she pulled the covers over her shoulders another inch, like a shield against his answer.

"I could stay. I'm here so often anyway."

"I don't think that's a good idea."

Her lips twisted into a frown, as if she'd expected that things would suddenly change between them. As if he hadn't made things abundantly clear.

"Should I plan to come over after the game on Saturday?"

It was their first home game, so theoretically, she could, but he wasn't sure seeing Raegan again was a good idea. "Not sure. I'll let you know."

"Next week?"

"Look, Raegan. You're great and we have a great time, but I think you're getting this a bit twisted." Landon bent down and grabbed her clothes off the ground, setting them onto the bed beside her. "If I'm interested in fucking again, I'll call." The words felt harsh as they left him, but he needed her to get the message.

Ignoring the clothes, she slid up, her back against his headboard and her tits exposed. "I wouldn't care if you hooked up with other girls. I don't mind that. But I'm obviously the one you want to be with the most. What's so wrong with being here more? And staying the night sometimes?"

What was *so wrong with it* was that it would inevitably lead to something akin to a relationship, and despite all she said about not caring that he hooked up with others, Landon knew there was no way it would end well.

He pointed around the room to where most of his things sat in boxes. "Now's not a good time. I'm moving to another building, but I'll give you a call when things settle down."

Raegan held eye contact for a few seconds before she nodded, stepping out of the bed and into her clothes. Landon moved out of her way when she approached him, dropping his eyes to the floor. He tried not to flinch when she set a hand on his bare chest, and then she was gone, the sound of his private elevator the only noise in the dark penthouse.

A voice in his head called him an asshole, but he preferred it to the alternative.

Landon took a couple of minutes to clean himself and his room up before he went into the kitchen to make a quick dinner, turning on the TV as he tossed on an apron and began chopping vegetables. It was a shame his landlord was moving back, because he loved this kitchen.

The rhythmic sound of the knife hitting the cutting board and the smell of garlic sautéing in a pan grounded him in a way that nothing but cooking ever did. His mother had taught him before she had passed—the one thing they'd done together as he'd grown up. Every free second outside of school had been spent trying to prove to his father that he could be as successful on the field as his brother, but in the few moments after getting home, when his mother would show him how to make his favorite meals, he hadn't had to prove anything to anyone.

He could just exist, enjoying the same rhythmic sound of the knife hitting the cutting board.

Now that she was gone, it was the thing that made him feel closest to her. Not even the two tattoos he'd gotten in honor of her—the sparrow on his hand with the words *to the moon and back* underneath and the butterfly over his heart with her birthday—gave him that same feeling.

The low hum of commercials turned to a local broadcast, and when Landon looked up, his face was plastered on the screen. He set down the knife, wiping his hands off on his apron before turning up the volume.

"Sentinels fans will get a kick out of this one." The woman reporting laughed. "San Jose Sentinels tight end Landon Beaumont was spotted Monday evening at Savannah Blake's birthday bash. Blake, whose latest album has topped charts for the last fifteen weeks, had a real assortment of people entering and leaving her party, but this is not the first time Beaumont and Blake have been spotted together. John, do we think this is the start of something?"

Landon scoffed, moving his chopped carrots to one side of the board and starting on an onion. Savannah had planned for her California tour dates to coincide with her birthday so all her closest friends could celebrate with her, Landon included.

"Well, by these pictures of them leaving the party looking *very* happy, I'd say they enjoyed each other and *more*." The screen shifted to a picture of Landon walking out of the club Savannah had rented out with her wrapped in one of his arms. Beside them were two more women, arm in arm.

Landon chuckled. If only they knew that two of the three women had gone home together without him. What looked like the beginnings of a sordid orgy had been a cleverly disguised way of smuggling Savannah and her secret girlfriend out of the party.

Clearly, it had worked since these poor excuses for journalists were talking about it. Either way, he didn't mind the attention. Kind of liked it, even.

Plus, the pretty blonde beside Savannah's girlfriend had come home with him, and the sex had been as good as any other. She'd left as soon as it had been over—a perk of hooking up with Savannah's friends, who were all famous in their own right, or at the very least, knew how to act around celebrities.

Landon worked on his fried rice as they dissected the photo. Right as he turned down the heat of the burner, he heard the man say, "Speaking of football and Beaumonts, early predictions point to the Sabertooths winning the championship again this year. Headed by who some might call the league's greatest of all time, Colton Beaumont, the Sabertooths have won three times in the last five years, and after their first preseason win this weekend, they're looking like they could make it four."

Landon ground his teeth, turning the heat all the way off and smashing the power button on his remote.

Just what he needed. A reminder that no matter what he did, it would never be enough to outshine the league's greatest.

Landon yanked his helmet off as the final whistle blew on their second preseason game Saturday evening, pulling the nearest Denver player into a handshake and mumbling, "Good game."

Preseason games didn't count for much, but Landon had played a good one, and with the constant collapse of Denver's pocket, it had been an easy win. Even better, that win had come at home, which meant he could shower, do some media, get treatment for his aching muscles, and go straight to bed.

His whole body hurt from the second hit he had taken in the red zone late in the first quarter, but he forced a smile as he rode the sportsmanship train. When a reporter approached him—after talking to Ray Landers and Myles Young, the Sentinels' head coach and quarterback—Landon smiled charmingly at her, ready to answer her template questions. He recognized her, had probably hooked up with her once or twice, but her name eluded him.

"Landon, great game. I know this is only preseason, but you looked good out there. Can we expect some big plays from you and Myles this season?"

"Today was defense's day. They did a great job, got a lot of stops. We always hope for big plays, and we're, of course, hoping to improve our stats this season. Playoffs were good to us last year, but I think we have a shot at a conference final and championship." Landon wasn't sure he was sticking to the script anymore, but hopefully the bullshit he spouted would be enough to keep his agent and the Sentinels' PR team off his back.

"Speaking of championships, your brother is at the helm of a strong Sabertooths team. They won their second preseason game too and are looking for another ring. How does that make you feel?"

Landon took in the woman's short brown hair, her shoulders squared, head held high, and her face scrunched as she held the microphone in front of him.

He could've told her that it made him feel like shit to constantly have everything come back to Colton. He could've told her that he was tired of playing the game and getting nothing from it because nothing he did was good enough, not for *anyone*. He could've told her that, like a child, his feelings were hurt that his family was usually across the country at a Sabertooths game, when he played just as often. That no one ever thought to come to his games except for the few times his sister was already in Los Angeles for work and flew up.

He could've said all of that, but instead, he forced that charming smile he was known for wider and winked at her. "I love a good competition. Would the league be as fun without some sibling rivalry?"

She laughed, though it was clear it wasn't the answer she'd been looking for from the way her eyebrows stayed scrunched. "Thanks, Landon. Good game, and good luck next weekend."

"Thanks."

He jogged off the field and toward the locker room, showering and rushing through a brief press conference with more of the same questions. While one of the team trainers massaged his muscles, Landon finally checked his phone. Maya, his sister, had congratulated him on his win. When he scrolled down, he saw the one message from his father.

His eyes scanned the number over and over again, though he knew what it meant. He didn't need to check to see the number of receiving yards he'd gotten, but he knew if he did, it would read the same. Landon let out a bitter chuckle.

His father couldn't even give him a single word. Just a number, which, for a preseason game, wasn't that bad. The disappointment was clear, as it had always been. Landon was sure Colton hadn't gotten one of these.

When he'd been a kid, nothing he did mattered and it didn't matter now, not when Colton had three championship wins to his name.

"I'm good, thank you," he said to the trainer, who nodded and walked to one of his teammates. Landon grabbed his dress shirt, buttoning it until he reached his diamond curb link chain and running a hand through his damp hair a couple of times.

He might not have been the best player in the league or even in his family, but damn did the media love him, and the least he could do was give them something to talk about. Screw an early night.

Wondering where his closest friend had gone, he shot him a quick text.

Landon groaned. Running backs took far more hits than tight ends, so the Sentinels had decided not to play Ikaika in the preseason to keep him healthy. It made sense that he'd left so much earlier.

He thumbs-upped the message, then dialed Savannah's number. He knew she didn't have an event today, but it was unlikely she'd answer, so when she did, he was surprised. "Lando boy, what's up?"

"Hey, Sav. You, me, a bunch of hot women, and a ton of booze. Tonight. Even better if it's somewhere paps will be."

She chuckled. "I love the way you think."

Once again, Landon ended the evening with a woman whose name he couldn't remember and woke Sunday morning with a killer hangover.

It was a better feeling than the emptiness in his chest.

Chapter Four

Keala

The spawn of Satan, otherwise known as Heath, Keala's ex-boyfriend, must have had a paranormal ability to sniff out when she was at her worst. She hadn't spoken to him in months, and yet just as she threw herself into her car after getting kicked off the Sirens for being late to practice again—shocker—he decided to grace her with a text.

Heath

I see you're still shaking your ass for the masses, which means you're probably still killing yourself as a nurse.

Wrong, actually. She was killing herself as a nurse *practitioner*, not that he would know the difference. She'd gone through countless unpaid patient care and healthcare experience hours, shadowing, and a bachelor's and a master's degree to get to this point. Despite all she had done to explain that to him, he hadn't managed to get it through his thick skull.

Heath

> Sucks that the thing you love doing has so much in common with stripping. Except at least they make good money.

Then he sent a still of her on the field at the second preseason game a few days ago, side by side with a photo of him with a stripper.

Real classy.

Now that she had been out of the relationship for a while, she could see all the signs her Vixens teammates, and even Ikaika, had seen. But like her other two relationships, all Keala knew how to do was bend over backward to make him happy, something that, at least with Heath, seemed an impossible task.

She had to fight the voice in her head that told her not to burn the bridge as she tapped the block button under his contact information. Then, she switched to the contact for Josie, her former teammate and closest friend in Virginia, and pressed *call*.

"KayKay! How *are* you?" Josie asked happily. With Keala's schedule they'd only been able to exchange texts over the last few weeks, but it was so nice to hear her voice.

"I'm doing okay. Missing you and the girls. And I might be in need of advice."

"Oh no. Are the Sentinels not treating you right? I'm on my way home from practice and have a long stretch of highway to cover. Hit me with it."

Keala sighed. "The short version is that I've now been late to three practices because my shifts at work haven't changed, even though my boss told me they would, and now I'm off the team."

Josie gasped. "No." She drew out the syllable.

"Yeah," Keala responded miserably.

In a turn of events that, frankly, shouldn't have shocked anyone, Angelica had lost her mind when Keala ran in five minutes late. She'd told her through gritted teeth to leave and not bother coming to practice tomorrow or showing up for the final preseason game on Friday. Not even Cora's protesting had changed Angelica's mind.

In an instant, Keala's greatest passion had been ripped from her grasp because of five minutes and a job that drained her in every possible way.

"Well, let me think…"

"There's more."

"Oh, no. What else?"

"Heath texted."

"He *didn't*. Oh my lord. What did the miserable, small-dicked man have to say for himself?"

Keala read the text out, then explained the photo.

Another gasp. "God, he's so annoying. Imagine not being able to make a woman finish and then complaining that she's empowered and doing what she loves. What is *with* men?"

Keala hummed in agreement.

"First things first, block his ass."

"Done."

"Okay, what kind of advice do you want? Productive? Vindictive? No, probably not vindictive."

Normally, Keala would have gone home, had a good cry, and figured out how to move on. Maybe she would have called her mother so she could be asked about whether she was still sure about her choice in careers. That would've forced her to put on the act that she loved her job, and maybe in those few moments, she could have believed it.

But now, after seeing how spiteful he could be to her after all she'd tried to do for him, she was mildly pissed off. Mostly at herself. Keala had nearly quit dancing for the Vipers, a job she'd loved wholeheartedly, just because it made him uncomfortable.

Actually, he claimed it was because she didn't give him enough of her time, but she knew he hated that she was a professional cheerleader.

It had taken Ikaika threatening to fly out to kill him to realize that she'd entirely lost her backbone in the process of chasing the love story her parents had.

Like everything in her life, Keala couldn't just *take control* of things. She couldn't take or even ask for what she wanted because she was so terrified of rocking the boat.

"Tell me what you would do."

"Oh, honey. That's...I don't think it's something you'd be comfortable with."

"Tell me anyway?"

"I'd get drunk and burn his house down, probably. Or, at the very least, key his car."

Josie was right—there was no way Keala was taking control of her life in *that* way.

"Maybe a little less aggressive? And a little more something I could geographically accomplish?"

Josie was quiet for a minute. "I still feel like it's not you, but...a bar? I know it's a Wednesday night, but you might be able to find someone who needs a drink after a long day of work. Especially where you live. I bet that's where all the hotties in tech and finance are. At worst, you get drunk. At best, you have a one-night stand. Oh!" Her friend clapped her hands. "Use the dating app we made you get after Heath. See if you can find anyone on there."

Keala turned the idea over in her head. The alternative was going back to an empty apartment since Ikaika was in LA visiting his niece for the evening, or going to her parents' house, which sounded like a horrible idea. And maybe with a one-night stand, she could ask the guy for what she wanted instead of spending her entire time focusing on what *he* wanted. Because she'd never have to see him again.

Taking Keala's silence as reluctance, Josie said, "See, I told you it wasn't your speed. Let me think."

"No, I'm going to do it. Like you said, at worst I get drunk. And without a shift tomorrow, I might as well."

"There you go! I'm so proud of you. That's going to be so fun. Please *please* text me about it."

"I will."

"And hey, if things don't work out, you can always come back. You know we'd be glad to have you next season, whether on the team or helping choreograph."

There was no way she'd be moving across the country again any time soon, but the sentiment was sweet. Sometimes she lay awake, wondering why she couldn't have just told her parents she would join them in a year, once she'd finished her five years with the Vipers. Her work schedule had never clashed with her dance there, and if it had, no one would've cared because they knew she was the hardest working one on that squad. Which was why she had been one of the four line captains, and why she'd helped choreograph so many of their dances.

But Keala didn't have a no button, especially not when it came to her parents. And she'd truly been excited to be a part of a prestigious group like the Sirens.

But now that was gone.

"I will keep that in mind. Miss you so much."

"Miss you! We should do a trip during the offseason."

"That would be awesome. I'd love to see you guys."

"I'll work on logistics. Love you! And don't forget to text!"

"I will, and love you too!"

Keala typed *bar* into her navigation app, chose the nearest one, and drove.

Chapter Five

Keala

Keala set her glass down on the bar, and the bartender, a man who could win a contest for most number of piercings, smiled at her as he took it. "Want another?"

"Could I get an Ocean View instead? Thank you."

She turned around, taking stock of the few people around the room. The space was dimly lit and smelled faintly of stale beer, with worn, faded posters on the wall and sticky tables, which had led to her sitting at the bar. A flickering neon sign cast a garish orange glow over the chipped wooden bar, where a few older men sat, nursing their drinks and taking turns eyeing her. In a darker corner was a group of both women and men laughing around a pool table.

So maybe she could've found somewhere better, but she'd never looked for bars before. Any time she went out, someone else chose where they went. The prospects here were not great, something that was about as surprising as the sun rising in the morning, considering it was a Wednesday evening at an aging bar. Still, she was glad she'd made a different way for herself than she usually might have, and with a drink's worth of courage in her body, she redownloaded the dating app and started swiping.

Sure, it would be Keala's first one-night stand if she was successful, but she was feeling good about this whole new version of herself. She'd gotten herself here, hadn't she? Maybe she would finally be able to come from something besides her own hand or vibrator.

That'd be the day.

The man dropped the drink off and she thanked him. Two small sips later, someone said, "I imagine the options right in front of you might be more interesting than the ones on there." His voice was velvety and deep, and something sparked up her spine at the sound of it.

The clatter of her phone on the bar top as she startled and whipped her head in his direction only served to make the stranger grin wider. He slid onto the tall stool beside her.

He was handsome with strong, dark features. Potentially Mediterranean? She wasn't sure. But there was something familiar about him as she looked a little longer.

She took in the rings on his fingers, the tattoos across his knuckles that crept up his left hand and disappeared under the sleeve of the nondescript sweatshirt, his skin tone close to hers, maybe a shade darker. And as she drank in the strong set of his jaw, the dimple beside his bemused grin that grew wider by the second, his strong nose, and thick locks of black hair, she realized exactly who had taken a seat beside her.

The hood that only left a bit of his hair exposed couldn't fool a woman who had grown up watching the Sentinels and had followed them closely since she'd moved away from home. Certainly not a woman whose cousin played for the team and who'd had to memorize the information and faces of every single player in case tailgaters felt like talking about them.

She made a move to stand because Landon Beaumont, hot as he may have been, sitting beside her was absolutely the last thing she needed as a Sentinels Siren with strict instructions not to fraternize with Sentinels players—outside of Ikaika of course.

But then she remembered Angelica's sharp words, the heavy feeling in her chest she'd hoped alcohol might chase away and she stayed seated. She wasn't exactly a Siren anymore.

"Um...huh?" she asked dumbly.

Landon nodded to where her phone now lay, the dating app still open. "Was just saying I can't imagine you're going to have much luck there."

Keala clicked her screen off. She wanted to agree with him, but trying to do the opposite of her instincts, she said, "That's...awfully presumptuous of you. How do you even know what I'm looking for?"

He shrugged. "I don't. But doesn't matter what it is, that can't possibly be the best place for it."

Channeling Josie, she asked, "And you're implying that this dingy bar is? That *you're* what I'm looking for?"

"I find that often, yes."

She ignored his self-satisfied smile, the right side of his mouth quirking up higher than the left. "What are you doing here? Don't you usually look for a place that's more, I don't know, high profile?" It was a genuine question, but it came out with a bit of an edge.

He looked around, setting an arm across the back of her stool. There wasn't even skin contact, just his sweatshirt-covered arm against her sweatshirt-covered back, and yet she felt the heat of his touch sear her spine and surge through the rest of her body. "Hey, there's no need to be mean to Ole Faithful."

"I'm just saying, it's a little depressing and miserable for a star like you."

He grinned. "You think I'm a star?"

Keala snorted but took another couple of sips of her drink instead of responding. She didn't know if it was the touch of alcohol in her body, or if her filter was gone thanks to the hellish day she'd had, but fighting her instinct to put him at ease was easier than usual. She couldn't read what type of person he wanted her to be, and that may have helped too.

"Maybe I like miserable. Maybe I'm seeking out miserable."

She cut her eyes to him. "What do you have to be miserable about? You guys won Saturday."

Landon's smile slipped to a fraction of what it'd been before, and he drummed his fingers on the bar. "Just an overbearing parent and a brother who can do no wrong." His mouth quirked up again, like he was joking.

Keala nodded because now he was speaking her language. She matched his smile. "It's like looking in a mirror."

Their eyes met, and Keala knew neither of them were joking.

Landon leaned back, and she hated the way his eyes traveled over her features, then down to her sweatshirt, and finally to her drink before meeting her eyes again. Hated even more how her whole body warmed at the look, as if it knew what she was planning and had set its sights on him.

"While I know I'm hot, I'm not the smoke show you are."

She fake gagged. "Please."

"No good?"

"Could definitely use some work. Not sure how you pull as hard as you do with lines like that."

"Aw, sweetheart, do you keep track of my dating life?"

Why was the way he was looking at her so hot? He was presenting himself as an intriguing option, even if a very loud voice in her head told her it was a horrible idea. But wasn't the point of tonight to ignore that voice?

"Trust me, I'm much too busy for that." Though she suspected the next time she saw a headline about his antics, she'd be more inclined to pay attention.

"Right. Well, I live down the street, and this is a good place to get a drink when I want to go somewhere low-key and don't want to be chased down. And a good place to meet beautiful women, apparently." He paused for a second, then rapped his knuckles against the bar. "Anyway, if you have any interest in someone of a slightly higher caliber than"—he looked down at her phone—"and you haven't had too much to drink, I'd be more than willing to oblige."

Keala opened her phone and glanced down at the finance bro, aptly named Chad, who she'd spent too long debating about. Siren or not, it wouldn't look good if she were photographed with Landon Beaumont. But then again, with his sweatshirt hood pulled over his head, he appeared to be flying under the radar.

She felt the thread of her resolve coming undone, fraying and unraveling. She wanted to be a Siren again, that she knew, and sleeping with a player was a horrible idea, even if he was hot. He was on the team with Ikaika, and doing anything with him could be uncomfortable for her cousin and for her if she had to see him again.

Then again, she'd been living at Ikaika's for a couple of months, and Landon had never been there. Either they didn't hang out much, or if they did, it wasn't somewhere she'd have to interact with him again.

And when had playing by the rules ever worked out for her? Tonight was about doing things she normally wouldn't, and she wanted to have a story to tell Josie tomorrow. She couldn't let her friend down.

Keala finished the drink, enjoying the burn as it flushed through her body. Then she tossed a few bills onto the bar and stood, tucking her phone and wallet into her small purse.

Landon watched her closely, and he must have caught the subtle jerk of her head, because when she'd made it past the group by the pool table and to the darkest part of the already dark bar—a hallway with a couple of unisex bathrooms—he was only a few feet behind her.

She didn't need anything more from him than sex, she reminded herself. She didn't need his love or his affection the way she did from others. She didn't need to please him any more than he did her, didn't need to go out of her way with him. Keala could ask for what she wanted without feeling like she was asking too much or stepping on anyone's toes. She chanted it in her head like a prayer.

Landon leaned against the wall, waiting. Like he wanted her to make the first move, which was rather unexpected. Keala had assumed he would take charge.

She stepped forward. In the interest of taking what she wanted, she pulled him by his sweatshirt and kissed him. He brought one hand up to cup her face, hands rough and calloused like she'd hoped they would be. The other slipped into her hair, twisting just enough that excitement shot through her body.

It was slow at first, but she wanted more, and their height difference was quickly becoming a nuisance. As if Landon understood, he took over, hands on her waist, picking her up and allowing her to wrap her legs around him.

Smart man.

He pushed her against the wall. And then, suddenly, it was the best kiss of her life. His large palm on her back arched her into him, his stubble scratched against her, and when she opened her mouth, he grunted, suddenly greedy. Her hands moved over his arms and shoulders frantically, floored by the feel of his muscles beneath her palms, even over his sweatshirt.

His hand slipped down to cup her ass, and when he bit her lip gently, she couldn't help but moan. Her hips rolled, trying to create friction, and she could feel the hard press of him between her thighs. She grinded against him like she was a beast half unleashed and was rewarded with another throaty groan.

He pulled away a touch, whispering, "I don't mind fucking in the back of a bar, but you seem like the type of woman who should be spread across a nice bed."

Keala reared back. "What is that supposed to mean?" Did she look like a princess? She was dressed in an oversized sweatshirt and tight workout shorts—she hardly thought so.

"I just mean you're too pretty to be fucked like you're a mistake."

She rolled her eyes at the way he said it so plainly, like it was obvious.

His lines seriously needed work. "Fine. But not at my apartment." That would be too strange, even without Ikaika home. She'd have to figure out a way to get back to her car tomorrow, but she knew she was close enough to her building that it wouldn't be a problem.

He set her down. "I live down the street."

Right as Landon moved to put an arm around her, she pulled his hood farther over his head. "Do a better job of hiding who you are."

"Don't worry. The media does less fawning here with all the celebrities and tech people nearby. Plus, it's not like my team is particularly good." There was a flash of something in his eyes before he dropped them away from her, eyebrows drawn. Still, he allowed her to pull the hood as far as it would go, then guided her out of the bar. "I want to make it super clear—"

Keala shook her head. "If you're going to say this is a one-night thing, I'm going to stop you right there. I promise you I am *not* gonna want to see you ever again."

He gave her that cocky, lopsided, dimpled smirk. "I think I might like you the best."

Chapter Six

Keala

The pair just missed the start of a thick storm as they walked a block down the street and rode the private elevator up to Landon's penthouse apartment. It was bigger than Ikaika's, with an open floor plan that allowed her to see the large kitchen, where Landon stood, on the left and the larger living room to the right. Boxes littered the floor.

A wave of anxiety crept over her, though Keala couldn't put her thumb on why. To try to shake off the feeling, she asked, "Moving?"

Landon gave her a lazy smirk as he tossed his keys onto the kitchen counter. "I'm impressed you noticed. Most people wouldn't catch on that quickly." He leaned back, clearly enjoying himself. "I like an observant woman."

My god, he's an ass.

Still, as he pulled his hood down and the dim overhead light hit his face, it took monumental effort not to inhale at how beautiful he was. His cheekbones were so stunningly defined, and his lips were still swollen from their session at the bar. She wondered how he would want her to respond, how the women he usually took home would have responded.

Not important. She wasn't supposed to be caring about that. This night, this hook up was for taking what she wanted, not caring about his impression of her.

"I'm a lot of things, most of which are not relevant right now," she murmured.

Landon's eyebrow raised, but he nodded, stepping toward her. "One of those things is a great kisser, which is both relevant and incredibly exciting." His voice dropped, more gravelly. "I wonder what other things you can do."

He picked her up again in an instant, her back against the door and his lips on hers. Resuming where they'd left off, he nipped and sucked. Keala tried to keep up with him, but her brain refused to turn off.

What would he like? Should she drop to her knees first? Did she look like his usual hookup? She doubted it. What if she did something wrong? And on and on and on it went—far too much thinking for what this was supposed to be. She'd been so confident when they'd been at the bar, but now that it was happening, that confidence was waning. Quickly.

Landon pulled away but stayed rooted to the spot. "You seem uncomfortable. Do you want a safe word? I wouldn't say I'm the kinkiest, but it might be more than you can handle." Her eyes widened, and he let out a soft chuckle. "I'm kidding. All the kinky stuff happens with my regulars." He winked.

Oh god, now I'm thinking about what his regulars look like. What would they be doing right now?

They'd inevitably do better than her in the bedroom; she wasn't the most experienced. How could she compare? Maybe this was all a bad idea. Maybe she wasn't cut out for one-night stands.

The look of alarm must have still been on her face, because he set her down and ran his hands over her arms, tugging on the fabric of her sweatshirt. "Hey, I'm sorry. That wasn't the right thing to say. If you *are* uncomfortable, we should stop. Let me take you home."

Keala wanted to protest. She couldn't help but feel guilty that Landon would be let down if she stopped now. She'd gotten him riled up. She glanced at where she'd felt him against her before, then looked away.

Her mind ran for a couple more seconds, Landon seemingly growing more concerned as she thought through it all.

Instead of protesting and telling him she'd be happy to continue, she blurted, "I'm sorry, it's just that I lost one of my jobs and my ex-boyfriend is an ass and I hate my other job but my parents think I chose to work in medicine so I can't do anything about it and I thought I was in a place where I could do a one-night stand but I'm starting to think this was a bad idea."

Oh, the word vomit. Keala cringed, a hand over her mouth and her eyes on the floor as she caught her breath. She couldn't bear to look at Landon after that most utterly embarrassing confession. Warmth bloomed in her cheeks, and she closed her eyes, taking a breath in, then out.

One-night stands were officially off the table.

As was ever, *ever,* seeing this man again.

Keala heard Landon take another step back, and she chanced looking at him, squinting one eye. He shoved up the sleeves of his sweatshirt and fiddled with the watch on his wrist that probably cost more than everything she owned. "Ah, uh...do you want to talk about it?"

His eyebrows were drawn, and he was looking anywhere but at her, probably uncomfortable by her oversharing. Keala released a breath, stood up tall, and pulled down the black athletic shorts she'd thrown on for practice. "I think I should go."

"Sure, I can take you. Let me just—"

"No, no. That's alright. I can get back on my own." The very last thing she needed right now was to spend *more* time with him. The embarrassment began to fester like a wound, and she hoped that the further she removed herself from the situation, the quicker it might heal. She turned, reaching for the doorknob, her hand shaking.

"It's storming like crazy out there. I don't know how much you had to drink, but you don't seem okay. Let me get you home."

"Oh, that's alright. I don't feel the alcohol at all. My car's at the bar anyway."

Keys sounded against the marble of his counter, and then he was behind her. "Again, I must insist. Let me get you safely out of this storm, and then, if you want, I can make sure your car gets to you tomorrow morning."

She battled herself, still facing away from him, before she finally sighed. "Okay."

Keala followed him to the garage, but when he unlocked a Rolls Royce, she stopped short. "Don't you think that's a little flashy? Do you have a less obvious car?"

Landon blinked at her, locked the car, then turned back and got into the elevator. Keala waited a minute, looking around the private garage. If this was just for him, the only other car was an Audi RS7, and while it was certainly less obvious, she was still worried.

He appeared again, clicking the Audi unlocked. "I've never met a girl who wanted so badly not to be seen with me that she wouldn't let me impress her with my Rolls Royce."

There was a joke in there somewhere about overcompensation, but based on what she'd felt pressing against the fabric of his pants earlier, she wasn't so sure it would apply.

Keala gave him the address and he punched it in, an odd expression on his face. The storm was far worse than she'd been expecting, and as an anxious driver, she agreed that her driving home would have been a bad idea.

The drive was quiet, and she was thankful he understood she was too embarrassed to talk. Sure she'd ruined his night, she sighed, watching two raindrops battle it out on the passenger window as he drummed his fingers against the wheel.

"I'm sorry about your job. And your ex-boyfriend. Seems like an idiot to me, but what do I know?"

Keala glanced at him. "We don't need to talk about it. I'm sorry I said anything."

Landon nodded once.

She'd thought that he would pull up to the front of her building, but instead, he parked by the private side entrance for residents.

When he opened his door, she squeaked. "You don't need to come in!"

"No, no. I want to walk you up."

"I don't want to put you out."

"It's no trouble."

Keala held back a groan but allowed him to open her car door. They dashed through the downpour to the private entrance, where she scanned her fob to get into the building and then again to get into the private elevator, waving as she passed Richard at the security desk. She couldn't fathom why Landon wanted to walk her all the way to her apartment, but she also didn't know how to stop him without feeling rude.

Conversation in the elevator was nonexistent, and she was sure she'd made him monumentally uncomfortable with her confession.

She still couldn't figure out what his plan was.

"I meant what I said. We won't be seeing each other again, definitely not hooking up again. If we do ever run into each other for some reason, we can pretend this never happened. You don't have to prove to me that you're a good guy."

He smirked. "Noted."

When they reached her floor, Landon's eyes flicked to the apartment across the hall, then slid back to her. "Nice place. Must cost a fortune."

Keala slid the key into the door and then slipped in, leaving only enough room for herself to enter. When she was comfortably inside, she turned to look at him. "Thanks...for this. Hope you get home safely."

"Do you want me to take your keys and bring your car over tomorrow morning?"

Keala thought about having to see him again, having to look him in the eye in the light of day and act like she hadn't admitted some of her most important secrets. Was he purposely ignoring what she'd *just* said about not seeing each other again?

She shook her head overenthusiastically. "Nope, all good, thanks!" Even though it was a three-mile walk to get it. Luckily, she didn't have anything going on tomorrow.

Only as she closed the door did she realize he had never asked for her name and she'd never offered it. Thank goodness for small mercies.

Chowder's screaming laid waste to Keala's eardrums the next morning. The menace was outside of Keala's bedroom door, and when she checked the time, Keala realized it was two minutes before the cat's feeder would go off.

That damn cat knew exactly what she was doing. At least Ikaika would be home for a few hours to calm her before going to the hotel the team stayed at before home games.

When Keala scrolled through her notifications, she saw a text from Cora. Immediately, she sat up.

Cora

> I talked to Angelica after practice and this morning. She knows she can't cut you.

> Please come to practice tonight, and I beg of you: be on time.

> I know you're struggling with work, but we all want you at the game tomorrow.

Keala sent a quick message back and jumped straight out of bed, crossing the hall to the bathroom so she could start on her skincare. She would be so early to practice, she'd beat Angelica there. Without a shift at the hospital, nothing would stop her from taking advantage of this second chance.

And she'd make sure to send another email about getting her schedule changed before the season opener in September.

Her phone buzzed as she finished splashing water on her face.

Josie

So?? You never texted me!

Keala

I'm back on the team!

Josie

That's great! But not what I'm asking about.

Keala

Couldn't go through with it and instead recounted all my darkest secrets!

Josie

Oh my. Was he ugly?

Keala

I wish. Hottest man I've ever met.

Josie

Do we think you'll meet up with him again?

Keala

Hope not. I never want to see him again.

Josie sent back a sad face, and Keala set her phone down as regret shoved through her chest, finally letting her thoughts fall on the turn her evening had taken.

Rationally, she recognized it probably wouldn't be an issue. Keala had been good about making sure they had stayed hidden. She'd made it clear she hadn't wanted to be seen with him, and he seemed like a semi-decent guy based on the way he'd treated her after her little freak-out. Still, she flipped through any recent news articles about the Sentinels and Landon to see if she'd been included in any of them and breathed a sigh of relief when she saw there was nothing. At least not yet.

But what if Angelica and Cora found out? Landon *did* seem like the type to flaunt this sort of thing, but he'd also been hiding when he'd found her at the bar. Keala hadn't seen anyone following them or cameras taking photos. Plus, if Cora said she could come back, she and Angelica must not have seen anything, and they were always privy to information about the Sentinels, almost before the media.

Keala set her hands on either side of the bathroom sink, resting her weight on the counter. She took a breath in, then let it out. It was probably okay. Sure, it had been embarrassing. Sure, she regretted it. But at least she'd chickened out and let him take her home instead of trying to keep at it.

Her no-fraternization clause was back in full effect, and while kissing Landon went against it, there would have been no going back from having *sex* with him.

Screw her *doing the opposite of what I would do* philosophy from yesterday. What had she been thinking, trying to take control? That sort of mentality was for the Josies of the world.

No. Keala would show up to practice early. She'd prove to everyone, but especially Angelica, why she'd made it through the rigorous tryout process and why she was an asset to the team. It would be like it never happened.

Consider it under the rug.

She would see Landon on the field tomorrow during their last preseason game, he wouldn't recognize her, and that would be the worst of it. Once the season started, it would all be forgotten.

Because she was *that* lucky.

Chapter Seven

Landon

> **ESPN notification –** Week One is only a couple of weeks away: Here's what Colton Beaumont and his Sabertooths have to fix for another championship run (hint: it's not much!).

> **Bay Area News 5 –** Fight breaks out at downtown San Jose bar—Myles Young and Landon Beaumont among Sentinels players kicked out.

Landon listened to the sportscasters discussing statistics and predictions for the last preseason game, which signaled two short weeks until the start of the season in September. A couple of seasons ago, that wouldn't have meant much for Landon's after-dark activities, but since Landon had gotten closer with Ikaika, who almost completely stopped going out during the season, Landon's partying had decreased too.

Somewhat. He was still easily convinced to go out with Myles and the rest of his teammates occasionally.

The change meant that Landon spent more of his evenings playing video games or watching other teams at his or Ikaika's apartments instead of hitting their favorite club and finding two—or more—willing women to take home with them.

Hence why he was at Ikaika's that evening, waiting for the Pittsburgh game to start. He looked around Ikaika's apartment with fresh eyes now that he knew who his Wednesday evening had been spent with. Or at least half an hour of his evening.

To be fair, Ikaika had been adamant that they not go back to his apartment the last couple of months of the offseason. They'd been partying a lot and coming home at odd hours, usually loudly, and Ikaika hadn't wanted to disturb his cousin. Landon just hadn't realized said cousin looked...as good as she did.

His friend was very family oriented, and pictures with his family in Hawaii sat on the kitchen counter by the sink and along the TV stand. Landon had never looked at them too closely. Only one frame featured the woman who Landon had spent an inordinate amount of time scrolling through Ikaika's social media following looking for. All he'd found was a rather innocuous private profile that had given him no information but her name.

Keala Lōkahi-Price.

The only reason he'd known it was her was because her last name was hyphenated with Ikaika's last name, and the profile picture featured what was likely a younger version of the woman he'd met.

San Jose was huge, filled with tons of people. It was no surprise he hadn't recognized the similar features until she'd been in his car, giving him her address. That was when the pieces had begun falling into place.

Now that he was looking at the photo of them with their cheeks pressed together and big smiles on their faces—or as big a smile as one could pull from Ikaika—Landon could see the resemblance even clearer. Their eyes scrunched the same way when they smiled, and both their noses hooked upward slightly at the end.

But her hair was lighter, brown with a bit of blonde, like she'd gotten highlights. Her eyes were lighter too—hazel that nearly tipped over into green. Freckles dotted her smooth cheeks and the bridge of her nose, and when he'd met her, Landon had thought she was the prettiest woman he'd ever had the privilege of *almost* hooking up with. Even if she *had* been drowning in a sweatshirt and overthinking the entire time.

He'd liked that she hadn't treated him like a celebrity, and now he knew why. He hadn't been able to stop thinking about her and what arguably may have been the best kiss of his life. But the things that kept buzzing around in his head were the words that had tumbled out of her mouth like rocks down a hillside.

It was clear she had let him in on pieces of her life that were immensely private, and now that he'd had a taste, he was intrigued. He wanted another shot with her. Something in that kiss had left him more out of control than usual, and he desperately wanted to finish what they'd started.

For closure's sake.

He couldn't imagine she would be too happy when she realized how close he was with Ikaika and how much time that meant they would be spending together.

A part of him was excited to see what she would say when she found out. If she would get angry. If those pretty lips would pout.

"What the hell are you doing?" Ikaika asked as he brought a bowl of food into the living room, Chowder rubbing against his legs as he walked.

"Huh?"

"Why are you staring at that picture so intently?"

I should tell him. It was the right thing to do. He wasn't sure Ikaika would care, especially since he hadn't known until after, but...

The front door opened, and Landon jumped away from the stand, slamming his leg into the coffee table and garnering an odd look from Ikaika.

"My shift was awful and practice at Zoe's ran *so* long. I need a shower immediately. Have you eat—" Keala had finally turned his way.

Ikaika placed his bowl on the coffee table, picking Chowder up with one hand as he stood and nodded between Landon and Keala. "Keeks, this is one of my teammates, Landon. Landon, this is my cousin, Keala."

She was stunning, just like he remembered, only now she was in a tight-as-fuck two-piece workout set that showed off how exquisitely toned she was. Her hair was in a ponytail, a little wet, and a few strands framed her face. Dark crescents were stamped under her eyes, made more obvious by her glare.

Keala walked toward Landon with a hand outstretched. Landon flashed a grin, sensing she was upset. Which was confirmed when she squeezed the ever-loving hell out of his hand.

Screw pouting. He liked when she glared. A lot.

"Ah, so this is why we haven't been coming back here for the last couple of months."

She stepped away, her glare morphing into a genuine smile as Ikaika approached her. They hugged, and Landon wanted to know how they seemed so close and yet he had no knowledge of her. Granted, he and Ikaika had only been good friends for about a year, but Ikaika's hot cousin seemed like a great topic of conversation. At least for Landon.

"Keala's busy. She's a nurse practitioner and a Sentinels Siren who barely sleeps as is. The last thing I wanted was to have us stumbling home drunk at odd hours when she was trying to sleep." Ikaika set Chowder down, and she gave Keala an unimpressed look before following him back to the couch.

A Siren? No wonder she hadn't wanted to be seen with him. If being a nurse practitioner was the job she didn't like, the Sirens must have been the one she'd mentioned losing that night. Was she still off the team or...

And now he was picturing her in those little outfits.

Keala grimaced. "Oh...that was so sweet of you."

Ikaika shrugged. "Now that the season is beginning, we won't be partying as much, so I didn't think it would be a problem if we started hanging around again."

"Right. Of course not. It's literally your apartment—you should do whatever you need to. Please don't feel like you have to change anything for me." Angry eyes found Landon's again, and he tried not to crack another smile.

"Have you eaten yet? There's pasta from the facility in the kitchen."

"I had a protein bar, but I'll grab some. Thanks. I'm going to take a shower and get to bed."

"You don't want to hang out?"

She looked at Landon for a split second. "I have to be up early."

"Your shifts still haven't changed?"

"Not this week. But they do next week. Monday, Friday, Saturday instead of Monday, Tuesday, Wednesday."

"Good. Hopefully Angelica will get off your ass now."

She hummed, disappearing into the kitchen. Landon found it amusing and even a little adorable how badly she didn't want to be in the room with him.

Landon knew he had said all the wrong things Wednesday when he was normally so good with his words, but everything about her confession had thrown him off. Her propensity for emotional vulnerability was jarring, the complete opposite to him. The thought of being open the way she had been made his skin crawl, and yet he wasn't running in horror the way he expected most people would if he were to ever express emotion like that. He had actually kind of...liked it, even if he hadn't known what to say.

When she had taken her bowl of food and bags into the hallway, refusing to look back at him, Landon finally took a seat on the couch.

Not wanting to go any further without being honest, he told Ikaika, "I'm going to be real with you. We almost hooked up a few days ago." Five, to be exact. "She was at Ole Faithful, and one thing led to another."

Ikaika knew Ole Faithful was the place Landon went on the few evenings he wanted to get out of his apartment but didn't want to be seen. Landon had discovered it a few years ago when he'd first started renting the penthouse and realized that being all the way across the country from Colton and his father still might not have been far enough. If the managers or staff knew who he was, they never said. And they never tipped off the media. So, in short, it was one of his favorite places and would be dearly missed when he moved.

Ikaika made a disgusted face, setting his empty bowl down. "That's why you've been acting weird."

"I didn't know who she was, and nothing came of it. I brought her home, here, and that's when I realized."

Landon waited for some kind of anger or, at the very least, a question about why he'd waited so many days to tell him when they had seen each other at practices since then, but Ikaika just shrugged. "What she does isn't my business. As long as she doesn't get hurt, I don't need to know about it."

Oh. That was a surprise, but it made him feel better about his desire to pursue her.

Ikaika continued, "Is it going to be weird with you moving in across the hall?"

With Landon's landlord moving back, he had finally decided to purchase his first luxury apartment. He'd thought it would be great to live across the hall from the guy he spent the most time with, so when the place happened to be for sale right around the time his landlord had messaged him a few months ago, it had seemed fortuitous.

"You know I don't care about stuff like that. Will it be weird for you?"

"Nah. And Keala's super busy. Even with her shifts changing, I don't know if she and *I* will see each other much, let alone the two of you."

Landon didn't know why that made his shoulders slump.

"But if she is around enough, are you planning on..." He waved his hand in Landon's direction.

Landon cleared his throat, trying to find the right words. "If you don't think it would make things uncomfortable."

A look of disbelief. "Wow, I expected you to say no."

"So it would be uncomfortable?"

"No, I mean I've just never seen you focus on someone after things didn't work out. Or even after they did. This summer, you had a new girl almost every day. The few times you took the same girl home more than once, it was because she was persistent as hell—low-key stalking you to know which club you'd be at—and there were no other prospects. I'm shocked."

Landon shrugged. He couldn't explain it either. If he could, maybe he'd have found a solution to push her out of his mind once and for all.

Ikaika turned to the television. "Again, she's an adult. If it's something she wants and it doesn't bleed into my relationships with the two of you, I don't care. But I don't want to hear anything about it."

Landon nodded in understanding.

Ikaika increased the volume, and Landon tried not to put too much stock into the fact that Keala was the first woman he had ever thought about after he'd been with her.

And she didn't seem interested in him in the slightest.

Chapter Eight

Landon

ESPN notification – Five best Colton Beaumont plays—Paving the way to the Hall of Fame.

ESPN notification – Top three preseason letdowns: 1. Max Clark. 2. Landon Beaumont...

Three days later, Landon directed the movers where to put the boxes and pieces of furniture, trying to listen to what his sister said to him over the phone. Failing. He glanced across the hall to where Ikaika had gone to shower and play video games; Landon had denied his offer of help since he'd already hired the company to assist him.

The apartment was the mirror image of Ikaika's, taking up the other half of the top floor. A long entryway cut to a hallway with a guest bathroom and bedroom. In the hallway was a set of stairs leading down to the owner's suite with a closet that could house his many suits and a bathroom so big, it was obscene. But his favorite part by far was the massive kitchen on the main floor with its island stove and space for sitting. He would have to get some bar stools for it.

Maya sighed, reminding him he was still on the phone with her. "Are you even listening to me?"

"No," he admitted.

"Landon! I was talking about how much therapy has been helping me the last few months and how I think it might benefit you too."

Landon frowned. That did *not* sound like something he would enjoy in the slightest. He was just about to voice that sentiment when one of the movers called to another one downstairs.

"Landon! Do you have people over?" Maya gasped. "Do you have a *girl* over?" He could practically hear her eyebrows waggling like she was getting the latest gossip, but alas, he hadn't touched a woman since...

He glanced across the hall.

The week-long dry spell was unusual for him but he wasn't about to talk to his sister about that.

"Also no. I'm moving."

"Oh, right! Text me your new address please. I'll send you some gifts."

"I don't think that's neces—"

"Consider it an 'I miss you and I'm sorry I haven't been able to come see you as much' present from me."

Landon sighed, knowing she wouldn't stop until she got his address. It had been two years since she'd moved to Charleston to live with her boyfriend, and because of it, their visits had become less frequent. He knew she felt guilty about it. "I'll text it later. Can I call you back when I'm done here? I can't focus on both things right now."

"Always pushing your little sister and biggest fan off the phone. Fine. Call me when you're free. Don't think I'm going to let you out of having a conversation with Colton that easily though. I need the hatchet buried immediately. I'm tired of all this division in the family."

"Yes, fine, will do." That was not a conversation he wanted to touch with a ten-foot pole, so the longer he could put it off the better.

"Love you to the moon," she said, their mother's favorite words and the ones inked on his left hand.

"Love you to the moon," he repeated.

Landon slid the phone into the pocket of his sweatpants. He wondered if Keala would catch him in the process of moving. He had planned to tell her about it since she seemed so annoyed at the prospect of him being friends with Ikaika, but he hadn't seen her since Monday. Ikaika hadn't been joking when he'd said she was very, *very* busy.

She would find out soon enough. He couldn't say he wasn't counting down the days.

Landon didn't like it, and he couldn't put his finger on what *it* was, but there was something about her that made him want to see her again. He'd thought after a few days the knowledge of who she was paired with her disdain for him would melt the feeling away. He wasn't the type of guy who fed off chasing women; on the rare occasion a woman wasn't interested in him, he was already looking at other options.

This was different. This was thinking about kissing her against the wall of Ole Faithful. About the needy moan she had let out when he'd bitten her lip. This was picturing her lips wrapped around his cock as he fisted himself in the shower. It was different, plain and simple.

The reason? Neither plain nor simple and entirely incomprehensible.

And he hated it.

"Where's this one go?" James, one of the movers, asked, holding up a labeled box. Landon gave him a charming smile anyway, pointing in the direction of the kitchen.

It was going to be another few trips before everything was in, and then he would take the weekend to unpack it all. There wasn't all that much anyway, and practice on Saturday and Sunday wouldn't be as long or as difficult as usual.

A part of him hoped Keala would come home soon so he could finally see her again.

Maybe he wanted to see that pretty glare trained on him too.

Chapter Nine

Keala

Keala had already lost a patient to a heart attack, had diagnosed and set the broken arm of a woman with fading bruises while her overbearing husband watched, barely letting her talk, and yet she knew *this* patient was the one who was going to haunt her two hours of sleep tonight.

There had been a soft lull before her—this little comatose girl with blonde ringlets, pale cheeks, and blue lips—and the emergency department nurses had been taking a much-deserved rest for the half hour when things were quiet. Then, out of nowhere, people had started running around, and Annie, a triage nurse and Keala's closest friend at Westfield Methodist, had radioed her with the exam room number.

She'd learned from the social worker, Trish, that Ella had been forced to drink milk that contained a significant amount of her mother's benzodiazepines. The mother had lost custody of Ella, and rather than allow her to live with her ex out of state, she'd decided it was a good idea to kill them both so they could be together. Permanently. Only, the mother hadn't taken enough to keep herself out long. After regaining consciousness, she had recognized what she'd done and called the police.

After fully assessing the situation, Keala prescribed Flumazenil to reverse the effects of the benzodiazepines. Normally, one of the nurses would administer it, but Keala couldn't bring herself to leave Ella's side. She wanted to monitor her vital signs and ensure she had adequate hydration as long as she could.

Her breathing had evened out after the last dose and her lips were no longer a bright blue, only tinged now that the medication was being flushed out of her system, but Keala knew she wouldn't be able to get the image of Ella struggling to breathe out of her head. No matter how many years Keala spent in the emergency department, she was sure she'd never get over these kinds of cases.

A knock sounded, and Keala looked to the doorway, where Annie glanced between Ella, Trish, and Keala, who was seated for the first time this shift. Annie's light brows were pinched, and Keala knew Annie was taking this as hard as she was. Keala walked over and stepped outside the room.

"I thought you'd want to know that it's seven so you can head to practice. I can monitor her and check with Melissa about further treatment," Annie said, referring to one of the NPs working the overnight shift.

Keala had forgotten about practice. Deirdre, one of the other NPs, had called her early this morning asking if she could take over her morning shift since her son had gotten sick. Keala had been up since five working on social media for the team, so when she'd gotten the call at six, she'd grabbed a protein shake from her fridge, changed into her scrubs, and rushed over to the hospital.

She nodded, taking another long look at Ella. "Thanks. I talked to Trish. The father is driving here as we speak. Hopefully he gets here before she wakes up," she whispered back, exchanging a hand squeeze with Annie before grabbing her stuff and heading to the employee lot.

It was days like today that forced Keala to confront her career choice. Her mental health was constantly at risk of shattering. Her body felt like it was falling apart from the physical toll of being on her feet for twelve hours a day, her back, neck, and calves aching. Her mind raced no matter how exhausted she was—to the point that she could never turn her brain off long enough to *rest*. Some days were easier, seeing patients with panic attacks, pneumonia, and other things she felt comfortable treating, but days like today...

If she was being honest with herself, she hated it. She hated the job, she hated working in healthcare, but it was what she'd struggled toward her whole life so her parents would love and respect her. Now that she was in medicine, with parents who were vaguely proud of her for it—though they would, of course, have preferred it if she were a *doctor*—Keala couldn't abandon it. She would fall right out of their good graces and become just like Nohea.

Plus, she'd dug herself a hole of debt to become an NP and she had no other marketable skills besides dance, which would never be accepted as her full-time job. No one would view her as successful if she left something meaningful like saving lives in order to teach people how to move to a beat.

So she'd put her degrees to good use, throw on a winning smile, and keep pretending this was what she wanted for herself.

Later that evening, after a grueling practice, Angelica allowed the girls to leave early. They wouldn't have any home games for nearly two weeks, but it was still a shock to learn Angelica was vaguely human.

The woman in question called her over as most of her teammates headed out, and Keala complied quickly. Len grimaced in her direction as she left, and Zoe stayed behind for choreography.

"Yes, ma'am."

"I need you to clean up the locker room. Make sure everything is picked up. We're allowed to have photos pinned, but the tours are starting back up again, so it needs to be neat."

Keala thought about how that was usually a rookie's job, a twenty-one- or twenty-two-year-old just getting their bearings. All it involved was collecting trash and making sure all the girls had taken their travel vanities with them. If they hadn't, she would have to lug the vanities to the lot, keep them in her car, and make sure they got to their owners before their next appearance.

It was hardly a job for a fifth year, even if that fifth year was new to the team. Keala was beat, her mental health had taken a few hard punches today, but fine.

"I can absolutely do that. Would you like for me to clean before or after Cora's choreography session?"

Angelica's frown deepened, as if any questions indicated Keala was talking back. "The tours aren't happening this evening, are they? But since you won't be here tomorrow before they start, get it done before you leave tonight." She turned on her heel before Keala could respond, the short, thinning hair she kept dying brown bouncing as she walked away to do more important things.

Keala let out a sigh but added it to the list of things she needed to do that evening. She should be thankful she was still on the team, she reminded herself.

Cora, Brooklyn, and the four line captains had begun the choreography session, and Keala jogged back over to join. There were a couple of new songs Cora wanted them to work through. Ever the innovator, she always wanted them to do something fresh to wow the crowd, and Keala loved it.

Keala couldn't remember when it was that she had fallen in love with choreography. Her parents had home videos of her at three dancing to any song that came on, from movies to commercials. But it wasn't *just* dancing that she loved—it was the *creation*. The act of choosing the right move to hit the beat perfectly, of telling stories through movement, making nothing into something. It wasn't a hobby but the thing that made sense, the space that felt like it was *hers*.

As much as her parents enjoyed her dancing, they valued academics above all else. For them, being successful meant getting good grades, earning degrees, going to medical school. Education was what opened doors, something that could easily be measured and celebrated.

Dance recitals and competitions were measured as well—she'd always pushed herself to be accomplished in that way too—but those were like grades on a report card, and while she loved dance, choreography was euphoric. It was a language she spoke fluently that no one in her family understood. It thrummed through Keala's veins more than anything else.

"Okay." Cora clapped her hands. "For this part, what do we think works best?" She played one and a half eight counts from a song that was topping charts. Keala closed her eyes, imagining what she might do with every beat.

When Cora played it a second time, Keala marked some new steps without the usual energy required of them, just to solidify what movements worked best with the music. When she opened her eyes, Cora was watching her with a smile on her face, and Zoe yelled, "Heck yeah, Kay!"

Cora nodded like she agreed with the sentiment. "Keala, why don't you do that again full out, and captains, please join her as you can."

Scuff right foot to jump out, feet shoulder-width apart into a demi-plié. Punch poms at an upward angle. Bring to chest. Punch at downward angle. Step to right foot, circle poms, bring left foot to meet the right. Right foot step back as poms break across chest, then slide down the sides of body. Feet back together, wrists cross over each other in a small X.

Everyone caught up, and the session continued like that, with someone coming up with an idea for the next eight count of the song and then all of them implementing it into the routine until a new song was completely choreographed.

Cora pointed to Brooklyn. "Let's do one full run-through now that that's done. Brooklyn can video it, and then you all can head home."

Keala lined up beside Zoe, poms ready, and when the song began, she sprang into motion. Every step, kick, twist, and turn was perfectly timed, focus unwavering as she kept her smile bright, loving the feeling that simmered through her as she felt more than saw how synchronized the five of them were. Like a well-oiled machine.

By the end, Cora clapped excitedly. "Great job, girls. When we have the whole squad here, we can figure out field formation, but this is great for tonight. We'll see you next Tuesday for practice, and Jordy, you'll be at the zoo appearance this weekend with your group, right?"

Jordy, one of the other captains, nodded.

"Angelica wanted me to talk to you about it so you can tell your girls what to expect. It's nothing..." Keala tuned out the conversation as she packed up her bags.

"Going straight home?" Zoe asked as she packed her stuff up too.

"I've got locker room duty, but then yes." Keala sipped down the last of her Pedialyte and took a bite of the protein bar she'd started eating before practice.

Zoe rolled her eyes. "It's ridiculous that she has you doing that. That's not your job at all."

They walked together toward the squad's locker room, and Keala shrugged. "I don't mind. I'm not working tomorrow anyway."

Zoe scoffed. "You know you would do it either way. I wish you would learn to say no to things."

Keala sometimes wished that too, but there was something so innate inside of her that would never allow it. Maybe it had come from trying to make up for the fact that she wasn't as smart as Akoni, or perhaps it had evolved to deescalate the tension that had built in her house when her older brother Nohea had started disappearing for days at a time; she couldn't say.

"It's okay. It won't take longer than a few minutes, especially if everyone took their stuff."

The pair walked into the entryway of their locker room. The space held a vending machine and a six-foot table, where their game day food was typically served. Taking a few steps past the table and a right into the actual locker room, Keala noticed the two black, hard-shell portable vanity tables that had been collapsed down into cubes, slightly smaller than a carry-on bag. They had an extendable handle and wheels like a suitcase, which Keala was grateful for since she would have to transport them.

She could guess whose they were.

Caroline, as sweet as she was, was one of the more scatterbrained of her teammates, and when Keala checked the one closest to her, sure enough, she found a sticker that read Thompson, Carol's last name.

Zoe, who had walked to the other one, shot Keala a smile. "Guess."

"Kennedy?"

Zoe nodded. "Kennedy." She laughed, hauling it up as if she were getting ready to help.

"Oh, don't worry! I can handle getting them." Keala was already tossing trash into the trash bin and wheeling Carol's vanity to the door.

"Don't be ridiculous. They weigh a metric ton and you'd have to make two trips. I'm going to the lot anyway." A bit of an exaggeration. They were likely twenty pounds, and if she could get doors figured out, she would be fine.

"But this is *actually* beneath your job description. Plus, I'm sure you need to get home to get some sleep before work tomorrow."

Tomorrow would be Keala's final "free" Friday before her work schedule changed. She would go to a workout class in the morning, practice most of the day, spend a few hours figuring out content ideas for the Sirens' socials for the next week, and then she would meet with a few of the girls to practice some more. If she was lucky and he was free, she would be able to hang out with Ikaika after. At some point in there, maybe on the way to her workout class, she would try to call Josie, but with the time zone difference and their dance and work schedules, it was nearly impossible to say for certain.

Zoe scoffed. "Again, I'm going to the exact lot you are any-way, and the more we talk about this, the less time either of us have to sleep. Plus, I live closer to Kennedy."

"Wait, no. You can drop it off at my car and I can take them both tomorrow or Saturday."

"You should have them come to you since they're the ones who forgot them."

"You know they can't with Ikaika living there. And I don't mind."

Zoe didn't say anything, but Keala could read the look on her face. She—lovingly—called Keala a pushover often, and while Keala knew Zoe meant well, something so fundamental to Keala wasn't going to change so easily. It was woven into the very fabric of her life.

As was made clear by the whole one-night stand attempt and subsequent fallout of trying to be someone she wasn't.

She moved right past that train of thought, having spent as much time as possible this past week away from the apartment or in her room so she didn't have to interact with the consequences of her mistakes.

The walk back to the lot was long, but Zoe told Keala about the trip to Yosemite she and her boyfriend had planned for the weekend. When they finally reached the parking lot, they said their goodbyes.

Keala had once again tried to take Kennedy's travel vanity, but Zoe hadn't been having any of it, so Keala tucked Carol's into her backseat and headed home.

Chapter Ten

Keala

When she got off the elevator to Ikaika's floor later that night, she heard some commotion and looked up from her phone. A few muscular men were taking boxes into the apartment across the hall, and Keala marveled at the fact that she hadn't known it had been vacant until now.

As she stuck the key in the door, she heard a voice behind her she had dreaded having to hear again. Velvety and deep as hell.

And quite frankly, maddening.

When she had to come to the realization that he was close friends with Ikaika, she'd been annoyed with herself for being so vulnerable. Also for being dumb enough to believe that he would just disappear from her life when they were both so deeply entrenched in the Sentinels franchise. And even though *she* had known who he was and not the other way around, the irrational part of her brain blamed him for this situation they were in.

Keala whirled around, dropping her bags as she did so and looking for the culprit. Landon stood just inside the apartment across the hall, a shit-eating grin on his face, though he had the good sense to hold his hands up in surrender when he saw her expression. His eyes drifted over the tight, all-black workout set the Sirens wore for Thursday practice, appreciation clear.

"You," she hissed, all her natural instincts jumping out the window when she started putting the pieces together. The boxes in his apartment last week. The same boxes now in the foyer in this apartment. Still, she asked, "What the hell are you doing here?"

"Well, I did buy the place."

"The building?"

"Sweet that you think I want to spend my entire contract and more to own a building of this size, but no. Just this apartment here." He hooked his thumb behind him.

Keala took an angry step closer to him. "Why wouldn't you have told me that? You literally forced your way all the way up here when you dropped me off. You'd think you might have said something about this."

That irrational part of her suddenly seemed more rational, because while she had known who he was, *he* had known that they were about to be living across the hall from each other, something he hadn't made her aware of. That pissed her off. Now she really did feel like she could blame him for all of this.

Landon stepped out of the doorway toward her. "For one, you were trying to get away from me as quickly as possible, which didn't exactly leave me with a lot of room for talking. I wanted to come up when you gave me your address so I could confirm my hunch that you were Ikaika's cousin, which I didn't put together until you gave me the address. And then we came up to the top floor, and...you weren't exactly honest with me either. Ikaika's cousin *and* a Siren?" He tsked, shaking his head, though that lopsided grin was still on his face.

"Yeah but—"

"Plus, you were all, 'trust me this isn't going to happen again,' so it shouldn't matter if we're living in the same building, right? It's like it never happened. I didn't think it was super important at the time, especially with you running away, but I was going to tell you after we talked Monday. You just haven't been around much. And to be fair, *you* were the one who knew I was on the team. *You* knew I was your cousin's teammate, and *you* knew you were prohibited from fraternizing. I didn't know a thing about you until we got here. So really, even though this doesn't matter because nothing happened, I think *you* have some explaining to do."

Keala's mouth opened and closed. So many things floated through her head. It mattered to *her* because it was the hottest kiss she had ever had, and it made her want so much more the longer she thought about it. And now, not only was she learning he was close with her cousin—and therefore she *would* see him here and there—he was *moving in across the hall.*

He was infuriating. She wanted to stab him with her keys.

The worst part was that there was a flurry of emotion going on within her, but the one that was most prevalent was utter and absolute embarrassment. This man had watched her struggle through her first ever attempt at a one-night stand. But more than that, he had been a witness to the catastrophe of things that had fallen from her mouth that evening. She had told him things she hadn't ever told *anyone* outside of Ikaika.

This man, who she was never supposed to see again—as dumb as that thinking might have been on her part—could not possibly live in her building, on her *floor*. She would have to see him as she came into the building, as she left the building, and more likely than not, in her apartment. And often.

Was she living in a nightmare? She thought about pinching herself but didn't want to give him that satisfaction.

"You're doing an awful lot of thinking," he said, smirking. "Get out of your head, *Keeks*. I think you'll find that I'm far more fun."

Shoving a finger into his chest, she said, "Don't call me that. You might not think it's important, but it *is* if we have to see each other every day. Especially with my no-fraternization clause. Which, by the way, wasn't in effect at the time because I'd been told I was off the squad."

"Oh, so you *are* back on the team." His smirk widened. "Good. I've been betting with myself about whether or not I'm going to get to see you in that hot-as-fuck cheerleader uniform."

"That's not—that's so not the point. I wouldn't have hooked up with you if I thought you were going to be living on my *street*, let alone *across the hall*."

"Well, we didn't exactly hook up, did we? We could remedy that if you want. My bed was delivered earlier." His dumb grin widened.

"I'm—Are you…Is that a joke? Are you kidding me right now? Did that seem like the right thing to say in this moment?"

"I'm not *not* joking. Unless that sounds like something you'd like? I don't have anybody else on the docket for today."

An image of her keys jabbed into his carotid flashed behind her eyes, and she squeezed them in her fist. She never got this angry with anyone. It was probably because she'd had a shit day, but Landon being an asshole wasn't helping any.

"Stay. Away. From. Me." She punctuated each word with a stab of her finger to his chest, but that only served to make him smile wider.

"You're doing an awful lot of touching for someone who claims they have no interest in me."

"For the love of…" Keala took a step away, realizing they were toe to toe and had an audience that was pretending not to listen.

Landon dropped his voice, suddenly serious. "Don't worry. They won't say anything."

Keala sighed, picking up the bags she had abandoned on the floor. "Dance is important to me. I don't need to lose my last year because you're an arrogant ass. I know you're Ikaika's friend, as bizarre as that may seem to me, but leave me out of it."

She turned around, about to open the door, when he said, "Okay, but in the interest of full disclosure, which it seems you want, I *did* tell Ikaika about us."

Keala closed her eyes, rolling her neck and pushing the door open. She slammed it behind her.

She knew his type. He was conceited and a total slacker. She had looked him up. His whole family was in sports, including his parents, and she could tell he got by on talent alone. She had watched him at the last game, showboating when he'd barely been trying, barely playing. All he seemed to care about was partying and women.

He was the type of person who had things handed to him and didn't have to work like she and Ikaika did.

"Hey, Keeks. You okay?" Ikaika stood from the couch, a video game controller in hand and his curls wet. He gave her a hug as Chowder turned her nose up.

"I do *not* like Landon."

"You hide it so well." Ikaika pulled away, a small playful smile on his face. "Does that mean I have to stop playing with him? Do I have to find another friend?"

Keala tried not to, but she let out a small chuckle.

"Wow, you *really* don't like him. You're all tense."

"I'm always tense," she mumbled.

He nodded solemnly. "Very true."

"Why did you never talk about Landon when I was in Virginia? It would've saved me tons of trouble."

"We only got close last season after I moved up to first string. The few times you and I talked, it was about important stuff, not our daily life."

Keala grimaced, looking down at the floor. She hadn't been the best at communicating with how busy she'd gotten, so it wasn't a surprise he hadn't felt comfortable talking to her about his day-to-day life. "I'm sorry I didn't tell you about what happened. I was embarrassed."

"I'm not going to lie and say I wasn't surprised. But I don't care what you guys do. Just be careful with the Sirens and everything, and don't hurt each other. I trust you to be adults about everything so things don't get weird."

"Trust me, nothing is going to happen. Nothing even happened. I didn't want to come back to the empty apartment while you were in LA. I made a dumb mistake, but all we did was go to his place for a couple of minutes and that was it."

"Don't hurt each other." Keala scoffed internally. There would be no opportunity for that. It was clear that Keala wasn't programmed for one-night stands, and it wasn't like Landon would ever want more. Relationships took work, and he wouldn't know work if it smacked him in the face.

Not that she would want a relationship with him anyway. He was the last person she would be willing to bend over backward for.

"Gross. I don't need to know that."

Keala shoved him. "Shut up. All I'm saying is, you have nothing to worry about. I made it very clear to him that I have no interest in him."

Ikaika's eyebrows raised. "So you actually told him how you felt? I don't think I've ever seen that."

"Oh, yeah. You missed the show." She crossed her arms. "I can't believe you didn't tell me he was moving in across the hall."

If she didn't love him so much and if he hadn't done so much for her, she would be mad at him. Instead, she was just peeved.

"Hey, I hardly saw you this week!"

"Right, 'cause it would've been so hard to say, 'Hey, just so you know, Landon is moving in across the hall.'"

"And what would you have done if I had?"

Keala blew out a breath. What, indeed. Torch the place, maybe.

"Exactly." He waved the controller. "Now, stop pretending to be mad at me and come race me."

Chapter Eleven

Keala

Setting her head on her steering wheel, Keala stifled a sigh. She was running later than she would have liked. Their call time for the first real game of the season was in an hour, and most of the girls got there far before that. Traffic was practically at a standstill, and her mother, whom she'd called to ask about a pair of heels she'd left at their house, had completely taken over the conversation.

"It's so nice he's in Los Angeles. We're so close to our babies." Her mother's voice grew excited, pitching up. "He's applying to medical schools now, you know?" Keala didn't need to have been paying attention to know she was talking about Akoni.

"It *is* nice that he's close," Keala murmured, trying to keep the conversation away from medical school. Someone honked, and she whipped her head up, pressing on the gas as she waved an apology to the car behind her. She hated lying to her parents, and that was only getting more uncomfortable now that she saw them once or twice a week. Medical school and doctors were all her mother wanted to discuss—her subtle, and sometimes not so subtle, way of pushing Keala to go back to school and become a doctor.

"Dad and I think he'll be a shoo-in for Texas, but we're hoping he goes to Geffen or UCSF. Wouldn't it be amazing if he were that close? We could have family dinners every week like we used to."

A long time ago, before Nohea had begun acting strangely and coming home disheveled every few days, before her parents had sent Akoni and her to their rooms while they yelled at Nohea, family dinner had been an important part of their lives. It held some of her strongest memories of her older brother and the family dynamic before everything had changed. Thankfully, a few months after Nohea had gotten kicked out, Ikaika had moved in and joined those dinners. Keala had always glanced at that empty seat at the table though, wondering if she'd ever see her brother again. If she would suffer his same fate if she, too, upset her parents.

"Yeah, it would be great," Keala answered quietly. She loved her younger brother, but every moment she spent in his presence was a reminder of all that she wouldn't be able to achieve in comparison. When they were together for the holidays, she had to push that feeling deep down. Akoni was a great brother, always making sure he got her something for Christmas and her birthday. Always wishing her well when big things happened in her life or texting when he saw something that made him think of her, and she tried to do the same for him.

But it was a struggle not to blame him for her own shortcomings.

Traffic began to thin, and Keala sped up. She hoped her mother's silence meant she was thinking about something, *anything*, else. But she had never been that lucky.

Hesitantly, her mother asked, "Sweetie, you know Dad and I will help pay for your medical school, right? Is that why you decided to get your master's instead of going to med school? We don't mind. We want you to be happy."

"I am happy."

"Of course. But don't you think you'd be happier if you were making half a million a year? You're smart enough to be a surgeon."

Would she think that if she knew Keala hadn't gotten into medical school? She doubted it. Anyway, it was unlikely she'd make that much as a surgeon. Even if she did, malpractice insurance would take up a big chunk of her money.

"I don't know what I would do with that kind of money," she answered, recognizing she couldn't placate her mother completely but not wanting to get into a discussion about the financials of being a doctor. Things were very different from when her father had gone to medical school.

"You would live in a beautiful house and would want for nothing. Everybody would know you're successful."

Ouch. Keala sighed. The only thing she wanted was to dance, choreograph, and be paid enough to live off it. But if her parents didn't consider being an NP successful, she couldn't fathom how her life as a dancer would be viewed.

Her mother wasn't trying to be mean, but this was what she had always believed. With a doctor for a father, all the Lōkahi-Prices had grown up knowing they would follow in his footsteps. It hurt to know that, after all the work she had put into getting where she was, society and her parents didn't recognize her achievements.

Noticing her exit approaching, she said, "Mom, I'm running late and need to go. Please let me know if you find the shoes. And you're coming to the game, right?"

"Oh! The shoes. Completely forgot. I'll look tonight. And yes, of course we are! We have to cheer you and Ikaika on."

And that was the difficult part. Her parents were so supportive of her dancing, so proud of her in general, that she knew they wanted the best for her. She didn't have it in her to tell them that medical school was *not* what was best for her.

"Great. I'll see you both after. Love you."

"Love you, sweetie."

Keala let out a deep breath as she switched lanes, trying to put the conversation out of her mind. It wasn't a new one, but it *was* a reminder that Akoni was knocking on the door of success, and soon, Keala would be the one left behind.

The Sentinels' first game of the season was at home on a beautiful, sunny, mid-September day, and they had decided to make it a throwback game. All the players wore retro uniforms and all the Sirens wore varying outfits from the past too.

Keala touched up her makeup, preparing for the pregame dance. She had already handled social media for gameday, filming a few videos before and after practice. That was one thing she could cross off her mental to-do list. Her group had just gotten back from taking photos with fans, so she only had a couple of minutes until it was time to go out and warm up the crowd.

It had been entirely by chance that Keala had been given the exact uniform she'd been hoping for: a black, long-sleeve dress with cutouts at the shoulders, a high neckline, and a very short, ruffled skirt that was shorter at her hips and longer in the front and back. It had silver accents and the Sentinels logo on the front.

Growing up, if the Sentinels were playing, her family was watching. Her father was a San Jose native and had been a fan since he'd been a kid. Keala and her brothers had been no different. While Keala had loved watching football, she'd loved seeing the cheerleaders dance on the sidelines more. When she'd been six or seven, she remembered seeing a throwback game and a cheerleader wearing this style outfit. Keala had always wanted to wear it just once.

After she took one last look at her makeup in the mirror, Cora pulled her into the meal room.

"Is everything okay?" Keala asked worriedly.

"Yes, yes. I'm just checking on you. You look tired."

Keala's eyebrows pinched. She'd worked late last night and had woken up early to quadruple check that everything she needed was packed. Then they'd had a rigorous two-hour field practice, so she *was* tired, despite the energy drink. She had put on a ton of makeup after practice to hide the bags under her eyes, but maybe she hadn't done a good enough job.

"Oh, I can add more makeup if you think I need to. I was going to wait until after we finished appearances before our pregame dance, but..."

Cora clasped her shoulders, a small, genuine smile on her face. "Hon, I'm not worried about that. I'm worried about you."

"I'm okay, I promise. I stayed at the hospital late after my shift and didn't sleep as much as I should've." It had been a product of changing her schedule, but at least she hadn't been late to practice once since she'd been pseudo-fired. Though, it almost felt like she had gotten *more* busy since the change.

"You seem to be overworking yourself. When was the last time you had a good night's sleep? Are you eating well? I don't want Angelica to comment about your energy levels. She's not in a good mood today. Some of the throwback uniforms are—" She shook her head, cutting herself off.

Falling asleep had always been a struggle for Keala, a thousand and one thoughts flitting through her head when she tried—tasks she needed to get done that she couldn't stop thinking about. Sleep was rare, and she woke often. But that wasn't likely to change. She'd been eating as much as she could remember to, but with so much going on, she sometimes skipped meals or had a full day of snacking. If she had to cook or feed herself, she fell apart because she couldn't find the time to prioritize making anything.

Again, all things she had gotten used to over the years.

"I promise I'm okay." Game days meant she got two full meals provided, so today was better than most.

Cora looked at her like she could see every little thing Keala thought. "Workaholism is an addiction, you know. It works the same way that alcohol and drugs do, only, society rewards us for it. They tell us that it's good to work ourselves into the ground, that it's good to hustle your whole life away, but its repercussions can be just as deadly. People applaud when you work yourself to death, and so workaholism becomes acceptable. But it's not, and you're hurting yourself in the long run."

She said it like she had personal experience. Keala wondered why. She didn't have anything to say though. Keala didn't think of herself as a workaholic. Yes, she always needed to be busy, but not in a sense that was hurting her. Being busy was a comfort from the anxiety she felt pressing against her sternum when she sat still for too long.

Before she could voice once again that she was fine, Cora continued, "If you find that you can't sit still, that you always need to be doing something or you don't feel like you're fulfilling your side of the bargain with the world, know that rest is necessary, okay? Please make sure you're eating, staying hydrated, and getting enough sleep. Take care of yourself, because nobody else will do a better job of it than you."

Keala nodded, though, internally, she was already brushing it off. She'd been like this her entire twenty-six years. In grade school, when she wanted her parents to know she was working hard, trying to play catch up with her younger brother, she took on extracurriculars and extra classes to prove she was a good student. She pushed herself so hard for every achievement, in dance *and* in school.

College and graduate school had been the same way. Hell, she'd simultaneously worked at the hospital, gotten her master's degree, and cheered for the Vipers, so she had less on her plate now than before.

She would be fine.

The pregame dance and first half flew by since she danced for most of it. The few times she wasn't dancing, she was doing her best not to watch Landon, focusing on Ikaika and Myles, the Sentinels quarterback, or literally anyone but her loathsome floormate.

Keala had spent a little over a week trying to stay away from him, throwing herself into practice at the field and hanging with the girls when she wasn't at her parents' house or at the hospital. Avoiding Landon felt like the best course of action, but that meant that she had spent a lot less time with Ikaika, and it was a loss she was beginning to feel.

Unfortunately, ignoring Landon at a game wasn't so easy. He had been targeted an inordinate number of times. The two times he'd gotten a touchdown for the Sentinels, he had been showboating in the end zone, and she'd had to smash her teeth together hard enough to keep her eyes from rolling.

The crowd ate it up though. He might not have been a team favorite with his well-known shitty attitude and constant media presence, but anyone putting them on the board and up above Pittsburgh was going to get some love.

The halftime show came and went just as quickly, and Keala held back tears at the thought that this was her last first dance. Never again would she start a season in the center of the field in front of this many people, dancing like it was her body's purpose. It was a heartbreaking thought, and having to force a smile through it made it worse. By the end, her feet were falling apart, her arms were tired from holding up her poms, and her cheeks were numb from smiling, lest she let it drop and get fifteen lashes from Angelica.

A joke, though she couldn't imagine the consequences for not being perfect on the field.

The Sentinels slashed through the Pittsburgh defense easily in the second half too. Keala exclaimed along with the fans when the Sentinels offense got another couple of touchdowns. Landon had tried, on many occasions, to make eye contact, and as badly as she'd wanted to glare him down, she'd just cut her eyes away, ignoring that smug grin.

Keala had never spoken to anyone the way she had the night she found out he was moving in, and yet instead of running away, he'd stepped forward, a challenging smile on his face as if he *liked* that side of her. There was something freeing about letting someone see the real her. The version of herself that she hid beneath so many layers of pleasantries, happiness, and willingness to do things for others that even *she* didn't know her. She wanted to push it, see how far she could be herself with him before he decided enough was enough.

It was a scary thought.

Maybe that was the real reason she'd stayed away.

Chapter Twelve

Landon

> **ESPN notification –** Sabertooths wreck Minnesota 42-6. Colton Beaumont comes away from week one with six touchdown passes and 50 rushing yards.

> **ESPN notification –** Colton Beaumont's brother, Landon, scores two touchdowns in Sentinels home opener.

Landon was exhausted and his body felt like it'd been hit by a train. He'd played well, despite what some people said. No surprise that even his good days weren't good enough.

As long as he didn't spend too much time on his own, he wouldn't have to think about how that made him feel, allow those emotions to seep into him like storm clouds gathering on the horizon until they turned darker and angry.

He jogged up the stairs from his bedroom, grabbing his phone from the kitchen counter.

Myles

> Ikaika, I know you're probably not coming out tonight but open invite. Landon, are you?

Will

> Don't come. If you do, none of the women will even look at me.

Myles

> That's a you problem.

JJ

> We can make bets about how many women hit on you before you go home with one.

Will

> Are you talking to me?

Myles

> He's obviously not. And my money's on one.

> Dude hasn't been out in weeks. He's gonna be quick.

Landon

> Just because I haven't been out doesn't mean I'm not getting what I need.

That was a complete lie. Keala's moan tormented him every time he thought to text Raegan or his other regulars.

Landon

> But not tonight. Next time.

He'd already agreed to play video games at Ikaika's.

JJ

> Lameeee

Myles

> Boooo

Will

> Thank God.

Landon laughed.

Outside of the apartment across the hall, he knocked once, and when he heard an, "It's unlocked," from inside, he walked in. The moment he saw the large L-shaped couch, he noticed Keala lying across one side, wearing a tight, black T-shirt that read "Vipers Vixen" in red lettering and a pair of short red-and-black plaid shorts. Funny that her last team had the same colors as the Sentinels, black and red.

Landon was surprised to see her here. She'd spent so much of the last week either busy with her jobs and whatever her social life looked like or avoiding the place because of him.

Even now, she glared at him. Ikaika shot him a wave.

Knowing how much his presence seemed to needle her, Landon smirked. "Nice PJs. I'm sure if we tried hard enough, Ikaika and I could come up with a Sentinels shirt between the two of us so you don't have to wear another team's merch. We have *some* sway with the team, I'd think." He turned to Ikaika. "Right?"

Keala stood, her features steadfastly held in that glare of hers. Eyebrows drawn, cute lips pouting, her nose scrunched adorably as if he smelled like the garbage outside a fish market.

She moved toward the hallway, and Ikaika called after her, "Where are you going?"

She turned, focusing her attention on her cousin like Landon wasn't there. "I could be fired if I'm caught fraternizing with anybody besides you. Plus, I have work tomorrow. I should get some sleep."

Ikaika frowned. "It's like nine. We haven't eaten yet, and I barely get to see you despite living with you." He glanced over at Landon, who still stood in the archway that connected the foyer hallway to the living room. "I certainly won't say anything to anybody, and I promise Landon won't either. That rule is unfairly placed on your shoulders, and I'm not going to let you lose dance because of something stupid like that."

"You know if Angelica caught a whiff of this, it would be over for me."

"Keeks, come on. Landon, swear on something important to you. Tell her you won't say anything so I don't kick you out right here and now."

He thought his friend was joking, but he wanted Keala to feel comfortable in her own home, even if he did like getting under her skin. "I swear on my little sister, I won't tell a soul," he said like he was in elementary school, promising to conceal the location of the secret hideaway he and his friends had found.

Keala looked unconvinced, probably not a fan of the way he'd said it, though, when her attention was back on her cousin, Landon saw her wavering. It was clear how much love was between them and how hard Keala found it to say no to him.

A problem she did *not* seem to have with Landon, which Landon liked.

"Look, I won't ever invite any of the other guys over. If we want to hang out with them, we'll go to Landon's or somewhere else. Nobody will know. It stays between these walls. Just hang out. I don't want to choose between my best friend and you." Ikaika looked at him, and it was obvious that if he did have to choose, Ikaika would choose her.

"I can go. If you'd rather me not be here, I don't mind." Landon hoped he sounded as sincere as he was trying to sound. She glared at him but was becoming more convinced by the second, as evidenced by her brows separating and the corners of her lips tipping up.

"Fine," she relented, walking back to the couch and throwing herself where she'd been before. She grabbed the controller and laid her body in such a way that Landon had to sit on Ikaika's other side, away from her.

That made him grin wider.

"What are we playing?" he asked as he sat down, grabbing the controller Ikaika handed him.

"I'm teaching her Smash."

"You've never played Smash?"

"Do I look like someone with my own gaming console or with any interest in video games where my character gets the shit kicked out of them?"

Ikaika snorted.

"You realize that you aren't supposed to let your character get the shit kicked out of them, right?" Landon asked.

"Ikaika, if you don't kick the shit out of *him*, I'm leaving."

Ikaika smiled at her. "No, it's fun. I promise."

He pointed to a couple of buttons, explaining what they did. She tried each of them, her character throwing out items and hitting Ikaika's character. After a few seconds, he tested her knowledge of the buttons and Landon watched as she scrambled to choose the right ones, a panicked look on her face as she darted her eyes to Ikaika when she got something wrong.

A few minutes later, he said, "I think you're ready to play a real one. What do you think?"

"Whatever you want, but I'm not going to win no matter how much I play."

Landon shook his head. "Giving up so easily? With all your talk about having Ikaika beat me up, I would have thought you'd want to at least try."

Keala didn't deign to look in his direction. "Start the damn game."

The moment the game started, it was clear all Ikaika's training had flown right out of her head. She was mashing buttons and muttering to herself as she tried—and failed miserably—to get any points against him or her cousin.

"Keeks, you have to remember what I taught you."

"I don't remember any of it! The game is called Smash. Why can't I smash all the buttons?"

Ikaika laughed as he moved his fingers so quickly over the controller, it almost looked like he, too, was smashing buttons. But Landon knew better. "Because it's clearly not working."

When Landon looked over at Keala, she was biting her lip in concentration, and the image was so disastrously attractive, he had to look away.

By the end of the first game, Keala was miles behind and grumbling about not being on a level playing field. Still, she shoved her hair into a ponytail and focused her frustrations on the controller once more.

Ikaika leaned over to her and said something so quietly that Landon couldn't hear it, but the instant the second game began, he figured it out.

"Now it's *really* not a fair fight." Landon chuckled as he tried to fend off Ikaika's character. Behind him, Keala's character was doing everything in her repertoire, until finally he began losing health, and then Keala was laughing maniacally as she shoved him off the platform. Ikaika held out a hand for her to high five, and she did so gleefully, a smirk on her beautiful lips as she looked at Landon smugly.

"And what exactly *is* a fair fight? Both of you with your years of experience beating up on me until I'm out of lives?" When he didn't respond, she muttered, "Exactly."

After another few games of Landon getting his ass kicked, Ikaika's phone dinged. "Food's in the lobby. I'll be right back."

Keala sat up. "I can grab it. Don't worry!"

"Stop it. It might be heavy, there's a lot to carry."

"Now you're being sexist."

"I can go," Landon piped up.

Ikaika stood. "Both of you shut up. I'll be right back."

When he was out the door, Keala mumbled, "You would think in a fancy place like this, they would deliver food up here."

"Kind of have to balance that with security, I guess. Nobody's supposed to be able to access this floor. Though I guess someone from the building could bring it up. But that doesn't seem right."

Keala looked at him like she hadn't been talking to him.

"How much of the game were you able to watch?" he asked.

She glanced down at the controller. "I danced most of the time, but I saw some of Ikaika's plays."

"Did you see my touchdowns?" He grinned.

She rolled her eyes. "I told you; I watched *Ikaika's* plays."

"So you didn't see how amazing my touchdowns were?"

"I saw you run an easy route and come away with a touchdown." A little dismissive of the work he'd put in and a bit too close to what his father had said, but where his father's words were meant to fuel him, hers were entirely uninterested. It didn't upset him like he would have expected it would. If anything, it made him want to prove to her that he did more than run defensive backs in circles.

"Go out with me." The longer he'd thought about it, the more he'd recognized she was the reason he hadn't been able to close with anyone else. He wanted, needed, to finish what they'd started at the bar so he could move on. Get her out of his system. When she'd told him off in the hallway, all he had been able to think about was how out of control he'd felt that first night and how badly he wanted to feel that way again.

She scoffed. "You're insane. Those DBs hit you too hard."

"Why? No commitment. We could finish what we started and then move on."

"You do *not* know how to read a room, do you? On what planet does me saying you had an easy game or that I want you to stay away from me mean I want to go out with you?"

"The planet where that was the hottest kiss of my life and deserves to be finished."

Her cheeks pinked. "Not even in your dreams."

"Oh, I promise you it's been happening in my dreams." Constantly. When she didn't respond, he shifted gears. "How are you and Ikaika related? Like, on which side of your families?" Ikaika hadn't given Landon much information on the cousin who was staying with him, even after making introductions. Landon hadn't wanted to ask and potentially make his friend uncomfortable with his obvious interest.

Keala lay back down, looking up at the ceiling thoughtfully. "His dad is my mom's older brother."

"Ah, so that's why your last name is hyphenated." That was a slip up, and by the way her head whipped to look at him, he wasn't getting away with it. To rectify it, he added, "To keep the cooler name." It was no help and didn't make him look any less creepy.

"Excuse me?"

Landon shrugged, feigning indifference. "Had to do some research after I dropped you off on my best friend's doorstep. Your dad's white, then?"

"What is this? Twenty questions? Are you trying to steal my identity? Because I promise there is nothing I have that you want, and while I'd love to see you handle my mountain of debt, I highly suggest you don't."

"Nah. Just wondering. I'm also a member of the White Dads Club." When she squinted at him, he waved a hand over himself. "You think I put work into this perfect tan?" He shook his head. "My mom's Indian." Or rather, *was*.

It was sometimes weird acknowledging that other part of his heritage, knowing he hadn't experienced anything relating to her culture until long after her death, when Maya had reconnected with their grandparents and introduced the siblings to it all. It was one of the many ways he had failed her. While his mother may not have seen him as the disappointment that his father had and did, he *had* failed her, especially near the end. She'd been the one source of love and comfort from his parents, and the moment she had gotten sick, he'd found every way imaginable to fuck things up for her more: partying, drinking, smoking, skipping school. That was his way, after all.

Landon looked away for a few seconds, then glanced back at Keala. "So you liked what you saw on the field then?"

Keala's head cocked, but as she began to answer, Ikaika opened the door, paper bags in both hands. "I come bearing gifts." Chowder bounded up the stairs from Ikaika's bedroom and ran to him like she thought he was talking to her.

Keala stood up to help her cousin, and they all moved into the kitchen to plate their food. She didn't speak to Landon again as they watched reruns of *Survivor* but gave him a strange look when she turned in for the night.

He couldn't help feeling as though, somehow, without him having expressed any of the pain in the content of his thoughts, she had picked up on it.

He wondered if that would change the way she treated him. He desperately hoped not.

Chapter Thirteen

Keala

The feeling of undeniable exhaustion swept over Keala the next day, and she regretted playing video games with Ikaika and Landon instead of trying to sleep. Though who knows if she would have even been able to.

She sat in the supply closet she often used for breathers throughout the day, finishing the last few carrots she'd brought for lunch. As she tossed the plastic bag into her purse, a couple of beats of choreography floated into her mind, tapping against the door in her head like they did when she had a breakthrough. She clicked record on her phone, setting it on a stool and leaning it against the wall.

From center, step right, hands punch to the right, step left, hands punch left. Circle arms overhead, small C-jump. Left leg crossed over right and chest folded over, torso down. Drag left arm up leg before whipping head up to smile at the crowd. Arms shoot up, then drop back down to sides as—

A knock and then Annie stuck her head in. She didn't comment on the state of Keala, giving her a soft smile. "Sorry, I know you started your break ten minutes ago, but you have a patient."

Keala nodded, stopping the recording and tossing her phone into her purse. She was the only NP on shift, and even if that weren't the case, she didn't get set lunch breaks. Following Annie to their desks, she placed her purse under hers. "What do we have?"

"The patient in room twenty-six is a seventy-two-year-old presenting with several months of vaginal bleeding despite having gone through menopause twenty-one years ago. They also state they've been feeling fatigued."

Keala thought on that. "Got it. What's their name?"

"Vivian."

"Perfect, thank you, Annie." Keala pulled up the patient's chart to look through the notes. A lump formed in her throat when she narrowed down the possibilities. She just hoped Vivian had come in soon enough. She headed to the exam room and knocked before entering. After confirming the patient's name, date of birth, and preferred pronouns, she asked, "How are you today?"

"I'm okay, I guess." Vivian's posture was straight, her gray hair cropped close to her head, and she wore a youthful smile despite her surroundings.

"Annie tells me you've been having some vaginal bleeding. Tell me about that."

"Yes, it's been four months now. I've been feeling more tired than normal recently, so I tried to get an appointment with my gynecologist, thinking it might be related. They don't have anything for a couple of months, so I thought I'd come here in case it's something serious."

Keala asked some follow-up questions to better understand Vivian's medical history and current condition.

The symptoms Vivian described, as well as her history of menopause, aligned with endometrial cancer. Chronic blood loss led to anemia, which could have explained her fatigue. Keala's heart hurt for Vivian, who appeared so strong. She hated that this always seemed to be the case—the strongest always had to battle the hardest.

Keala put in an order for a CBC to check Vivian's blood count. "I ordered some lab work, but I'd like to perform a pelvic exam so I can better visualize the bleeding. It can be hard to determine where blood is coming from in the pelvic area without an exam. Do you mind if I take a look? The exam should only take one or two minutes, and I promise to talk you through each step as I go."

"Okay," Vivian responded softly.

Keala moved around the room, collecting her supplies, and performed the exam without difficulty. She found a large amount of blood in the vaginal vault, which was clearly coming from the opening of Vivian's cervix. This furthered Keala's suspicions, but she didn't let it show on her face. No use adding to Vivian's worry just yet. She helped Vivian clean up and get comfortable before taking a seat. "I'm going to go speak with a colleague who works in gynecology and see if they can drop by to consult so we can get you taken care of. One of the nurses will be in to draw your labs, and I'll be back in a few minutes, okay?"

"Thank you so much." Vivian smiled, reclining against the seat.

Keala returned to the desk where she'd left her purse, grabbing her phone. She'd made it her mission at her last hospital and at Westfield Methodist to befriend the gynecology staff.

Almost six years ago, Ikaika's sister Malia had experienced some vaginal bleeding in her third trimester. Knowing she had placenta previa, her obstetrician told her to go to the hospital, and after spending the better part of a day on the maternal and fetal medicine floor with a heart monitor for the baby, she'd been transferred to labor and delivery for further observation.

After they'd run the usual tests and performed an ultrasound, they'd discovered her placenta previa had worsened. The part of the placenta with the blood vessels that connected Malia to her baby girl had shifted, covering her cervix and making it difficult for the baby to be delivered vaginally. The bleeding stopped, and Malia and Ikaika's family prepared for the possibility of a C-section. After a few days of normal activity, she'd been sent home on strict bed rest and told to return immediately if the bleeding came back or if her blood pressure spiked.

A few days later, she'd been rushed to the hospital in the middle of the night with spiked blood pressure and more bleeding than before. The baby wasn't moving and her heart rate had dropped. The on-call obstetrician was in an emergency C-section, and the hospital was short-staffed with no advanced practice providers like a nurse practitioner or physician assistant to help in the emergency department. They'd done the best they could, but while waiting for another obstetrician to arrive, Malia had died from blood loss and kidney failure as a result of HELLP syndrome she had developed suddenly.

Her baby girl had barely made it and now lived with the father.

Keala had only been twenty-one at the time, still in college. She had never been close to Malia, who was seven years older—they'd seen each other once or twice a year when Keala's family went to Hawaii to visit—but the news had still shocked Keala. After two weeks at home with family, Ikaika had shown up in Virginia completely distraught. Keala had never seen him so devastated, eyes glazed, guilt that he hadn't been there for Malia clear in everything he said and did. Keala had taken a few days off from school, dance, and her shadowing at the hospital to stay with him, her heart breaking all over again while she held him.

Maybe that was one of the reasons she'd decided to work in the emergency department. Either way, because of that, she'd made certain that as long as she was at the hospital, she would do everything in her power to prevent something like that from happening to anyone else. A piece of that was keeping an open line of communication with gynecology.

"Saw the order for room twenty-six's CBC. I'll get on that now," Annie called as she walked past the desk.

"Thank you!" Keala found her friend's contact information, knowing Genevieve would be able to put her in touch with a gynecologic oncologist.

"Hi, Keala. You doing okay?" Genevieve asked.

"I'm great, thank you. How are you?"

"The usual. Tired beyond belief." They shared a laugh.

"I wondered if you know anyone in GYN-ONC? I have a patient presenting with postmenopausal bleeding, a family history of gynecologic cancers, and fatigue, and I'd really appreciate a consult."

"Sounds like it could be endometrial cancer. Glad the patient came in. There's a PA, Camila. I can call and see if she'll head down to you."

"You're the best. Thank you!" After hanging up, Keala turned to Aaliyah, who sat at one of the desks. "I'm going to follow up with the patient in room nine. Could you let me know when a PA named Camila gets down here?"

"Of course!"

Keala continued her rounds. Although healthcare wasn't her passion, moments like this made her proud to be here. She was glad she could hasten the process for women like Vivian and Malia to get the care they needed swiftly.

Chapter Fourteen

Keala

Keala had two big reasons to be stressed about practice that evening. The first was that she'd stayed long after her shift ended yesterday and hadn't made it to Zoe's for an extra practice, which meant she might not be perfect today. The second was that Angelica would be at the choreography session tonight after practice, and all Keala had been able to come up with was what she'd thought up in the hospital closet yesterday plus a couple more beats.

Cora forgave unpreparedness to a certain extent. Angelica did not.

Attempting to meal prep, she seasoned her chicken while twirling around the kitchen, completing the choreography she'd strung together so far. She hoped if she continued working through it, the next steps would reveal themselves to her. So far, she hadn't had much luck.

"One, two, three, four, five, six, seven, eight," she muttered as she moved, rolling her hips and looking side to side. Picking up the baking sheet with the seasoned meat, she put it in to broil.

Keala put a fifteen-minute timer on her phone, like the online recipe told her to do. She figured she should prep her meals for the week to make sure she ate enough to keep her energy levels up. She wasn't the biggest fan of chicken and vegetables, but she also wasn't the world's greatest chef by any stretch of the imagination, so her choices were limited.

Back in her room, she ran through the first dance they would practice tonight from start to finish before going through the other three. The pregame dance was the same every game, but the other three were new pieces, which meant they had limited time to perfect them. Keala put in her wireless headphones and started moving.

She was beginning their halftime dances when a piercing, high-pitched noise sounded somewhere in the apartment. It was so loud, she could hear it clearly with headphones in, and when she took them out, she all but collapsed onto the floor as she attempted to cover her ears again.

"Ow, ow, ow, ow," she whispered, trying to figure out what could possibly be making so much noise. Her brain moved slowly, but finally she realized.

Her vegetables.

She had left her vegetables in when she'd started broiling the chicken. She was supposed to have taken them out.

Shit.

Keala stood, rushing into the kitchen. Sure enough, smoke billowed inside the oven, and she was certain she saw a hint of flames.

"Oh god. Oh no. This is so not good." What if she burned down Ikaika's apartment? He was going to throw her out and she would have to live out of her car. Or worse, with her parents.

She grabbed the oven mitt, ripping the oven door open as the front door slammed. Ikaika had come home from the facility early and was going to see the mess she'd made of his apartment, and that was going to be it. Trying to fix it any way she could, she pulled the baking sheet out and threw the vegetables into the sink, turning on the water to put out the small fire.

Her eyes burned. Her nose burned. She was glad Chowder hated her presence so much that she was probably downstairs in Ikaika's bedroom, well away from the smoke.

Keala turned, coughing, and took in Landon's tall form in the entry of the kitchen. All he had on was a pair of shorts and socks, thighs on full display.

My god. They were thick as tree trunks, and she could just make out the start of a tattoo disappearing underneath the hem of his shorts. She didn't know what she'd expected, but he was the most muscular man she'd ever seen. Strong forearms turned to stronger biceps, a full sleeve of tattoos from his left hand to his heart, where a butterfly and a date were located. Her eyes dropped to his abs and the trail of hair that disappeared into his shorts.

"Keala!" Landon waved a hand to get her attention. The fire alarm still screeched overhead, and she half read his lips. "Are you okay?"

She nodded. He walked around the island, taking stock of what had happened. Turning off the tap, he frowned at what had once been sweet potatoes, carrots, broccoli, and cauliflower. It was nothing but a charred lump now.

"What the hell happened?" he yelled.

"I was baking my veggies and forgot to take them out when I started broiling my chicken."

"You didn't smell them burning? They must have been smoking for a while before this."

Keala glared at him, not liking that he'd flown into her apartment to berate her. Something told her to be nice, but it was easier to let out her stream of consciousness. "Not that it's any of your business, but I was practicing because, unlike *you*,

I'm not a slacker. What are you doing here when the rest of the guys are at the facility?"

Something she couldn't identify flashed across Landon's face as he pulled on the oven mitt, taking out the chicken and setting it onto the island. If she could have heard over the sound of the smoke detector, she might have been able to discern her phone alarm going off. He grabbed a towel and used it to waft the smoke out, opening balcony doors while Keala stood in the kitchen, waiting for an explanation. Though she regretted being so rude to him when he was trying to help.

Even if he could have chosen his words better.

In an effort to assist him, she tried unlocking the large windows behind the kitchen sink, but nothing she did worked. After a few seconds, Keala felt Landon behind her, a hand on her lower back as he gently moved her out of the way, murmuring, "I got it."

It took him all of a couple of seconds to get them unlocked and open.

Landon turned to her, a small smile on his face. "Tuesdays are typically our day off. A lot of the guys go in to get food, but I like to cook my own meals when I get the chance, so I don't go in."

"Oh."

Now she felt bad, but where she might have apologized to someone else for jumping to conclusions, she couldn't bring herself to do so with him.

Over the last few days, Keala had been trying to figure out why she felt comfortable enough to be direct with him. To be a less perfect version of herself. Someone who didn't have to do everything right, who could lash out like others did, make mistakes and not worry about being left behind. Who didn't need to placate him for fear of escalation.

Maybe it was because he'd proved that he would stay in her life despite her messiness, despite the blunder she had made their first night together. Maybe it was the knowledge that he was aware of some of her darkest secrets and didn't seem to think less of her because of them. Whatever it was, she felt perfectly comfortable telling him exactly how she felt when she'd never been able to do the same with anyone else.

Testing the limits, checking to see how much of herself would end up being too much.

Keala did feel bad for calling him a slacker though. At least in this instance. She knew she should apologize.

She remembered how she'd felt when he had mentioned his mother on the couch a couple of days ago. Landon hadn't said much, but the way the light in his eyes had shuttered after a few moments—sputtered out as if the thought of her had blown out a burning candle—had unsettled her. He'd raised walls she hadn't known had come down, then thrown out a joke to cover his emotions, and she hated that it had made her want to know more about it.

About *him*.

"Doing an awful lot of thinking again," he said, tapping a finger against her temple gently, smiling down at her without any of his usual cockiness. "Climb out of there and come hang out with me."

Keala searched his face, watching his smile widen when she still didn't answer. "One second," she responded, realizing the smoke detector had stopped. It reminded her to turn off her alarm and close Chowder in Ikaika's bedroom to prevent her from going out on the balcony.

When she came back, Landon asked, "Do you want some help cooking?"

She wanted to say no, to keep pushing, but even she could see that she was wrong for what she'd said.

"Okay," she mumbled. Clearing her throat, she nodded. "Sure. Thank you."

"Do you have more veggies? I can order more if not."

Keala opened the fridge and pulled out the other half of the vegetables she'd purchased from the grocery store across the street. If things hadn't gone so poorly, it would have all been enough for a week's worth of meals, but now she would be lucky to stretch it for three to four days.

Landon chopped them swiftly.

"Do you cook a lot?" she asked, watching the deft movement of his hands, like a musician playing a familiar tune. The sparrow on his hand looked like it was taking flight, and the words across it that read "to the moon and back" were more tender than Keala could have ever imagined from him.

"I try to. I find I like the quality and taste better than the facility meals, and this way, I know my exact macros. Which, yes, we have nutritionists who are keeping track of that stuff but..." He shrugged. "I don't know. I like doing it myself."

Keala pulled the paper with charred vegetables off the baking sheet, tossing it into the trash before cleaning the tray. Her cheeks burned when she remembered that this was now the second time she had embarrassed herself in his presence. She hoped this didn't become standard practice.

She set the tray down, adding another paper liner to it.

"Did you teach yourself?"

Landon stepped beside her, and her breath caught for a millisecond as he added the chopped vegetables onto the tray. "My mom taught me. She was a great cook, and though I was always busy with football, the kitchen was the one place we got to spend time together."

Keala tucked that past tense "was" into a file in her mind. No wonder he'd seemed to shut down after his mother had come up in conversation Sunday evening.

"That's sweet, actually."

Landon smirked. "I *am* capable of being slightly less of an ass sometimes."

Keala rolled her eyes, pouring olive oil over the vegetables. "Sure. Like, two percent of the time."

"You make it so easy."

"To be an ass?"

He nodded, grabbing the spices she'd left on the counter and handing them to her. "Has anybody ever told you it's fun to get under your skin?"

"Never." But she'd also never let anybody *know* they were under her skin.

"You're telling me I'm special because I'm the only person in your life who bothers you like this?"

Keala seasoned while he took a knife to the chicken. "I wouldn't use the word *special*. You're just in my space all the time and love the sound of your own voice. Annoying me is inevitable with that combination."

"Ah, so you were sent to humble me."

"You do need a healthy dose of humbling."

"Don't worry. You running out on our one night of fun was plenty humbling. Job well done."

She glared at him, though he had that lopsided smirk on his face and was obviously joking. Keala remembered how forward he'd been when asking her out the other night, talking about finishing that "one night of fun." The thought excited her more than she could comprehend, but it was a bad idea.

"And you're back to being an ass."

He shrugged. "What can I say? You only gave me two percent. I'm running with it."

Ignoring him, she changed the settings on the oven, double- and then triple-checking that they were set properly for the vegetables.

"I'd better do that," he joked. Landon took the sheet from her and placed it in, reviewing the settings once more. "The chicken's perfect. Do you have containers I can put these into?"

Keala hadn't thought that far ahead. "Oh, I...damn. Let me run downstairs to get some."

"No need. I have a ton. Be right back." He turned, placing his hands on her shoulders. She stiffened at the contact and at being so close to his muscled chest, the scent of pine just poking its head through the smell of smoke. "Don't burn down the place while I'm gone." He turned and moved out of the kitchen.

"Shut up! And put on a damn shirt."

His head popped back into the room, dimple on full display as he laughed. "You might have been sent to humble me, but you can't deny the sway of my rock-hard pecs."

"I hate you." But she also couldn't disagree because her request had been a plea for her own sanity.

A couple of minutes later, he returned with a few glass containers, and to Keala's chagrin, an apron. It read *This guy rubs his own meat.* She started to ask about it but thought better of it.

"So, who taught you how to set a kitchen on fire?"

Keala added some rice from the rice cooker to the containers, then added the chicken Landon had sliced for her. "My mom is also a great cook. I didn't inherit the gene or the interest. I'm more of a premade salad or frozen meal person since I'm so busy, but I finished up some social media work early and decided to try." She smiled down at the counter shyly. "It went about as well as I'd expected, all things considered."

Even as a child, Keala had pushed herself to her limits, making sure she was always boasting crazy hours and achieving as much as she could to compensate for the fact that she wasn't as naturally smart as Akoni. It was no surprise that cooking had never been of particular importance to her.

"So should I expect the building to go up in flames any day now? Will this be a weekly occurrence? Because we do have Thursday games, you know. I might not always be off on Tuesdays."

"Don't worry, I'll find the fire extinguisher."

"Good. Because I have a vested interest in this place now, you know?"

"Yes, I kind of figured that when I walked into you mid-move."

Landon chuckled, opening the oven to check on the vegetables. "You were so pissed when you saw me, I thought you were gonna go full homicide."

"Yeah, 'cause I'm the type of person who would commit a crime," she muttered sarcastically.

"No? I could've sworn I saw your mugshot at the police station for arson. Very pretty, by the way."

"Oh my god, will you go away?" She shoved him, but he didn't budge. Her embarrassment meter was going to be full for the foreseeable future.

"I can't until the vegetables are out. You haven't proven to me that you know where the extinguisher is, and until then, I'll handle the veggies."

One of the three sets of balcony doors creaked shut from the September breeze, and Keala walked over to close them now that the smoke had dissipated. She was sure Chowder was most displeased at being closed into a room, so she made her way downstairs to free her.

Just as she'd thought, the moment Keala opened the bedroom door, Chowder went running up the stairs, upset meows drowning out the pitter patter of her paws as she found Landon and rubbed against his leg.

"Him you like? But the person who gives you food every time she eats gets screamed at?"

"Chowder's very particular."

"I can tell."

When the vegetables were finally in the containers and safely in the fridge, Landon shut the windows and locked them with a self-satisfied smirk. He shouldered past Keala, his hand just brushing against hers as he passed her in the kitchen entryway.

Pulling open the front door, he kept that smile as he said, "When you're ready for something more advanced that tastes a hell of a lot better, I'm across the hall."

And then he was gone. Chowder glared at her like it was her fault.

Chapter Fifteen

Keala

When Keala got back from practice the next evening, she was met with the smell of curry powder and something spicy. Chowder stared daggers at her from the couch, even after Keala made a silly face at her. Resigned to the fact that the little devil would never like her, Keala dropped her dance bag off in her room and headed to the kitchen.

She was surprised to smell *anything* cooking, since Ikaika exclusively ate what the facility provided them, and was shocked further when she saw her cousin sitting at the island, Landon stirring a pot on the stove in front of him. When their eyes met, Landon smiled knowingly, like they shared a secret.

Which she supposed they did.

"Hey, Keeks." Ikaika jumped up, wrapping an arm around her shoulders. "Practice go well?"

"Yep. Since you guys are away for the next couple of weeks, we get to work through new choreo a little slower than when you're at home." She paused, taking in the dishes on the counters. "What's up?"

"Landon has decided that I need to 'learn what real food tastes like,' a comment which Mom won't take too kindly to."

"Woah." Landon pointed at Ikaika with the silicone spatula. "I'm not insulting anybody's cooking. I've just been with you almost every day for the last fourteen months and haven't seen you eat anything but facility food. So I'm making yellow curry."

That was oddly...sweet.

Maybe she was reading too far into it, but she knew the Sentinels' food budget was absurdly large, which meant their food was very high quality. It sounded to her like Landon was trying to make Ikaika a home-cooked meal.

She was definitely reading too far into it.

"You hungry?" Ikaika asked.

"Oh, that's okay. I've got some food in the fridge already." Keala shared another look with Landon, his smirk only slightly less annoying to her than it had been a few days ago. "Plus, I'm tired, so I'll probably shower and sleep."

"I'm making plenty if you want some for tomorrow." Landon chuckled. "Or if you get hungry in the middle of the night."

"Why is that funny?"

"I don't know. I'm just picturing you in your Vipers pajamas, prowling through the hallway, trying to be quiet while you heat up food." There was a smile on his face as he joked, but something in his eyes made her feel warm.

Keala scoffed. "Don't picture me in my pajamas." She couldn't respond to the other part because he wasn't far off. When she hadn't been able to fall asleep a few nights ago, she'd gotten out of bed, made herself some popcorn, and watched a strange movie about aliens.

Ikaika tried to suppress a laugh, which was confirmation that he'd heard her the other night.

"It's not my fault Ikaika's such a light sleeper."

Ikaika laughed harder. "I don't know if I'd call it prowling. For someone who's so nimble and graceful when they dance, you're surprisingly loud walking from your room to the kitchen."

Keala's jaw dropped. "How...how dare you. I will not stand for this abuse. Good night!" she called over her shoulder. She disappeared into the hall, their laughter only intensifying as she left.

Thursday evening, they tried a Smash tournament, which ended with a lot of yelling and a spoon flying over Landon's head. Keala did *not* apologize.

By the time she returned from work and practice at Zoe's on Friday night, the guys had already left for Los Angeles.

The next week, they fell into an easy rhythm. When Keala came home from wherever she was—dance most nights—she found Landon and Ikaika on the couch, sometimes eating food Landon made, more often eating food from the facility, and almost always watching football or playing video games. She usually joined them after a shower, careful not to wear her Vipers pajamas for fear it would lead to a heated glance that would then end in some serious self care.

Which she was embarrassed to admit she'd been needing more of the longer she spent around Landon.

After her shower, she pretended to care about the teams that were playing, or that she knew what she was doing in the video game they'd chosen for the evening. Often, she found herself falling asleep on the couch.

Thursday night, right around midnight, she woke to the hallway light on, her legs across Landon's lap, Ikaika nowhere to be found. As she carefully extracted her legs from his sleeping form, his eyes opened drowsily, and the slow, easy grin he shot her made her stomach tumble.

"Good night," he mumbled. Keala felt his eyes on her as she walked away.

She was glad they were already on the way to New York when she got back from work the next night, thankful to have some space from him.

The week after seemed to drag. Their Sunday home game against Arizona meant practices were longer and more intense, and she barely got to see Ikaika, let alone Landon.

Friday morning, she tried starting her car but heard it sputter and then die. Noting her battery light was on, she called Ikaika.

"Hello?" he answered sleepily.

"I'm so sorry. I think I need a jump."

He said something quietly, and when Keala asked him to repeat himself, he said, "Chowder's lying on me. I don't want to move. I'll send Landon down."

Before she even had a chance to respond, Ikaika hung up the phone. A few minutes later, Landon entered their private garage using Ikaika's fob, a Sentinels sweatshirt hood pulled over his head.

Keala popped the hood of her car while he grabbed jumper cables from Ikaika's, then she sidled up to him while he got to work. "You're up early," she murmured. Keala had planned to go to a workout class at five thirty since she and some of the girls were only doing a run-through at Zoe's after her shift. But now she guessed she'd be taking her car to the shop.

"I exclusively wake up for damsels in distress. I shot awake moments before Ikaika called me." He chuckled when she rolled her eyes. "I don't know. Haven't been sleeping as well as usual. I guess it may be a product of wanting to do well during games. It's a new experience."

"Landon Beaumont gets anxious? I'm shocked."

He grinned, done attaching the cables. "I know. Tell no one. I like you too much to have to dispose of your lovely body." Landon glanced down appreciatively at the workout set that hugged her curves. "Your *very* lovely body."

"You're hopeless." Still, her stomach did that dumb tumble again.

"Hopelessly ready for you to finally say yes to finishing what we started."

"Landon, it's five in the morning. And if you think getting my car working means I'm giving you anything, you're out of your mind."

His face morphed to a look of disgust. "I would never expect something out of you for giving you a jump. My god. Who do you think I am?"

"Someone who shamelessly flirts with me before the sun rises."

Landon walked to the driver's side of Ikaika's car. Before he ducked down to start it, he glanced at her. "You're telling me I can shamelessly flirt with you as soon as the sun rises? Buckle up, Keeks. You're in for it now."

She snorted. "Just start my damn car." When he didn't move, she rolled her eyes again and sighed. "*Please.*"

His lips twitched. "Is begging not included in the flirting category?" Her eyes narrowed, and he ducked into the driver's side.

When her car was operational, he pulled the cables off and tucked them back into the trunk of Ikaika's car. Coming up beside her, he pointed to her dashboard. "Might just be your battery, but it could be your alternator."

Keala nodded, having assumed as much. "Yeah, I'll take it in so they can check it out."

"Do you want me to follow you to the shop? I can take you to work. Or wherever."

Here he was again, shocking her. Being sweet. It was unsettling.

"It's probably best if I find another way. With any luck, it'll just be the battery. It's so early that they might be able to get me in and out before work."

Reluctantly, he nodded. "See you tonight. Be safe."

They shared a look that lasted a beat longer than it needed to, and then she was on her way, shaking thoughts of him out of her head.

Chapter Sixteen

Landon

> **ESPN notification –** Colton Beaumont's undefeated Sabertooths take the league by storm. Can they keep their rhythm going throughout the season?

> **ESPN notification –** The Sentinels may be undefeated after three games, but Landon Beaumont's efforts on the field, or lack thereof, have been average at best. Which receivers could benefit San Jose more? See here...

Game four was supposed to have been an easy win against Arizona at home, but as the third quarter drew to a close, the Sentinels were still down three. The offensive line wasn't giving Myles enough time to get the ball out, and when they did, his receivers dropped or fumbled it, making it impossible to score.

Landon included. He had been no help all game.

What was worse? He had done something he'd promised himself he would stop doing.

Landon knew Maya and Colton had all but cut their father off, and Landon had made a real effort to avoid his calls after games, knowing it would only lead to more anger and resentment on his part. There was nothing good that could come of interactions with his father, but today he'd slipped up. That childlike part of Landon's brain that still held on to the hope that his father wasn't the monster they'd made him out to be had battled for purchase within him, leading him to make a mistake.

But old habits die hard, and Landon had found that out in the worst way.

Answering a post-game call from his father would inevitably snowball into conversations about his game that he didn't much care to discuss. While Landon enjoyed football, it wasn't the biggest, most important piece of his life the way it had always been for Colton. At least, before Lucia and their daughter, Lyla, had come into the picture.

But it was so rare that his father called *before* a game that a part of him had been clinging to the hope that maybe, *just maybe*, his father had been calling to wish him luck. To give him some kind of peace since he couldn't be there in the stands the way he always was for Colton.

He'd thought his father finally saw him, considered him more than the spare son in his back pocket for when the "chosen one" eventually retired.

It hadn't taken long for Landon to realize he'd been wrong. The conversation had started with his father griping about not being allowed to sit in Colton's family box but had quickly devolved into insults. Landon had heard them all before, but it hit harder because he'd gone in with hope. Like he had promised himself he would stop doing.

His father was merely looking for a puppet, and Landon had been trying to cut the last of his strings for years.

"Don't you ever get tired of being the second-best Beaumont child? Doesn't it bother you? You could at least try *to care."*

Sure, Landon didn't put his all into football. Why would he have? He had more to live for than a sport that never seemed to pay him back in kind, and no matter what he'd done, he had never been good enough anyway. Keala had said it herself, Landon was a *slacker.*

That word, spoken from the mouth of a woman he'd grown to admire in a way he wasn't yet comfortable digging into, had hurt worse than any of the venom his father had spewed over the years. It was salt in a wound his father had created, and it had *burned.*

He wanted her to see him as more. Had been trying harder on the field to prove to her that he *was* more.

The problem was that he'd tried so hard for so much of his early life until it had become clear it wouldn't pay off. His father didn't treat him any differently, and even when he made catches that were practically impossible to make, the quarterback would get lauded as the MVP. Especially when Colton was throwing it, like in high school and college.

So what was the point of trying?

At least if he didn't try, didn't give it his all and just continued with his self-destructive defensive mechanisms, no one would expect more of him and he'd never fall short of their already low expectations. And if he *did* do something well, it was a pleasant surprise for all.

It was better to disappoint people on purpose than to make an effort and miss the mark, failing them when he was trying to do anything but.

"Beaumont, get in there, damn it." Landon was shoved onto the field. He ran to the huddle, listening to Myles call a rush play, then got set on the line to block, face to face with an outside linebacker.

The moment the ball was snapped, Landon extended his arms to prevent the linebacker from reaching Ikaika, expecting a combination block with Jaxon, a Sentinels right tackle. Instead, Jaxon moved toward another backer up the field, and the one Landon had been blocking chopped his arms down, cut up into the backfield, and blew up the play, tackling Ikaika before he could cross the line of scrimmage.

The linebacker stood, flexing his biceps for the booing crowd before getting in Landon's face. "Too bad you got stuck with this shit team while your brother wins championship after championship. Maybe if you could block better, you'd be—"

The Arizona linebacker didn't have a chance to finish his sentence before Landon shoved him. In a matter of a few seconds, both of their helmets were off, and he was exchanging blows with the guy, getting in as many punches as he could as they wrestled each other to the ground. Ikaika had even jumped in, which was entirely uncharacteristic of him.

Landon felt himself being pulled up and away from Arizona's players, whether by a referee or a teammate, he couldn't tell. He was more than pissed. It was bad enough he had to hear that shit from his own father, from the media, constantly having it bouncing around in his head. The last thing he needed was to hear it on the field from a low-life, attention-seeking bastard on a worse team than him.

The flags that flew came as no surprise, and Landon was sure he was about to get thrown out of the game. It only took a second for the referee to confirm he was right. "After the play, personal foul, unnecessary roughness, San Jose Sentinels number eighty-three. Fifteen-yard penalty. Number eighty-three for San Jose has been ejected."

Coach Boyer, the tight-end coach, shook his head as Landon headed to the locker room to change out of his pads. He knew he would be in a world of trouble after the game, but unfortunately for the coaches, Landon didn't care in the slightest.

Ikaika stayed on the sideline, his face set in a scowl, and Landon wondered why he'd jumped in.

Ikaika and Landon were alike in many ways. They liked football, they liked partying, and they loved women. But where Landon dabbled in the occasional recreational drug and got into fights on and off the field when he got into these moods, Ikaika never joined.

At least he hadn't been ejected too.

Landon spent the remainder of the game in the locker room, his chin in his hands and his head a storm of thoughts roaring through him, each centered around being his family's greatest disappointment.

He wondered how much of that same disappointment he would detect on Keala's face when he saw her next, knowing she had witnessed it all from the sideline. Landon was always on high alert for that look, primed and ready to identify it in all the people in his life.

For some reason, the thought of it on her was worse. *So much worse* than anything his family or his team could possibly have thought about him.

Letting her down *meant* something to him, and he hated it.

Landon didn't remember how he and his teammates had ended up at this club despite knowing he hadn't had all that much to drink. He'd been in his head all night, isolating himself from his teammates who, he was sure, partially blamed him for their loss. If not entirely.

He went out with the guys after games sometimes, but he hadn't been as motivated to do so the last few weeks. The looks he imagined on his family members' faces and his coach yelling at him after the game had been enough to change that.

Maybe those things should have fueled him, pushed him toward a more straight and narrow path. Instead, it had the opposite effect. Landon wanted to drown his sorrows in the burn of alcohol, pushing himself toward the brink of blissful ignorance, even if just for one night.

Landon had expected Ikaika to go home after the game, already having participated in one entirely out-of-character thing for the night. But instead, he'd joined the team.

The pair were seated at a table with four women they didn't know, nor did they care to get to know. His friend's scowl hadn't budged since the game, and he'd hardly responded to the incessant line of questioning coming from the short woman with red hair next to him.

The brunette beside Landon inched closer and closer to his lap, and it took a moment of thought to know he didn't want anything to do with her. Sex was not on his mind at the moment, and if it had been, there was only one person he wanted. Maybe he could get this woman's number and call after he found a way to get Keala out of his system, but even the thought made his stomach turn.

Why prolong the inevitable? Might as well go home and get this over with, knowing Keala would become another person who couldn't bear the sight of him and his many fuckups. "Ik, you want to go?"

Ikaika nodded, and they said their goodbyes to their teammates before heading outside.

The chill in the air seeped into them, causing Landon to shiver as he dug around in his pocket, pulling his phone out. "I'll call a car."

"Don't bother," Ikaika said, waving a dismissive hand through the air. "I can drive back. That's why I drove here in the first place," he added, his voice gruff.

"Are you sure?" Landon had been sitting beside Ikaika most of the hour they'd been at the bar, and his friend had drunk at least a beer.

"Yes," Ikaika grunted, leaving no room for argument. Landon trusted Ikaika with his life, and if he said he was safe to drive, Landon believed him.

He followed Ikaika to his Porsche Panamera, and as Landon swayed on his feet through the parking garage, it was clear that while his friend might have been safe to drive, *he* most certainly was not.

He slid into the passenger seat, buckling himself in. Ikaika did the same and started the car with ease. Landon turned his attention back to his phone, checking notifications he'd missed over the last few hours.

His father hadn't deigned to so much as text him, not even to berate him. Even *that* would have been too much to ask for since he was obviously too disgusted to waste a single brain cell on his youngest son. There were, however, messages from Savannah, Maya, and his grandparents checking to see if he was okay.

His fingers shook as he formulated an answer to his sister, typing and then deleting the response only to start over again. *What does someone say after beating someone up on live television?*

The tell-tale sign of his sister's worry was evident in the three dots that appeared and disappeared. She was doing the same thing he was. Trying to come up with a response that would ultimately fall short because there was nothing to say. He sent a quick "all good" and switched to the conversation with his grandparents.

Nausea roiled in Landon's stomach as his body was thrust in the opposite direction of his head, his phone slipping from his fingers and falling to the floorboard of Ikaika's car. His eyes widened and he steeled his spine, pressing his feet into the car below him as he white knuckled the handle above his head.

One moment, they were on the road, Landon's head buried in thoughts that seemed insignificant now, the next, they were swerving, dodging a car and spinning out.

They barreled toward a concrete guardrail on the small stretch of highway, Ikaika slamming his foot on the brake, miraculously managing to slow the car down. It wasn't enough though.

A split second before they made impact, Ikaika's arm swung out, plastering itself to Landon's chest, preventing him from feeling the full force of the airbags deploying.

The wind was knocked out of his lungs, and he sat there panting, overcome with an uncomfortable mix of fear and appreciation that things hadn't been worse.

Landon's muscles ached, his neck sore and his head pounding as his pulse beat against his temples. The pain throbbed, radiating throughout his body.

"Fuck," Ikaika groaned, head in his hands.

"Are you okay?" Landon asked his friend, his tone frantic as the shock wore off.

"Damn it," he grunted. "I'm fine. Fuck!" Ikaika was frustrated, likely more with himself than anything else. Landon couldn't help but internally shoulder some of the blame for him.

A rush of relief swam through Landon's blood that Ikaika was okay enough to be frustrated, but so did the subsequent guilt making its way to the forefront of his mind. Why hadn't he pushed harder for them to call a car? He would have never forgiven himself if something bad had happened to Ikaika.

If Keala hadn't hated him before, she certainly would now.

Working in silence, they pushed the deployed airbags down enough to extract themselves from the vehicle. Once outside, Ikaika's face fell further, taking in the significant damage.

Landon had never seen so much concern in his friend's eyes. "Landon, I don't want to have another issue today. I'm fined for the fight and I know my family is going to see that. I can't let them see this too. It would kill them, especially right now."

Landon didn't know what Ikaika meant by "especially right now," but he didn't want to agitate his friend further by asking. He thought through their options. "I can have Seb work on it. Find us a ride and he'll get everything else taken care of," he responded, knowing his agent had dealt with far worse with far more difficult clients. Ikaika nodded and stepped away to make his call.

"Hey, Seb?"

"The hell did you do now, Beaumont?" Landon's agent answered, his no-nonsense tone more terse tonight after the fight Landon was sure he'd seen.

"Small car accident, run-in with a guardrail. No injuries and no one else involved. The car we avoided hitting is gone, so for now, it looks like we're in the clear." Landon glanced at Ikaika, whose shoulders were slumped, hand rubbing his brow as he spoke into his phone quickly. "It was my bad. Can you make sure the media doesn't catch wind of it?"

"That *is* part of my job," Seb grumbled, and Landon was thankful he had found such a gem of an agent who had done so much for him.

"You're the best. I'll send you the location. Just, uh…" He looked around nervously, clearing his throat. "Probably should get a move on before this gets any harder to clean up."

"Yeah, yeah. It's more important that you get out of there before people show up."

"Already on it." Landon inclined his head to Ikaika, and they walked down the side of the highway, making their way to the small gas station at the next exit. Landon texted the information to Seb as they walked, then waited for Ikaika to finish his call.

"Keala's on her way."

Landon nodded. He hadn't thought he'd be forced to see her so soon after the night had taken this turn, but it made sense that Ikaika had chosen her. Except now that the inevitable was approaching, Landon knew he wasn't ready to see her.

They'd fallen into an easy routine over the last few weeks. The night she had drifted off with her legs in his lap, he'd sat there waiting for her to wake up. When she hadn't, he'd decided to try sleeping upright. A part of him wished they could have slept like that all night.

And when he'd gotten her car started a couple of days ago? There had been something simmering there. Sure, he'd been overtly flirty, loving the way her freckled cheeks lit up in annoyance, but something else had lingered between them.

That would all be gone now. Surely, she'd be pissed, and that made him more upset with himself than anything else.

It was a feeling he couldn't fathom, so unfamiliar and terrifying, he was scared to look at it head on.

Chapter Seventeen

Landon

ESPN notification – Colton Beaumont leads Sabertooths to beautiful win over Atlanta in their week four game. Here are some key takeaways...

Bay Area News 5 – Landon Beaumont throws punches at Arizona linebacker in the third quarter of a devastating week four loss. Is head coach Ray Landers finally ready to accept Beaumont is a liability and needs to go?

Keala didn't say a word as she pulled up beside them, her face betraying nothing. They piled into her car, Ikaika in the passenger seat, Landon behind her, hoping to avoid her disapproving glare.

Several tense moments passed before Keala spoke, cutting through the thick silence. "Did either of you hit your head?"

"I don't think so," Ikaika mumbled.

Landon opted for humor in hopes of settling some of the building unease. "Nope. I couldn't have, not with how Ik hit me across the chest."

"So, to be clear, neither of you hit your head?"

"I didn't," Ikaika confirmed again.

"Me neither," Landon responded quietly.

"Good. Do either of you have a headache?"

"No," they answered in unison.

The next several minutes of the drive was spent with Keala calmly, if not tersely, assessing them for signs of shock, internal bleeding, or something equally insidious. She must have been satisfied with their answers, because by the time they arrived home and got into the elevator, her line of questioning had come to an end.

Once inside, Keala disappeared into her room. Landon sat beside Ikaika on the couch, his head hanging low. When she returned, she had a stethoscope, pen light, and blood pressure cuff.

"Landon, turn off the lights."

He complied. She shined the pen light in Ikaika's eyes with her hand split down the bridge of his nose, then did the same to Landon. He knew she was checking for a concussion, something he'd been assessed for many times after practices and games.

Next, she made quick work of inspecting Ikaika's injuries. His knuckles had bruised but, unlike Landon's, hadn't split open.

When Keala finished, Landon looked away while she hugged her cousin tightly, murmuring something to him. Ikaika hadn't spoken much since they'd left the scene of the crash, answering Keala's questions with clipped responses. Landon couldn't help wondering if his friend was upset with him. But maybe there was something more going on that Landon wasn't privy to.

Chowder hadn't left Ikaika's side since they'd gotten home. He picked her up, said a quick good night, and went to his room, leaving Landon and Keala alone.

Landon stood, heading to the kitchen to avoid the conversation he'd been dreading all night. To his dismay, Keala followed him, carrying her things with her.

"Get comfortable." She nodded toward the island, putting her hair up. As she washed her hands thoroughly and dried them with a paper towel, Landon hopped onto the counter. He tracked her movements, his spine rigid as he waited for her to yell at him. She refused to make eye contact, and all Landon could think was that the moment of truth was coming.

When she finally met his eyes, she said nothing. Like he had anticipated, he detected a level of disappointment mixed with something he couldn't discern. Landon couldn't imagine what she was thinking.

To break the tension, he joked, "Everything I touch turns to shit."

Leaning back against the other counter beside the sink, she sighed. "Okay, reverse Midas."

Was she joking? He couldn't tell, but if there was a way for him to use humor to prevent the conversation from coming, he would. "I'm not sure the opposite of gold is shit."

She pointed at him, her lips fighting to keep a frown on her face. "Don't. Don't you try to make me laugh when I'm upset with you."

There it is.

"Why are you upset with me?"

Keala rolled her eyes. "Take your shirt off. I need to check for injuries."

A joke was on the tip of Landon's tongue, but he thought better of it as her glare grew more irate. He tried to brush off her request, unsure of how he would handle the confusing concoction of Keala both upset with him and flustered by his near nakedness. "Nah, I'm sure it's nothing serious. Some bruising and a few scratches. My knees feel pretty banged up, but that's the worst of it."

When she crossed her arms, he shrugged, unbuttoning the linen shirt he'd put on after the game to expose the bruise on his chest. Keala took a couple of steps toward him, his legs on either side of her body. The bruise hadn't fully bloomed, a faint reddish purple whose shape mimicked the strap of his seatbelt.

Her fingertips trailed over it gently, as if she didn't realize what she was doing. Landon was acutely aware, goosebumps erupting in her wake.

"Why?" she murmured.

"Why what?" he whispered back, trying not to jump as her featherlight yet frigid fingers brushed over his chest.

Earnest eyes met his, and he was shocked by the concern in them. "I know why Ikaika acted the way he did today. Fighting and driving under the influence." She dropped her gaze to his hands, where they rested in his lap. She grabbed them, inspecting his knuckles. "What's your excuse?"

Her proximity was driving him crazy, the smell of vanilla lingering in the air between them. When he didn't respond, Keala gathered her first-aid kit from below the sink. She cleaned her hands with hand sanitizer, then pulled out a packet with a pair of gloves. "Are you allergic to nitrile?"

"No."

After setting gauze and other supplies onto the counter, she slipped her small hands into the blue rubber material. Busying herself, she sprayed his knuckles with a saline rinse, allowing it to sit for a few moments while she gathered pieces of gauze to wipe off the dried blood.

Landon's lips contorted in pain, the rough fabric pulling at his skin despite how gentle she was being. Once clean and dry, she used a cotton-tipped applicator to swipe the wounds with petroleum jelly. She laid the gauze across one hand and peered up at him, catching his intent stare. He didn't so much as blink, not wanting to miss a single moment of her so close to him.

"Hold here while I wrap," she instructed. He listened, and she repeated the steps on his other hand.

Landon was desperate to avoid the question he'd ignored. Instead, he asked, "Why did Ikaika do it? Is something going on?"

Keala glanced up at him, her face only a few inches from his. Realizing that, she moved away, backing toward the freezer. She pulled the door open, grabbing two small ice packs and saran wrap from the drawer beside him, returning to her place between his thighs.

As she wrapped his hands with the ice, she spoke. "Ikaika's sister passed away a few years ago. Six years ago today, actually." Her eyebrows rose, like the number surprised her. Like she still felt the pain, the sadness, like it had happened yesterday. "He didn't tell you?"

"No," he answered quietly. He and Ikaika were as close as they could be for two people who didn't talk about their feelings. He wished he had known.

She set his hands in his lap, her fingers brushing over his leg. Landon closed his eyes from the contact, reveling in the feel of her smooth skin against his.

"Sorry," she said, seeming to shake a thought from her head. She told him how Ikaika's sister had died in the third trimester of her pregnancy, recounting every detail as if she had been there for it all, her eyes glassy.

God, Landon was such an asshole. He'd had a fight with his dad and acted like a child; meanwhile, his best friend had been dealing with something so much worse.

He swallowed around the lump forming in his throat, choking out his next words. "I'm so sorry."

Keala gave him a soft smile. "It was harder on Ikaika. He'd been sent to live with us for half of his childhood and then stayed on the mainland for college, so he spent a lot of time away from his family. I think he blames himself for being away, but a team of highly qualified medical professionals weren't able to save her. There's nothing he could have done."

Landon sighed, looking down at his wrapped hands, numbing more by the minute.

"So, what's your excuse?" she repeated faintly.

"Doesn't matter. I shouldn't have done it. If I had known what he was dealing with, I never would've..." He sighed again. He could have done better, *been* better for his friend today, had he known. He could have avoided his father's taunting and focused his energy on Ikaika instead. Prevented the fight in the first place—the fight that had broken out as a result of Landon's poor attitude and desire to see the good in his father even when he'd learned long ago he shouldn't.

October third. He'd never forget it. He wouldn't bring it up though. If the roles were reversed, he wouldn't have wanted Ikaika to. And since his friend was even more emotionally reserved than him, he was sure it was for the best. Every year from now on, though, he would make sure he was there for his friend.

Keala studied him intently. Her eyes drifted over his features, and when he smiled, about to say something only a cocky asshole like him would, she held up a hand. "Don't. Don't be a dick. If you don't want to be vulnerable with me, that's fine. But don't act like nothing's wrong. That may work with Ikaika and everyone else in your life, but all it does is make me want to hit you."

Landon blinked at her in a daze. No one had ever called him out for his behavior except Maya, and even she allowed him his humor. It was his coping mechanism when things got serious because he was sure no one wanted to see the side of him that had feelings. He'd built his entire life, his entire personality, around that fact.

And yet here she stood, an inch or two from the counter where he sat, between his knees, her chest heaving with emotion. He didn't know if it was from anger or standing so close to him. What he did know was that he wanted her to stay there, maybe get closer, and he wanted to prove that he could let down some of the walls he'd spent so much of his life building up around himself.

"My dad called before the game. I always tell myself not to expect anything from his calls because, more often than not, it's a ploy to pit me and my brother against each other. Or to make me feel badly about not being as good as Colton. But he never calls me *before* games, so I thought maybe he had..."

Landon flexed his right hand, grimacing at the twinge of pain he still felt despite the soothing numbness the ice provided. "It was dumb. It *is* dumb. Now that I know about Ikaika, I feel like such an idiot. My dad said some shit about how I'm a disappointment to him. That's nothing new. In fact, it's old news." He shook his head. "I don't know why I do it. I don't know why I got pissed off and hit the guy. I think with him talking shit about me not being as good as Colton, it just pushed me over the edge when combined with everything my dad had said and all that I think about myself..."

Landon trailed off, realizing that not only was this his first time genuinely letting someone see the hidden, dark, and messy parts of himself, but he was telling her entirely too much. As a child, talking about emotions had, at best, ended in nothing changing for him. At worst, it'd ended with his father telling him how discouraging it was to have a son who was too emotional to focus on being the best he could be like his brother. And on the rare occasions Landon had spent time with his mother, it had been in the kitchen, relieving the stress of the day enough that he hadn't felt the need to talk about his feelings.

He didn't know why he'd said so much. He should have kept his mouth shut. Something about the way she'd been tending to him, or maybe it was the alcohol, made the confession feel easy. Like a breath of fresh air. Like walking out into the sun for the first time after being in the cold shade for too long. But Landon knew, right about now, Keala would back away slowly and say something about wishing he had stuck to being a dick.

To avoid that, he said, "I'm sorry for being an asshole today. I shouldn't have gotten into a fight. I shouldn't have let Ikaika join me. And I sure as shit shouldn't have let him drive. I should have insisted we call a car."

He held his breath, waiting for her to say good night. Knowing her opinion of him was probably getting worse.

Keala exhaled, and when Landon finally looked up at her, she was a step closer, breathing the same air as him. She pretended to examine the bruise on his chest again, but he knew there was nothing she could do but tell him to ice it.

"You're not an asshole despite what I may have said. You're human. You have good and bad days like everyone else. Being upset for how your father treated you is completely valid. Though, maybe you could refrain from punching people," she joked, lips quirking up into a small smile. It dropped as she stepped back, pulling off the gloves and throwing them into the trash. "And maybe you should stop answering your dad. He sounds like an ass."

Landon blinked. Then blinked again. Had he heard her correctly? Not only was she not confirming all of his greatest fears, but she was also validating his emotions in a way no one else had ever bothered to.

Maybe it wasn't the feelings themselves that were a problem but who he expressed them to.

And maybe Maya was right. Maybe therapy *would* do him some good.

Something new, completely apart from disappointment, shone in her eyes, and he wanted to bottle it and keep it for later. *Forever.* He wanted whatever she was thinking about him in this moment to eclipse all the bad that she'd seen in him.

And, *damn it,* he wanted to kiss her again.

After washing her hands, she gravitated back to him, like she felt it too.

"You're not mad at me?" he asked.

"I'm not happy with you. I wish Ikaika hadn't been brought into either of the things that happened tonight because I know he's going to regret it all tomorrow. Especially if anything comes out about the accident. It'll devastate his parents, and that will devastate him."

"It won't come out. I'll make sure of it."

Her eyes bounced between his. "But no." She paused. "I'm not mad at you. He's a grown man and is accountable for his own actions. Neither of you had a good day, and while that's not an excuse, it's you two who will have to deal with the consequences."

Landon nodded, gathering her hand in his. He had meant to give it a brief squeeze to thank her for what she'd done for him, but as if his hand had a mind of its own, he pulled her closer until she stood right against the counter. Her eyes, with that new emotion seeping into them, locked on his and held. Her chest heaved once more, and this time, he *knew* it was because of their proximity. He leaned forward an inch, eyes dropping to her lips, but he waited just a breath away, waited for *her* to make the move.

Her eyes closed, then flew back open a split second later. She took a step back before busying herself, tossing out the gauze packaging and double-checking there was nothing more she could do for Landon's injuries. Landon felt a strange melancholy crawl through him, residing thickly in his throat at the loss of her. He smiled sadly as he watched her.

Nothing and no one had ever made him feel this way.

"I understand more than you know," she murmured quietly as she worked. "About how hard it is to be overshadowed by a sibling."

"You? The person who, according to Ikaika, does everything everyone wants all the time? Except for me, of course." He grinned. "And who was, what? Second in her high school class and excelled in every avenue of school imaginable? Along with everything else he's mentioned you've accomplished?"

And he had. It was clear how proud of her Ikaika was, and Landon certainly hadn't minded learning more.

Her cheeks pinked, and she rolled her eyes. "He's so silly. He just likes to hype me up. More than I deserve."

"I highly doubt it's more than you deserve."

Keala put up the saran wrap and washed her hands. Landon wasn't sure if she was moving around so much because she found talking about herself to be an agonizing task, but he was starting to think it was more likely she felt keeping herself busy was how she stayed relevant to others.

And that made his heart ache for her.

"My younger brother is a certified genius. Seriously. Nothing I ever did was good enough in comparison to him. And my parents were never hard on me because of it, but...my older brother, Nohea, was different. He was always getting into trouble, doing things he shouldn't. Until, one day, he messed up so badly that my parents finally kicked him out of the house. I don't even know what it was. One day, he was there, getting yelled at, the next, he was gone." Her face took on a haunted look, shadowed and pale. Her freckles, which were quickly becoming Landon's favorite constellation, contrasted strongly against her skin.

"I'd never seen my parents fight like that, the way they did when they were trying to figure out what to do about him. I did everything I could to make things easier. After Nohea was gone, my mom sobbed for weeks, and I know my dad struggled with it too. But I thought, you know, that I never wanted to be like that. Never wanted to do that to them. I wanted them to love me the way they loved Akoni, my younger brother, not Nohea. So yes. I know what it's like to be overshadowed by my siblings."

No wonder she seemed to always do what others expected of her. Still trying to make everyone's life easier at the cost of her happiness.

"We really are two peas in a pod then, huh?" Landon asked, mostly joking, because Keala had gone down a different, much more productive path than he had.

They had come to entirely different realizations as children. He had decided that putting effort into anything was useless because he was never good enough, and she had worked herself to death just to try to get half of the attention she deserved. Were either of them happy with that? Was there a better way? A happy medium?

She smiled. "I wouldn't go that far, but I do understand where you're coming from. The difference is that you're always on your worst behavior, acting out to get the attention you never did, and I put my head down, do everything everyone wants, and push myself so I can, at the very least, be on the same playing field as my brother."

Keala had read his mind. She, who had known him for a little over a month, could read him so easily, knew him better than almost anyone else in his life. And though the last part of that sentence about pushing herself to be on the same playing field as her brother hadn't been directed at him, it may as well have been a lance from her hand directly into his chest.

Her knowledge of him, her awareness, scared the shit out of him, because if she saw the demons warring inside of him...

Well, he couldn't imagine she would want to stick around.

"So, the whole healthcare career...you're doing that to earn your parents' approval?" Ever since her confession at his apartment that first night, he'd wanted to untangle everything she had said, study her until he could make sense of the pieces she'd given him.

But, clearly, she was done sharing for the night because she scowled at him. "Good night, Landon." She walked out of the kitchen but called over her shoulder, "Ice your chest."

Chapter Eighteen

Keala

Stacked glass containers of food sat on the second shelf of Ikaika's fridge, which Keala found odd. When she looked closer, she noticed the sticky note on the bottom of the first container.

I worry about your ability to feed yourself after the kitchen fiasco, so accept this as a thanks for taking care of me yesterday – Your Favorite Asshole on his Best Behavior.

Inside the containers appeared to be beef and broccoli stir fry with noodles, and despite the early hour, Keala's mouth watered.

The guys were usually up early on Mondays for recovery at the facility, but there was no way Landon had made this this morning. She was up at five to go to her Pilates class before work, and when she double-checked Ikaika's door, it was closed.

Which meant Landon had gone home after they'd talked last night, made this for her, and brought it back so she would have it before work today.

It was so at odds with the person she'd originally thought he was. She had been learning over the last few weeks, and especially yesterday, that there was more to him than she ever could have imagined.

Keala hadn't necessarily been wrong about him, but she'd refused to let herself see the good side. The sweet side. And she'd certainly failed to see, or even think about, the potential reasons behind his behavior.

How must he feel with a father whose love he could never earn no matter how hard he tried? How must he feel with the words "you're not enough" stamped on his heart, all over his body, all because he was a second son who had never been given the chance to shine like his brother? How much of why he kept his emotions so close to his chest had been learned from a father who appeared not to care about him except when he could reinforce Landon's belief that he wasn't enough? How much of his media presence was for the attention he desperately craved from anyone who would give it to him?

Had he heard that again, repeated and reinforced, when she'd chastised him? When she'd called him a slacker?

His experiences didn't excuse his actions, but they did give her a new perspective. The two of them weren't so different after all.

Still, almost kissing him had been a mistake for many reasons, namely the fact that she wasn't supposed to be talking to him in the first place, and also because if she did allow herself to indulge in another mind-blowing kiss, it couldn't lead to anything more. It was abundantly clear she was no good at one-night stands or relationships. She had no time for the latter, anyway.

Keala placed the sticky note in her jewelry box, then grabbed the top container of food and one of the protein shakes Ikaika had gotten her from the facility.

Her workout flew by, and by seven, she was at the hospital, showered and ready to go.

"How was it?" Keala asked Deirdre, who usually worked the night shift so she could care for her young child during the day.

"Nothing crazy. There is a patient we admitted in five who thought it would be a good idea to"—she grimaced, and Keala braced herself for whatever tomfoolery was coming—"put a hamster stuffed animal up his asshole."

Keala sighed. "Of course he did. X-rays done?"

Deirdre nodded, hiking her purse over her shoulder and folding a sweater over her arms.

"I'll handle it. Have a good day!"

Keala jumped into action, running from room to room, diagnosing and treating until her sore feet ached more and her shoulders rose higher and higher. The only highlight of the day was the food Landon had made her, and once that was gone, the misery began all over again.

Keala wrangled the front door of Ikaika's apartment open later that evening, weighed down by four heavy tote bags full of groceries from the store across the street. When she noticed Landon sitting beside Ikaika on the couch, she bit back a smile, her heart jackhammering.

Which was entirely unwanted.

"Are you planning on feeding an army?" the man in question asked, a smirk on his face despite his eyes on the TV, where the Monday evening game played out.

Keala rolled her eyes, heading toward the kitchen. "No. Just trying to pull my weight."

She didn't hear his response as she set down the groceries and went into her bedroom to change out of her scrubs. She was in desperate need of a shower after staying late to help, so she grabbed what she needed and ran across the hall into the guest bathroom.

Once showered and feeling slightly less gross, she returned to the kitchen, scaring off a mischievous-looking Chowder. Based on the bite marks on the plastic bag of bread, Keala could guess what she'd been doing.

Landon appeared in the kitchen, grabbing a glass from the cabinet and filling it with water as she removed the items from her bags. "I hope you're not planning on cooking. I think my lungs are still trying to rid themselves of the smoke."

"Ha ha, very funny. How are your knuckles?" she asked, meticulously laying out each item in the order she would need it.

"Oh, testy today." He placed his glass down on the island in front of her, and she looked up at him. His smirk softened into something sweeter when their eyes met, and quietly, he asked, "Did you see the food in the fridge?"

Keala's hand stilled on a bag of flour. "I did. Thank you. It was delicious," she admitted begrudgingly. "What time did you make it? It was already so late when I went to bed."

He shrugged. "I knew you had to be up early, so I whipped it up after I went home. Only took half an hour."

"Well, thank you. It forced me to take a lunch break so I could enjoy it."

"Oh yeah? How long did that last?" he asked knowingly.

All of fifteen minutes, but he didn't need to know that. It was more than she typically took when she brought snacks for lunch, since she could eat them while getting through paper-work.

Ikaika walked in. Keala could read the sadness and regret clear as day on his face despite his attempt at smiling. "Hey, Keeks. Good day?"

"Always," she responded, leaning into him as his arm came around her shoulders. She rested her head on him for a few seconds, squeezing his hand before pulling away. He moved to the fridge to grab a protein shake, and Keala added liners to the cupcake tins she'd purchased before she preheated the oven.

"Oh boy," Landon muttered.

"Oh my god, be quiet. I know how to use the oven."

"Hmm, if I recall correctly—" He held up his hands when she shot him a glare. Ikaika still didn't know about the fire. "I'm just saying, I don't think Chowder can take any more of the fire alarm screaming."

Ikaika looked between them questioningly. "What did you do to Chowder?"

"Keala tried to burn down the place a few weeks ago."

Desperately, she said, "No, wait. He's lying. I was practicing and accidentally allowed my vegetables to broil alongside my chicken. Honest mistake."

"So, basically, one of us needs to keep an eye on her while she's in here doing whatever it is she's doing." Landon grinned, sitting on a barstool on the other side of the island.

Ikaika looked between them once more, but this time, his face broke into a small, genuine smile. "Seems like Landon's got you covered then. I'm going to keep watching Weston Colridge get his comeuppance, but I will want at least two of whatever it is that you're making."

"I do not need to be babysat! I'm perfectly capable of baking."

"Don't worry. It'll be like I'm not here." Judging by the cheeky grin on Landon's face, and the skeptical look on Ikaika's as he walked back into the living room, that was highly unlikely.

After a moment of silence, he asked, "So...cupcakes?"

"Wow, that lasted all of a couple of seconds."

Landon shrugged, leaning back and resting an arm over the barstool beside him, his Sentinels T-shirt stretching over his bicep as he moved, and the tendons of his hands straining as he flexed his busted knuckles.

"A bunch of the girls got together Friday to make some stuff for a bake sale on Saturday. For Breast Cancer Awareness Month, you know? They sold out fast, and since it was such a hit, a couple of the girls and I are going to do another one tomorrow."

Keala felt horrible that she hadn't made it either day. The girls understood, knowing she had long shifts, and had told her not to worry. But that was all she'd done since. The last thing she wanted was for the people she spent so much time with, and who she had grown close with, to think she wasn't contributing enough.

So she had bought enough materials to make an absurd number of red velvet cupcakes.

One of Landon's hands brushed over the freshly dressed knuckles of the other. Someone at the facility must have changed his bandages. "I guess the number of ingredients makes more sense now."

She nodded, grabbing a couple of large mixing bowls from a cabinet. "I have to make, like, twelve batches, so if you insist on being in here, I'm going to put you to work."

His grin was wicked as he said, "I'd love for you to put me to work. Give me one second."

He jogged out of the room, and then about two minutes later, Ikaika laughed in the living room. The sound made Keala smile. When Landon came back into the kitchen, he was sporting an apron. One different from the last Keala had chosen to ignore.

One that read *I like my butt rubbed and my pork pulled.*

Good to know the many blows he had suffered physically and mentally yesterday hadn't knocked the asshole out of him.

"You like? I have another one if you want to use it."

"Pass."

He chuckled, and Keala added butter and sugar to one of the bowls. "Mix please." She'd been too cheap to buy an electric mixer.

Landon took the bowl and silicone spoon from her, his arms flexing as he mixed. Keala averted her eyes quickly, knowing if she looked any longer, he would either catch her or she would lose all focus. Probably both.

"Alright, done."

It was creamy and fluffy, like the recipe said. "I'm going to add the eggs. Mix well after each." She added triple what the recipe called for.

When that was done, she added vanilla and food coloring. Landon continued mixing as she poured the buttermilk in. Her side brushed against his, her arm held steady against the arm he used to keep the bowl in place. He was warm everywhere they touched, and when she looked up at him, she found him already looking at her sans cocky smile.

He looked younger without it, and for the millionth time, Keala marveled at how breathtaking this man truly was. Her eyes flicked down to his lips.

"Careful, Keeks," he whispered.

She frowned. "What?"

"You're spilling."

Keala's brain was clearly in very sexual territory because it took her a second to realize he was talking about the buttermilk, and when she did, she jumped, spilling more onto Landon.

"Shoot, I'm sorry." She grabbed a handful of paper towels, her cheeks warming as she wiped the small spill on the counter and his arm.

"It's okay." He was still mixing. "You're cute when you're embarrassed. Actually," he amended, "you're cute all the time."

That forced more blood to her cheeks. She was sure she looked like a tomato. She'd been getting used to his flirting, but with their close proximity, she could hardly think.

The oven beeped, letting them know it was preheated.

Keala didn't respond to him, pouring the vinegar and baking soda into the first bowl while Landon stirred with a cocky grin.

"Next bowl." She pointed at the smaller green one.

"Aye, aye captain." He pulled it closer, keeping a hand on it as she added the flour, cocoa powder, and salt.

Taking great pains not to touch him, she slowly poured the dry mixture into the first bowl as he stirred. When it was all in, she cleared her throat and said, "Okay, you can beat it faster now."

He snorted, and in distress, Keala turned around, putting her hands over her cheeks. Her whole body was warm now, and she didn't know if it was all embarrassment or if some of it had to do with the thrill that shot through her at the thought of him...fucking his hand.

She was going to have to talk to Ikaika about not abandoning her when Landon was around.

Once the mixture was smooth, they divided it between cupcake tins, leaving the extra for another round.

"I didn't get enough trays," she stated the obvious.

"I would offer to go to my apartment to get some, but I'm not much of a baker." He moved past her with the two trays and put them into the oven.

Keala hummed. "Well, you're a great assistant baker."

Landon turned, placing a hand on either side of her and grinning down at her. "Oh, I'm great at listening to instructions." His voice was low, and it was the only piece of the situation that reminded her that her cousin was in the other room, still in earshot if they talked loudly enough.

"That's astonishing," she answered somewhat breathlessly, looking anywhere but his lips, the dimple carved in his cheek, or the look in his eyes that she worried might be mirrored in her own.

"I know. Just depends on who's ordering."

Keala cleared her throat. His smile widened, and there was now no safe place to look. He was, quite simply, too damn handsome, and he knew it. "And if I tell you to move away from me?"

Not because she wasn't enjoying this. Based on the fluttering in her stomach and the feeling that stretched down between her legs, she most certainly was and would probably need to do something about it later. Alone. She had asked the question because she couldn't think straight.

Because if she *was* thinking straight, she would have recognized that this was a horrible idea.

"I would ask if you're absolutely certain you want that, because by the way you're looking at my lips, I'm not sure you do." He paused. "Don't you wanna lean forward and see if it feels the same as it did that first night? Don't you want to do us both a favor and finish what we started? Or are you too perfect to slip up again?" he taunted.

Damn him.

It took great effort, but she placed her hands on the parts of his chest that weren't bruised and pushed gently. She knew if he'd wanted, he wouldn't have budged, but he listened to what she was unable to say and removed his arms from around her.

Seemingly unaffected, he checked the recommended time on Keala's phone screen and then moved to the clock app. He set a timer for sixteen minutes instead of the twenty the recipe called for, and when Keala frowned at him, he smiled.

"In case you want to go take care of yourself. Building in some time for cleanup." He inclined his head in the direction of her room, chuckling to himself while he walked back into the living room.

Keala stood, stunned silent, and not convinced he wasn't a mind reader.

Chapter Nineteen

Landon

> **ESPN notification –** Beaumont's one-loss Saber-tooths prep for their week eight game. What do they need to do to beat Washington?

> **ESPN notification –** Landon Beaumont had three touchdowns in the Sentinels' week eight Thursday evening game. Has Ray Landers finally figured out how to turn the tight end's attitude around?

Shifting in the leather seat of his car, Landon looked away from his phone screen uncomfortably. After a couple of weeks of going back and forth post-accident, he'd decided to try therapy. Online, of course, so no one found out. But even with the distance it provided between himself and Dr. Esposito, he felt the discomfort of talking about his feelings like a physical weight pressing against his chest. He was desperate for air, and it was only the end of his second session.

"Landon?" Dr. Esposito said his name softly, and Landon's eyes snapped to his phone. She smiled kindly. "Where did you go just now?"

He drummed a finger against his steering wheel. Cleared his throat. "Was just thinking about how uncomfortable I'm feeling right now...sharing."

"That's completely understandable. The fact that you sought professional help is already a step toward healing, so I commend you for that. And remember that this is collaborative. You can share as much or as little as you'd like in these sessions, okay?"

The feeling clawing at his chest dissipated a bit at the reminder. "Okay."

"We've done some great work today. If it's alright with you, I'd like to do a quick recap before we close, and then we can pick up again next week. Would that be okay?"

He nodded.

"Great. So last time, we explored a little bit about how your dad's focus on football may have shaped how you view expressing your emotions. This time, we dove into it a bit more. You're not answering most of his messages, and because of that, you've been feeling less pressure from him. You've also found some more intrinsic motivation to try harder on the field."

Landon wasn't sure that could all be attributed to not talking to his father. Finding someone he wanted to prove himself to had helped as well.

Like she'd picked up on his thought, she asked, "Is that right? Or did I miss something?"

"No, no. That's correct." He wasn't ready to talk about Keala. Didn't know what he would say even if he were.

Dr. Esposito smiled again. "Finally, we touched briefly on your relationship with your mother, specifically the out-of-control feelings you had around the time of her passing, as well as your search for attention in places that you believe might not have been best for you."

Right. Namely drugs and fighting. The attention he'd gotten from women over the years hadn't hurt.

"I know you expressed concerns about wanting tangible changes throughout this process, and I just want to point out that opening up the amount that you have already is remarkable. It's clear you've been holding a lot in for a long time, so being able to talk about it, even just to name the feeling, is progress, okay?"

"Okay, thank you." He didn't feel like he'd made much headway, but she seemed excited about it, so he tried to be too.

"Do you have any questions for me before we wrap up for today?"

"Did you still want me to try being vulnerable with others like last week? As...homework or whatever." Landon didn't understand how this all worked, but he was paying a ridiculous amount of money for it. At the very least, he could try.

Dr. Esposito nodded. "I'm so glad you brought that up. Yes, see if there are any opportunities for you in your daily life to open up to even one person. About anything. We can talk about it next week."

"Okay, I'll do that." He'd told his sister on the phone that he missed her this past week. Landon didn't know what other opportunities he might get, but he suspected they would be coming soon, especially since he would be with Keala and her family this evening. "Thank you, Dr. Esposito."

"Of course, Landon. Take care."

"You too."

He grimaced as soon as the call disconnected. Landon knew it was for the better, but man was it uncomfortable.

Keala's parents' two-story house was situated on a nice, tree-lined street in a southern San Jose suburb. It was painted a soft light-gray with white trim around the windows and doors, somehow both modern and warm. A small porch jutted out with a couple of chairs, and the lawn was neat, with flower beds along the edges that looked like they were cared for daily.

Landon couldn't explain why he felt so nervous even with Ikaika by his side. Keala's parents had invited the three of them over for what they called "Halloween Eve," which was apparently an important event in the Lōkahi-Price household.

"Keeks is close," Ikaika said, pocketing his phone as they walked up the driveway. "Her parents asked her to get the pumpkins. I wish they would've asked me—she just got off work and had to rush to the store." He sighed. "I don't think it's on purpose, but they always do this. Ask her for things when she's busier than anyone els—" He frowned, looking back at where Landon had stopped. "What's wrong?"

"I feel like I shouldn't be here. This seems like a family thing. Plus, I know she hasn't been hanging out as much, and I'm not sure if that's my fault." It had been three weeks since he'd helped with her bake sale. Though he knew he'd read the signals correctly and she'd been as affected by their proximity as he had, she hadn't been around as much since.

Ikaika shook his head. "You're always welcome here; my aunt has made that clear. And the Sirens have been busy the last few weeks with a ton of new choreography. They had back-to-back home games to prepare for. She's been at practice or practicing with her teammates every single day."

That may have been true, but any time she did hang out with them at the apartment and Ikaika got up to use the restroom or call his family, or do anything that left Keala and Landon alone, she jumped up and ran out of the room, claiming she needed to go to bed.

Maybe she worried that the tension between them would break into something more if they were left alone again. Or maybe he had ruined things.

Ikaika, taking his silence as hesitation, continued, "Seriously. I like hanging out with you, don't get me wrong, but it's gotten more fun because you bring out a side of Keala I've never seen before."

"In what way?"

"With everyone else, me included, she's always like, 'Yes, I'll do whatever you want whenever you want me to.' I mean, look at her running to do her parents' bidding despite being the busiest of us all. But whatever you did when you guys first met, you clearly bug her so much that she's going against her instincts, and I love it. I've never seen her like this."

Maybe she hadn't been fighting her instincts with him. Maybe she'd been letting him see the real her, the one she hid from everyone else so they'd always need her around.

Though, that may have been an absurd line of thinking, because why him? What was it about him that would make her feel she could let go and be her real self? Was it the same thing that had allowed him to be unguarded about his emotions in a way he'd never been able to with anyone else?

Nah, Ikaika was probably right. She was fighting her sweet, people-pleasing instincts to spite Landon. And Landon didn't mind one bit.

"Glad to be of service," Landon joked.

He followed Ikaika to the front door. A few seconds after his friend knocked, a woman with short wavy hair and Keala's smile greeted them. "Come in, come in, please!" She pulled Ikaika into a tight hug, then did the same with Landon.

A tall, lanky man with thin glasses and graying hair stood in the living room, his eyes focused on the TV, where a couple of college teams played.

"Adrian," Keala's mom scolded him. He tossed the remote onto the coffee table and joined them, sheepishly smiling at his wife before shaking Landon's hand.

"It's good to meet you. We've enjoyed following your career."

"Thank you. It's good to meet you both too." Though, if they were following his career, that likely meant they knew some of the worst things he'd done. Not a great start, but they didn't seem to care.

The most remarkable thing Landon noticed about Keala's parents was how much they touched. Her father's arm around his wife's back, her hand resting on his arm or stomach. It seemed so natural, as if they spent all of their time like this.

It was a dynamic completely opposite to his parents'.

The four of them made light small talk as they migrated past a small dining room to the living room. Behind the couch was a hallway with many doorways and a set of stairs.

Just as they sat down, Keala burst into the house, a big smile on her face, cheeks red from the cold, and arms full.

In an instant, Landon and Ikaika were up again, helping her with her bags.

"Ma, I got the groceries you asked for."

Ikaika grabbed the bags she held out to her mother. "I can take these to the kitchen."

"Thank you, Ikaika." Her mother followed him to the first room that split off the hallway.

Landon assisted Keala with the three medium-sized pumpkins she'd purchased, setting them onto the coffee table. "Thank you," she murmured, her eyes stilling on his face for half a second before she pulled out three carving kits and placed one beside each pumpkin.

"So, is this the family tradition?" he asked.

"Yes! Pumpkin carving. We do it every year." She turned to her dad. "Dad, is Akoni not driving up? I thought he said he was coming, but when you only asked for three pumpkins—"

Her mother's voice drifted to them as she and Ikaika returned to the living room. "Akoni had a medical school interview today at UCLA. He promised to send a picture of his pumpkin before tomorrow morning." Pride was clear from her eyes to her smile.

Landon looked at Keala out of the corner of his eye. Her face fell imperceptibly before she smiled. "Same rules apply this year."

"There are rules?" he asked, eyeing the pumpkins.

"Pumpkin carving is a big thing for our family. When we were younger, we would all sit around the table and Dad would carve whatever we asked him to. Then, when we got older, we began having family competitions."

Adrian smiled fondly. "Keeks got so excited the first year we let her try, she cut her hand open and we had to take her to the emergency room."

Keala laughed, holding up her palm. A small, faded, white scar curved under her thumb. He'd never noticed it before. "Dad got me a baby pumpkin, and the moment he left the room, after expressly telling me to wait, I grabbed the knife and went to town. Cut clean through the pumpkin and into my hand."

"Maybe that's when she fell in love with emergency medicine," her father said, pleased.

"Maybe," Keala responded weakly.

"Don't be silly, Adrian. The kids have wanted to be in medicine since they were little and you let them use your stethoscope. Akoni especially, right, Keala? I remember, when he was young, he would sit and listen to your dad talk for hours about his day."

Keala shifted uncomfortably, sharing a look with Landon. They'd come to a kind of understanding after learning about each other's family dynamics. "Yeah."

"So who won last year? And who wins most often?" Landon asked.

Keala looked at him gratefully. "Surprisingly? Always Ikaika." She shrugged. "Man's got a gift."

Ikaika smiled. "Mom always said if football didn't work out, I'd be a good artist."

"Why are you leaving out the best part?" her mother asked.

"Because it's the best part for Ikaika and nobody else," Keala grumbled.

"What's the best part?" Landon questioned.

Ikaika grabbed one of the pumpkins, examining it from all angles. "Winner gets a favor from the losers."

Landon smirked at Keala. "Really? You don't say."

Keala rolled her eyes. "Yes, yes. Whatever. Ikaika, stop cheating. We draw numbers to see who gets to choose first."

Each of them picked a small slip of paper with a number from one to three out of a hat. Landon, who drew the number one, chose first, then Keala, then Ikaika. Once chosen, they spread out. Landon settled with his back against the wall of the dining room, where he had a clear view of Ikaika beside the TV stand and Keala beside the couch.

Immediately, Ikaika and Keala got to work. They seemed to not only have an idea of what they wanted to carve but also how to execute it. Landon frowned down at his pumpkin, waiting for an ounce of creativity or an idea to jump out of him.

Keala pulled her hair into a ponytail. Over the last couple of months of getting to know her, he'd figured out that meant she was focusing hard. There was a small crease between her brow as she drew on her pumpkin, tilting her head back and forth, squinting her eyes.

Like with football, with expressing his emotions, and anything else where he knew Keala was watching, Landon wanted to *try*. Even if it was for a dumb pumpkin.

That's when the idea hit him. The thing that connected them all—the Sentinels.

The red-and-black logo featured a medieval knight with a helmet, its visor down and plume flowing behind him. He held a sword with both hands and appeared to be in the middle of driving it down into someone or something. Landon's drawing skills were mediocre at best, but by the time he had finished, it looked surprisingly like the symbol painted all over the facility and fields.

Landon had only carved pumpkins once, so he wasn't sure about his abilities off the dome. He desperately wanted Keala to owe him a favor, so he pulled up a video with step-by-step instructions on how to carve the Sentinels logo and muted it.

Was it cheating if it was for a good cause? He pretended the answer wasn't yes.

The three of them worked diligently for over half an hour. Keala's parents stayed seated on the loveseat, not wanting to see the pumpkins before they were done since they were judging. They asked questions, checking in with Ikaika and Keala, and sometimes Landon, on their lives, but most of their attention was on each other. They whispered to each other, laughing together like teenagers in the honeymoon stage. Mr. Price had an arm around her waist, her legs in his lap, and more often than not, their eyes were on the other as they talked, engrossed in conversation.

Their love was palpable.

Every time Landon noticed, he looked over at Keala. Often, he found her smiling at her parents, a wistful look in her eyes. A rope tightened roughly in his chest, seeing how badly she wanted something like that for herself.

At one point, wanting to see how Keala was doing, Landon had gotten up and pretended to go to the bathroom. She'd been working on something familiar, with a long, creepy smile, but he couldn't pinpoint what exactly it was.

"Hey! Cheater! Get out of here," she'd said, pointing at him like she was scolding him, a poorly hidden smile peeking through.

Finally, Keala stood, hands on her hips. "Are we all done?" Landon surveyed his pumpkin one last time, then nodded. "Everyone hold them up in three"—Landon hoisted his up, still facing him—"two, one." They all turned theirs to face the center of the room. Keala's was a more cleaned-up version of what he had seen when he'd walked to the bathroom, and Ikaika had gone for a silhouette of a cat.

Keala's parents looked at each of the pumpkins, and Keala's brows furrowed when she looked at Landon's.

"What the hell is that?" Ikaika asked him, cracking a smile. He probably thought he'd won.

Landon walked to the coffee table, set down his pumpkin, then turned the flashlight of his phone on and placed it inside. He put the top of the pumpkin back on.

"Oh wow!" Keala's mom traced the carving with a finger, and her father looked impressed.

Keala's jaw dropped. "Oh. My. God."

Landon smirked at her. "That good, huh?"

She ignored him. "Ikaika, put your flashlight in yours so we can compare." She did the same, placing hers beside Landon's on the table. Keala's mom flicked off the lights.

Admittedly, Landon's wasn't perfect, but when taking into account difficulty, he was pretty sure he had them both beat. By miles. He grinned.

"What is yours supposed to be?" he asked Keala.

She glared at him. "*Supposed* to be? It's obviously Jack Skellington." When he didn't register who that was, she continued, "From *The Nightmare Before Christmas*?"

"Oh, right. Hey, that's not bad." Her glare intensified, sharper and more angular in the light of the TV and their flashlights, her arms crossed.

"Very impressive work, Landon. Ikaika has some serious competition this year," her father said, picking up the top of Landon's pumpkin to look inside, then putting it back.

"Damn, man. Did you used to carve pumpkins as a kid too?" Ikaika asked.

"Only once."

Keala looked intrigued, so he started to explain. Realizing there were others in the room and not sure he wanted to be vulnerable in front of all of them, he closed his mouth. Like she had heard his thought process, her face dropped, turning back toward the pumpkins.

Screw it. It was his homework, after all. "My sister needed to carve one for class one year. She wanted it to be a sparrow because they were my mother's favorite. Maya thought it would make Mom feel better since she was sick."

He'd wanted to help, but both he and Colton had been tied up with practice and games. When he'd mentioned to his dad that he felt bad for not helping, his father had yelled at Landon and told him to stop being such a baby. Two nights before it was due, Maya had gone to bed with red-rimmed eyes, and the next day, Landon had purchased a bunch of pumpkins and gotten to work.

"I carved a ton before I got good at it, and around three thirty in the morning, I finally finished one I knew she'd love."

That strange, unidentifiable look was back in Keala's eyes. The one he had wished for more of when she'd cleaned his knuckles in the kitchen almost four weeks ago. He hoped it was something good, something like admiration.

"Well, you got real good," Ikaika mused.

Landon's eyes were still on Keala's, and she didn't look away. It made his chest clench and shudder in a way he was sure it never had.

Her parents took photos of the pumpkins before turning the lights back on. Her mom motioned in the direction of the door. "Sweetie, would you mind putting them outside on the porch? It'll be the perfect décor for when kids come by tomorrow."

"Of course," Keala answered, pulling her phone out of her pumpkin.

"I'll help." Landon grabbed the phones out of the other two, then picked the pumpkins up from the bottom, leaning them against his body as he followed Keala outside, where a blast of cold air hit them. Keala shivered, and he wished he'd brought a sweatshirt.

They placed them beside each other near the door, and when they were done, Keala took a step back to survey their work.

Landon gestured at his pumpkin. "I think we all know I won."

Keala grimaced like she knew it too. "We'll have to see what my parents say."

Landon took a step toward Keala, and she looked at him warily. "So, if I do win, you'll do anything I want?"

She heaved a beleaguered sigh. "Landon."

"What? It's a genuine question. I want to make sure I understand what's allowed here."

Her eyes narrowed. "Nothing sexual."

"Oh, Keeks. Ikaika and I aren't like that."

She shoved him, and he grinned as his back hit one of the wooden posts holding up the porch.

She hadn't mentioned any rules forbidding dates.

Chapter Twenty

Landon

Bay Area News 5 – Landon Beaumont seen entering Off the Grid, out for the first time since game four. Latest lady under wraps as Beaumont arrives alone, but the night is young.

Sav

You okay?

I've been keeping up with you by see-ing what you were up to in the news, but there's barely been anything on you. Have you fallen off the face of the earth?

Trick question because I know you've been playing.

Landon had not expected to see a clown with their tongue down Albert Einstein's throat when he exited Off the Grid's VIP bathrooms. He stepped around them to get back to the couches where the rest of his teammates were, taking his seat beside Ikaika and JJ, a Sentinels wide receiver. He was thankful they weren't downstairs on the dance floor, packed together in pockets of people in various Halloween costumes.

A woman dressed in scraps of gauze sidled up to him with a smile. If she was up here, she was either an athlete, had been brought in by an athlete, or had paid an insane amount of money.

"Landon!" she yelled, like they knew each other well.

"Hey…"

"I told my friend you'd be here! She didn't believe me. She's—" The woman cut herself off, looking around the many tables and chairs on this level. "I don't know where she went."

Landon took a sip of his beer, the neck portion of the apron he'd chosen for his chef "costume" tonight chafing against his bare skin. Kayvon, one of their younger tight ends, had insisted they all wear some form of costume, so Landon had nothing but his apron and dress pants on. Ikaika, who was half asleep beside him despite having had nothing to drink, was wearing a cropped football jersey.

Landon didn't want to be here, but even Ikaika had been game, so they'd come to Off the Grid—the only bar in the area that made everyone who came in leave their phone with phone check downstairs. They'd been here for over two hours, and he'd turned away at least fifteen women in favor of his beers.

Basically, he was having a miserable time.

There was something to be said about the haven he, Keala, and Ikaika had created in their apartment over the last two months. For possibly the first time ever, Landon had looked forward to going home after practices instead of going out, getting wasted, and finding someone to hook up with for the evening.

"Well, it was good to meet you." He had no interest in going down this avenue tonight. Probably not for a while. He couldn't remember the last time he'd looked at another woman with the intention of hooking up with them, but it had been before he'd met Keala. He knew that for sure.

"Wait! I'm looking for her because we were wondering if you might want to go home with us tonight."

He sighed, emptying his drink. A part of him hated that he'd ever started things with Keala, because she'd ruined this experience for him. Completely. But that was dumb because he would have given all this up again to keep what they had going. To have the possibility of kissing her again.

"Appreciate the offer, but not looking tonight." He inclined his head to JJ, who'd been eyeing the woman since she'd come up to Landon. "JJ's available though."

She pouted her bright-red lips but turned to JJ anyway. "How would you like a threesome?" His tongue practically lolled like the dog he was dressed as.

Landon stood and headed to the bar, asking for another beer. To his right, the balcony overlooked the downstairs portion of Off the Grid. He noticed a woman in silver boots, knee-high bright-green socks, and a silver bodysuit over a matching green see-through turtleneck. Her straightened hair looked familiar, pushed back with a headband that held up two balls attached to springs.

She was the hottest alien he'd ever seen. And the star of every one of his fantasies—sans alien outfit. Usually in his fantasies, she was wearing her red-and-black plaid pajama shorts, no top, and she was looking up at him as she—

Fuck, he had to stop.

Keala was surrounded by a group of women, who were all laughing. Already, heads turned in their direction despite them having just arrived. Landon watched raptly, even after the bartender brought him another beer.

The music pounded, and if it hadn't been clear before, Landon knew now they were Keala's teammates, all moving perfectly on beat to the song.

She looked so happy and free. He was glad she was going out, proud of her for not allowing work to rule her life entirely. She deserved to let loose like this.

A guy approached the group. Landon didn't think much of it, but the man pointed in Keala's direction, and her friends pushed her toward him. She smiled, nodding and responding to whatever he said. After a few minutes, he pulled out what looked like a pen and handed it to her, holding his arm out, and that's when Landon felt a hand gripping tight to something inside of him.

Had she agreed to give him her number? It wasn't like she and Landon had done anything since the end of August, but he'd thought she'd felt a fraction of what he did.

Landon thanked the bartender. One of the guys had put down their cards for the tab, so he grabbed the beer and headed downstairs. Ikaika was still asleep. He'd be fine for a few minutes.

It took what felt like a year to get to the bar downstairs, where Keala stood waiting for drinks, sweaty bodies writhing against him as he moved. Either the people down here were so drunk they didn't recognize him, or they were just very interested in dancing.

Finally, when he reached her, he leaned his side against the bar and smirked down at her. She was trying to get the bartender's attention, with little luck. He tapped one of the balls on her headband. "I won't lie, this costume is doing things for me."

Her eyebrows raised, then raised higher when she realized it was him. "I don't know why I'm surprised you're here. Makes sense for athletes."

Landon nodded. Not having to worry about people taking his picture was a definite perk. Her eyes dropped down his body until they landed on the words on his apron. "I cook as good as I look," she read. A small giggle told him she'd had a couple of drinks.

He inclined his beer in her direction. "It's true. Are you having a good night?"

"Yes. But if you want to talk to me, you have to face the bar and look straight forward."

"I'll admit, your rules are unorthodox, but if it means I get to keep talking to you..." He turned, setting his beer down and leaning his arms on the bar.

"I know nobody has their phones, but even being *seen* next to you is a bad idea."

"I got it, Keeks. My ego doesn't need to take any more hits."

Keala snorted. "We agreed I'm here to humble you. And you're lucky I'm letting you stand next to me."

"Fair enough."

"Are *you* having a good night?" she asked.

"It's okay, I guess."

She turned, frowning, but he shook his head. "Ah, ah, ah. Face the bar. Your rules."

Keala sighed, listening. "Why is your night just okay?"

"Because it's been three days since the game and you haven't congratulated me on any of my touchdowns. And I saw you *yesterday*."

She giggled again, and the sound wrapped around him, crushing any semblance of control he'd had over his feelings for her. It made him want to pull her into his chest and hold her tight.

"Hm, I'm not sure what you're talking about. As you know, when I'm at home games, I, too, am working."

"So when I turned to smile at you, you weren't watching me after one of my biggest plays this season?"

He saw her shake her head out of the corner of his eye. They were being jostled, and the side of her body pressed against him. He brushed his pinky against hers and heard her small inhale.

"Right. And if I told you that I scored for you? That if you'd looked at me long enough, I would have dedicated it to you?"

"I would tell you not to be an idiot because if Angelica caught us making eye contact for a moment, she would have been onto me. That woman can sense things before they happen, I swear." The bartender was still down the bar, moving fast as hell as he made drink after drink. Keala glanced around before turning to Landon, her voice dropping. "I'm proud of how you played. You finally look like you're trying out there." She elbowed him lightly.

Something burst in his chest. He didn't know if he had ever heard that before, and even if she was needling him at the same time, the knowledge that him putting in effort could finally be rewarded was...revolutionary. Ever since the night of the accident, he'd been focusing more at practice, working harder than he ever had. It felt like it was starting to pay off.

Landon looked away, wanting to make a joke but knowing that she had created a safe space for him. He didn't have to use humor to cover his feelings, and more than that, she wouldn't have wanted him to.

"Thank you," he responded genuinely. "That means a lot." And then, because he couldn't help himself, he said, "I guess I'm not the slacker you thought I was."

"Landon..."

"I know. I hadn't shown you any differently then."

Keala tapped a couple of fingers on the bar. "They're so busy. I don't know why we're here. We're never going to get served. I'm tired. I want to go home and change into comfy clothes, but the girls are trying to get me drunk even though I have work tomorrow."

Landon thought about her pajamas and his dick twitched. What was wrong with him? When had he become this guy who was more turned on by a woman in her pajamas than the sexy Halloween costume she was wearing now? And not any woman, *this* woman specifically. The shift from never wanting to see someone he'd fucked outside of the bedroom to wanting to spend all his free time with her had snuck up on him so quietly, happened so gradually, he hadn't noticed until now.

Scarily enough, he was pretty sure he liked her.

He liked that she challenged him when few others did. That she didn't take his shit. That she pushed him to be vulnerable and then listened and validated him. That she felt like a kindred spirit because of their shared experiences with their siblings. He liked how hardworking and driven she was, and that that made him want to work harder too.

"Want me to smuggle you out of here? If you do, though, you have to confirm what a little birdie told me about winning the pumpkin carving contest."

"Ikaika told you?"

"A little birdie."

Keala sighed. "Fine. Fine. Yes. You won. My mom loved your pumpkin and, to Ikaika's dismay, said you won by a mile. Akoni sent a photo of his last night, and she texted this morning about it."

"That's interesting because I seem to remember that I win a favor from you."

"And what do you want?" she whispered. When he turned, she was looking up at him, eyes searching his face.

He wanted to kiss her. He wanted to kiss her so badly, it was taking effort not to lean forward the last few inches. But then *she* was leaning forward, her eyes fluttering shut, and he didn't know if it was the alcohol in her system, or because they were standing so close, or if she was finally giving in to the tension that had been building between them.

As their lips brushed, Keala was jostled into him. He wrapped an arm around her waist to steady her, glaring at the person who'd pushed her. They weren't even paying attention.

Keala, dazed, extracted herself from his grasp. "I should go."

"Kee—"

"Kaykay! What are you—" Her friend's dark eyes widened underneath her pirate hat, her eye patch flipped up. "Oh."

"Hey, Zoe. This is Ikaika's friend. He was trying to help me wave the bartender down, but I think it's a bust. Too busy." Her words came out fast, one pressing into the next so they were almost a jumble.

Zoe nodded slowly, eyes still wide and focused on Landon. "Uh-huh. Well, as you've noticed, the team is here, so we need to leave. I know you wanted to go home, so now's our chance while Kennedy figures out where we should hit next."

"Sounds good. I'm ready." Keala grabbed Zoe's hand, pulling her through the throng of bodies, Zoe glancing back every few steps.

Keala did *not* look back.

Landon sipped his beer by the bar until he saw Keala get her phone and walk out with the rest of the Sirens.

With less of a desire to stay now that he knew Keala was gone, he went upstairs, grabbed a tired Ikaika, said their good-byes to the few teammates who weren't participating in various activities, and headed to the VIP section's phone check.

He would have no fun here knowing she was at home.

Chapter Twenty-One

Keala

It had been five days since Keala had allowed her judgment to crack at the club. She'd spent every free moment since actively avoiding Landon once again, reminding herself that the one-night stand hadn't worked with him. She didn't know if there had been too much pressure riding on it because it'd been her first attempt or if she'd been holding back because he was a Sentinels player. Either way, bad idea.

Considering his history, it seemed unlikely that a kiss would lead to more than a hookup.

And if it did, then what? In the past, she had been so desperate for love that she'd bent herself until she'd broken in two, cut pieces of herself off to fit whatever mold her partner wanted. In chasing her fairy tale, she had conformed to theirs, and she didn't want that for herself again. Sure, things were different with Landon. She didn't feel like she needed to be anyone special for him when they hung out around the apartment, but who was to say that wouldn't change if they became more?

Avoiding him felt childish, especially when he'd left more containers of food in the fridge for her, but she worried her self-control was in dire need of work. The chances that she broke and kissed him were increasing by the day, especially as he proved more and more that he wasn't the man she'd thought he was.

Her mind was a muddled mess, and the note tucked into her jewelry box from the food he had made after Halloween wasn't helping.

Hope you didn't have any Halloween/horror-induced nightmares last night (I have one nightly where you burn down the apartment). And thank you for including me in pumpkin carving. My family hasn't ever done anything like that. Sorry it took me so long to say.

PS I like knowing that you owe me something ;)

Keala had decided right then and there, to the sound of her thudding heart, that the only thing her slipup meant was that it'd been a while since she'd been touched. She needed *something* even if, inevitably, she'd find herself unable to ask for what she wanted and the experience would end without an orgasm for her. As they usually did.

She could try again with someone different, someone who *wasn't* on the Sentinels or her cousin's best friend. Keala was removing the pressure from the situation.

Which was how she found herself rushing to change in her car and throwing on a light dusting of makeup in the parking lot of the bar and grill where she'd agreed to meet Adam.

Adam, the thirty-year-old orthopedic surgeon specializing in feet, of all things, who she'd met at the club on Halloween.

Initially, she'd said no when he'd asked for her number. But Zoe had kept pushing her to do it, so she'd written it on his arm and then offered to get the group drinks so she didn't have to keep talking to him.

He seemed nice enough, but what had pushed her to agree to his second text asking her out was Landon. She had to get whatever this was out of her brain. If she'd known he was a surgeon before she'd agreed, well, she never would have agreed. She would never willingly date a doctor. She already felt like she was lesser for not getting into medical school. She didn't need them telling her to her face that her work wasn't important.

Landon never made her feel lesser.

Stop it. Keala slammed the sun visor closed and forced herself out of the car. *Keep thoughts away from Landon*, she reminded herself. That was tonight's mission.

When she saw Adam seated at a booth, she pointed him out to the hostess and sat in front of him. His brown hair was short, clean, and styled. His features weren't as strong as...

Damn it. *He's handsome*, she reassured herself. Based on their brief conversation, she thought Adam was looking for someone who was very positive with a lot of energy and had an interest in golf. Or rather, in learning more about him playing golf.

"Hi," she said brightly, hoping to radiate the vibes of the woman he was no doubt searching for.

"Hey." He smiled, and she was slightly dispirited to see there was no dimple.

"Sorry I'm late. Work." She grimaced but hoped bringing up her job would make for an easy icebreaker.

"No worries at all. You're a nurse, right?"

"Nurse practitioner." She hated to correct him, so she moved on quickly. "How was work for you today?"

"That's cute."

Keala stifled a sigh, already knowing how her night would be ending.

"Don't get me wrong, being a nurse who thinks they're a doctor is admirable and all, but...come on."

There it is.

"I'm literally the person people come to when their feet are in any sort of crisis. I'm talking about *structural integrity*, you know? Bones, tendons, ligaments. You get it. The foundation of the human body. How can you fix someone's health without addressing the foundation, right?"

Something sharp prodded at her temper, but she kept a smile plastered on her face. "Right," she gritted out, nodding. She couldn't believe she was missing her group's casual practice today for a date with the pushy guy from the club—something Zoe had been very excited to hear. After she'd asked *many* probing questions about her relationship with Landon.

Which Keala had shut down immediately. There was no relationship, so she hadn't technically lied to her.

Keala tuned Adam out as he continued talking about himself, trying so hard not to think about Landon. She could picture him now, making fun of her for sitting in front of this arrogant man.

Really? Him? he would ask jokingly. *You think this guy can give you what you want? I bet he doesn't have a single sexual apron. What an asshole. Do you seriously want someone like that in your life?*

Keala grabbed her water, taking a long sip of it as she nodded along with Adam. Her salad showed up as he talked about plantar fasciitis, and she focused on cutting her lettuce into little pieces so she could be the perfect lady.

She didn't know why she was trying with this guy. It wasn't like she would see him again after this. The part of her that wanted everyone to like her, to need her, told her to shut up and keep cutting.

"Don't get me wrong, I'm sure you're helping people. But I've worked with a lot of nurse practitioners and I've never seen one who gets the *nuance* of genuinely complicated musculoskeletal conditions. I assume when you deal with basic symptoms and assessments, it's easy to feel like you're diagnosing a ton of stuff, right? I don't know."

Keala took a big swig of water. "I'm in the emergency department and handle more than basic symptoms and assessments, but I see what you're saying."

She didn't. Not at all. But that was the safe response that balanced both the voices warring inside her.

"So what do you do outside of nursing?" he asked.

Keala angled her head so he didn't see her eye twitch. "I'm a San Jose Sentinels Siren. A cheerleader for the pro team," she added in case he didn't know who the Sirens were. His face scrunched, dismissiveness and disgust clear in equal measure. So similar to Heath's expression when he had asked her to quit the Vixens.

"That's...a shock. That seems beneath what a healthcare professional should be doing in their free time, no? Do you plan to do that for much longer?"

What had she expected here? Her friends in Virginia had agonized over how bad the dating scene was. She didn't know why she'd thought this would be a good idea. No amount of shit sex would make this more bearable. She wasn't sure the best sex in the world would make this more bearable.

Screw this guy, she heard in her head, but it was Landon's damn voice. *You don't owe him shit. The chances of you working with him any time in the future are ridiculously small. San Jose is huge. Say how you feel.*

She hated that she couldn't get away from him, no matter how much she tried.

"It's a very athletic job, and fans love it. *I* love it. I don't see how my being in healthcare has any bearing on it." In a small act of rebellion, Keala didn't tell him this was her last year. She didn't want to give him the satisfaction.

They made more small talk until he grabbed the bill and paid it. She kept shoving Landon and his advice out of her head, reminding herself that this whole date was about releasing the sexual tension *without* him.

"Would you like to come over? I live about fifteen minutes away in a great two-story. Hot tub and everything."

Barf. Seems all his medical training hadn't taught him about pseudomonas aeruginosa.

"Oh, wow. That sounds amazing, but I have an early shift tomorrow, so I'll have to see it another time. Thank you so much for dinner."

His demeanor changed significantly, but he still smiled as she gave him a side hug and ran toward her car.

During the short drive back to her apartment, she kept hoping that Landon and Ikaika would be out. It was bye week, and though it seemed they'd stopped going out as much after the accident, she deluded herself into believing they wouldn't be home.

The date, unsurprisingly, hadn't accomplished what she had hoped. It wasn't like she'd been looking for a boyfriend, and even a mildly interesting hookup might have been fun, but the fact that she couldn't get Landon out of her head, continually drawing comparisons to him, left her feeling more frustrated than ever.

When she noticed Ikaika's cars were both in the private garage, she assumed that meant Landon was home too. She thought about texting Zoe and Len to see if they were free after dance or if she could come over halfway through practice. Keala was sure they would say yes. But she had work tomorrow, and it was time to bite the bullet and deal with the situation.

Or rush into the apartment and go straight to her room.

Chapter Twenty-Two

Landon

ESPN notification – Sabertooths head into week nine with one loss. Click here for playoff and championship predictions.

ESPN notification – Six and two Sentinels are looking good going into their bye week. Here's what's been working well for them: 1. Landon Beaumont's hands!...

Landon rinsed his and Ikaika's dishes, adding them to the dishwasher when Ikaika's apartment door opened.

"Hey, Keeks," Ikaika said from the couch.

"Hi!" Keala called. Landon turned off the tap, shaking the excess water off a plate. She was back earlier than usual for a Friday. She typically practiced at one of her team-mates' places for at least another hour.

"How was your date?"

Landon frowned. He knew she'd likely been avoiding him the last few days, as seemed to be her move when things got too intense between them, but he'd had no idea she'd gone out with someone else.

The only thing that made him feel better was that she was already back, which he hoped meant it hadn't gone well. They'd been out for a couple of hours, max.

"You went on a date?" Landon asked as he walked through the doorway of the kitchen, plate still in hand.

"Uh, yeah." She refused to meet his eyes. Landon turned around and walked back into the kitchen.

That pang in his chest was far more than jealousy. It was knowing he had feelings for her that were different than anything he'd ever allowed himself to feel for anyone else. It was coming to the realization she didn't feel the same way.

Landon wanted more than whatever they were. He wished she would stop avoiding him at every turn and just be honest with him. Maybe he could have made sense of his feelings before she'd gone out with whoever this chump was.

But that wasn't fair. She didn't owe him anything.

Was this because of what had happened on Halloween? Landon knew she'd wanted to kiss him. After all, *she* had been the one to lean in.

"So? Was it good?" Ikaika asked. Landon placed the plate into the dishwasher. It rang louder than he'd meant for it to.

"It was...not great. The guy had a serious superiority complex and was clearly upset when I decided to come home instead of going back with him."

What an asshole. Good riddance. Landon hoped she'd told him where to shove it. He wasn't necessarily proud of it, but he was glad the date had gone poorly. He wanted her to see what was in front of her.

"Sounds like an ass," Ikaika said dismissively. Landon stayed in the kitchen, turning on the tap to pretend he wasn't listening.

Keala sighed. "Very much so."

"Not that I want to know details, but were you hoping it would lead to something more in the future?"

"Not really..." She laughed uncomfortably. "I don't have all that much time for dating. Was supposed to be a one-time fix."

Which likely meant she'd gotten riled up at the club and hadn't known what to do with herself. Landon grinned. That was great news.

"Hear you loud and clear." Landon listened as Ikaika stood up and walked past her. "I'm going to run to the restroom, but if you want to join me and Landon, we're playing Smash."

Landon stepped out of the kitchen and into the hallway, watching Keala walk to her room. "Keeks..."

She turned, trepidation stamped in the crease of her brow and the curve of her bottom lip. Had he been obvious earlier? Slamming the plate into the dishwasher had probably given away the fact that he was bothered.

He checked down the stairs to make sure Ikaika was gone, then took a step closer to her. When she took a step back, he stepped toward her again until her back was against the wall. Landon leaned forward, his familiar armor—his charming smile—hiding how he felt. He needed to parse it himself first, and she'd *just* said she wasn't looking for anything more than sex.

Twirling a few strands of her hair around his finger, he spoke in a hushed tone. "If you need to use someone for that pent-up sexual energy, or you're looking for stress relief, use me. You don't need to go out with assholes from clubs or wherever else you found this guy."

"That is..." She laughed, but it sounded strange, higher pitched than usual. "That's insane. I wanted to try out the dating scene in a new place."

Landon gently pushed her head to the side so he could whisper beside her cheek. "Really? So when you leaned in and kissed me at the club, that was, what? The alcohol? You had no interest in seeing where it would go?"

His lips ghosted over her jaw. Her response was shaky. "Landon, I could—I could get in—in trouble just for talking to you. The last thing I need is to—Jesus," she breathed. Her head tilted more. Landon pressed his lips where her neck met her shoulder. "The last thing I need is to complicate—*oh*—everything more by going down that path."

Landon smiled, pulling back so he could look into her eyes. They were half lidded and hazy. "Good deflecting."

"I'm not—"

"You are, but that's fine. We spend all our free time together anyway. We both know you're attracted to me, and I think I've made it pretty clear what I think about you." Actually, he hoped *not*, banking on his attitude to keep his feelings under wraps. "The more we see each other, the worse this tension is going to get. Why not try it out and see what happens?"

She sighed softly. "I don't want to jeopardize what I love for an orgasm."

"Give me *some* credit. It'll be two at a bare minimum, and that's assuming we only do this one time." She was so flustered, she couldn't fight the smile, hard as she seemed to try. "Have you gotten in trouble for hanging out with me these last couple of months?"

Keala shook her head once.

"Then they won't find out now. It won't leave these two apartments. Nobody will know. And with how hard you work? Damn, do you deserve to cut loose a little." Landon leaned back more, dropping the cocky act. "So use me. It doesn't have to be anything more than sex."

He just wanted her to realize what she needed was *him*.

A throat cleared from a few feet away, and Keala pushed Landon. He moved out of the way, back to his cheeky self. "Sorry 'bout that. Needed to clear something up with Keeks here." He turned to Ikaika, who approached the top of the stairs. "Ready to play?"

Landon thought he caught the hint of a suppressed smile on his friend's face. He would have felt more uncomfortable about the compromising position they'd been in if he hadn't been getting the feeling Ikaika was purposely leaving rooms to give them time alone. Landon had a hunch his friend wanted them to get together.

"You in?" Ikaika asked Keala, who was wringing her hands, her cheeks rosy.

Keala cleared her throat. "Not tonight. Early morning."

She disappeared for the rest of the evening. After Landon and Ikaika played a few rounds, Landon checked their fridge and headed home to make her lunch for the next day.

Cooking, as usual, gave him time to think and de-stress.

He focused on how he'd felt when Keala had gotten home. He didn't understand the feelings yet, but he recognized that he felt good when he was with her, and he didn't when he wasn't. And he felt worse when he thought of her with someone else. While he was struggling to deconstruct everything after spending so long shoving his emotions down, he understood that what he felt now meant that, in some capacity, he wanted her in more than a sexual way.

Dr. Esposito would be so proud of him.

He had no regrets about telling her to use him. Landon knew he was in uncharted territory with this relationship, but he also knew the one thing he was good for was sex. If she took him up on his offer, at least he would have her, even if not to the full extent of what he'd hoped for. He didn't know if he wanted to give her any more of himself anyway, terrified of disappointing her further than he already had. So, by all accounts, this seemed like the best option.

Running with that logic, he added the meal to a glass container, then grabbed the sticky notes he'd purchased for this purpose. On the top one, he wrote:

My door's always open for you. I'd love to be your dirty little secret – Your Favorite Tight End on his Best Behavior

He stuck it to the underside of the container in the hopes that Ikaika wouldn't see it, put it into her fridge, and fell into a deep sleep, dreaming of the pretty cheerleader across the hall.

Chapter Twenty-Three

Keala

Bye week meant Keala had Sunday to herself, so naturally, she was choreographing and practicing in her room. Ikaika had gone into the facility for a few hours, and he was just getting home. The sound of the door closing and her cousin calling to Chowder drifted through the apartment. Luckily for her, it didn't seem as though Landon had come over yet.

She could usually tell when they were together. They always seemed to come through the front door with boisterous laughter.

As Keala ran through all their dances and eight counts, her thoughts flitted to Landon's offer. Between work and dance practice with the girls yesterday, she hadn't seen him since he'd had her against the wall.

She'd scurried into her room like a coward and hadn't come out that evening, frantically texting Josie about her options.

Josie had called immediately. "Excuse me?" she'd screeched. "Who *are* you and what have you done with my innocent KayKay?"

"So it is a bad idea?"

"Hell no. You never do anything for yourself. If you know you can keep it under wraps, *please* do it. And I want every sordid detail."

That had been when Keala had finally admitted he was the man from the bar months ago. They'd gone back and forth on whether she should do it—mainly Josie talking her into it—and it made Keala feel better that someone in her exact position, with dance on the line, thought she could feasibly get away with it.

She wanted to talk to Zoe about it too, but she was worried that, as another Siren, Zoe might get in trouble for keeping the secret for her. She couldn't ask that of her friend.

"Keeks, you home?" Ikaika asked, knocking her from her thoughts.

"Yeah! Going to take a quick shower and then I'll be out," she called back. After her shower, she found Ikaika on the couch, watching games, Chowder curled up in his lap.

"Hi, how was practice?" she asked.

"Not bad. Glad it's bye week. My body needed it."

"I bet." Running backs got thrown around and slammed down by defenders more than most other players. It was something she'd always worried about when it came to him.

And Landon too, though with how strong and tall he was, defensive backs always struggled taking him to the ground.

That thought devolved into more about him. She couldn't get him off her mind no matter how hard she tried. Ikaika had turned back to the television so, feeling antsy, Keala got to work in the kitchen, needing something to do with her hands. She washed the few dishes in the sink, then began deep cleaning the counters.

"Keeks."

"Huh?" She whirled around, noting the amused look on her cousin's face.

"If it helps, he's a good guy. And if you're worried about people finding out because of dance, he'll make sure nobody ever does."

Keala dropped the sponge. "Uh...he told you about—" She waved her hand like that would finish her sentence.

"No, but I'm not an idiot. I know things have been tense between you two and I know you get fluttery and busy when you're trying to work through a problem. Based on how I found you two the other day, I'm guessing Landon is that problem."

Indeed. A very big problem.

When she didn't answer, he said, "I know you're worried about becoming someone you're not, but with him, you're different. That's what I think is so great about the two of you together. Something about him allows you to relax. You don't need to be worried you'll do whatever he wants at the risk of losing yourself."

Keala took a step back, her spine hitting the counter. Ikaika knew some of what she'd experienced in her relationships, especially since he had been the one who'd told her not to quit the Vixens and to break up with Heath instead. She had never fully expressed these deeper feelings though.

But that was all irrelevant. It wasn't like Landon was asking for a relationship.

Just sex, he'd said.

"This isn't weird for you?"

"I'm rooting for you guys. I think you work as a couple. Landon and I have football, you and I have family and the roommate moments we get. This will be his and your extracurricular separate from me."

"Sure, if that extracurricular were se—"

"Correct," he said, holding up his hand and biting back a smile. "You kids will figure it out. And Landon knows if he hurts you, he'll get his ass kicked."

Keala hadn't thought much about getting hurt. She knew Landon wasn't interested in more than the physical, and she wasn't sure she wanted anything more than that either. Plus, with dance and work, it wasn't like she had much free time.

She didn't know what Ikaika saw that had him rooting for them, but he was the person who knew her best. She took his endorsement as the closest thing to gospel.

He left her with her thoughts, and after a few more minutes, Keala washed her hands, changed into her best lingerie—though she covered it up with a T-shirt and sweatpants because she didn't need to impress him—and marched to the front door. Ikaika didn't make eye contact, smiling and turning up the volume on the TV.

Keala took a few grounding breaths before she knocked on Landon's door. When he didn't immediately answer, she rethought everything. As she turned to go back, the door swung open. Landon stood in his sweatpants, his muscled abdomen and chest on full display, his sleeve of tattoos completely visible.

He smirked, probably knowing there was one reason she would knock on his door.

Landon didn't speak, and words clogged Keala's throat. He leaned against the doorframe, grin widening as he waited.

"Don't make me say it," she managed to get out.

"Ask for what you want."

"Rules. We need rules. The most important one is we can't make things weird for Ikaika, no matter what happens. We act like we're all good, always."

Landon nodded once.

"No flirty eyes at games, either. I don't want anyone suspecting a thing. Like you said, just sex. No more kissing or almost kissing outside of this arrangement."

Something shifted in his eyes, but his smirk stayed strong as he nodded again. "You still haven't asked for what you want."

Keala didn't have it in her, so instead, she took two steps forward and kissed him. Like he'd been anticipating her move, he pulled her closer by the waist, shutting the door and pushing her against it. It reminded her of their first night, desperate and unhinged, devouring kisses and an intensity that heated her insides. Immediately, her *I don't need to impress anyone* mentality flew out the window. She followed his lead, trying to gauge what he wanted.

"Stop overthinking," he growled, trailing kisses down her jaw until he got to the spot right below her ear. Keala allowed her head to fall back against the door, enjoying his lips and warm breath against her neck.

Her hand moved over the hard planes of his chest, dragging down to his waistband. Landon pulled back, a look on his face Keala had never seen.

"Is this good?" she asked. "How do you want me to—"

"You don't care what I want most of the time, so stop caring now. I offered myself up to you so *you* can get off. Tell me what *you* want." Tenderly, he pulled her face to his and whispered against her lips, "You don't have to be the perfect person you are with everyone else. I thought I made it clear I like you the way you are. Take what you want from me and let me be the one who pleases you for a change."

Keala threw her arms around his shoulders, kissing him deeply. He picked her up and walked her across the room as she grinded against him until he was cursing and groaning into her mouth. He set her down on something hard and when she opened her eyes, Keala realized she was on his dining table.

Landon grabbed a throw pillow from his couch, setting it behind her and grinning. "Too many clothes." He wrenched her T-shirt up above her arms, thumb tracing over the lace of her bra. She arched into his touch, and he used his other hand to cup the back of her neck, tangling his fingers in her hair. He kissed her hard and played with her nipples through the lace.

Liquid heat shot through her whole body and then sank down to where his hand was slowly drifting. "Is this what you want, baby? Tell me what you want."

Baby.

She nodded, but that wasn't good enough for him. "Use your words."

Breathily, she responded, "I want your fingers inside me until I can't take it anymore, and then I want all of you."

"Now, was that so hard?" His fingers slipped beneath the waistband of her sweatpants, tracing over the lace that covered her. Landon groaned, surely because she'd soaked the fabric. "How long have you been waiting for this? How many times have you thought about this while you fucked yourself?"

Too many.

He didn't wait for a response, moving the material aside and sinking a finger into her.

Keala gasped. "Oh."

Landon lowered to kiss her again, his other hand still holding her up by the back of the neck.

His finger was slow at first, then he picked up his pace. When she asked for more, he added another and a third until she was wrapped around him so deliciously, she couldn't help but cry into the kiss, little sparks shooting across her vision. The movement of his hand rubbed her thong against her clit so perfectly, she knew it would only be a few more seconds before she lost herself in the feel of him.

"You like the way my fingers stretch you?" he breathed into her ear. Keala nodded. "Come for me, Keeks. I want to watch you fall apart before I fill you up."

So she did, writhing against his hand while he smirked down at her. When she finally found words, she blinked up at him. "Landon, please can you—" Another wave rolled through her, and she clenched around him again.

"What was that?" His dimple appeared, as it always did when he tortured her.

"I want you to fill me up," she panted.

The smirk dropped, lust taking over. "It's so *fucking* hot when you ask for what you want." He pulled his fingers out, then ripped her sweatpants and thong off, tossing them to the floor beside her shirt. He gripped her now bare thighs, dropping to his knees and licking a path from where his fingers had stretched her to her clit, sucking it into his mouth as she gasped and writhed, still a little sensitive.

"Holy, oh, *oh*."

Landon stood, pulling his sweatpants down. "I'm so glad you think this is a religious experience too." The thighs Keala had hardly been able to take her eyes off at her apartment were more distracting up close. They had to be bigger than her head, and the right one had a large triangle with palm trees, a sun, and the beach tattooed inside it.

She hadn't realized she was a fan of tattoos until she'd met Landon, and now she didn't know how she would go back.

"Sorry, I need one more." He dropped back to his knees and sucked her clit back into his mouth. All thoughts disappeared in a cloud of smoke.

When she felt like she could come again, she begged, "Landon, please. Stop teasing me. I want you."

Landon grinned, finally taking off his black boxer briefs. "Look at you asking for what you want without me telling you to." He disappeared for a second, then came back, pushing a condom on and spitting on his dick. "I need you to grab onto the edge of the table with both hands. Can you do that for me?"

He was so gentle, and the whole experience felt oddly intimate. She nodded, and he kissed her softly. Keala grabbed a table edge in each hand, resting on her elbows. Landon kissed her reverently, positioning himself at her entrance. "Ready?"

"Please," she begged once more. It was all he seemed to need, one thumb circling her clit, the other gripping her thigh as he sank into her slowly. She gasped, slightly uncomfortable, and like he could read her mind, he slowed down.

"Tell me when it feels good." He looked so determined, so handsome, and then he closed his eyes like it was all too much.

Her body was beginning to stretch for him, but she slipped a finger down to help him. With everyone else, she'd always had to help if she wanted to finish, especially because she would get so in her head that she needed to be doing something to ground herself.

Landon moved her hand back to the table. "I told you it's my job, my *privilege*, to give you what you want. So let me. And grab the table like the good girl I know you are."

Keala complied, surprised he was such a giver. She'd known he'd be good, but she hadn't realized *how* good. She'd also expected he would be opposed to eye contact and kissing, but he seemed to want that more than any of her exes had. The stretch around his cock no longer felt uncomfortable, and she whispered as much, embarrassed by how desperate she sounded for him.

Landon pulled out, then pushed back in slowly. His thumb played the perfect rhythm against her, and she arched up, knowing his promise of two orgasms hadn't been a lie. She was heading that way as he picked up the pace, drilling her so hard, she *did* need to hold on to the table. Keala whimpered as she felt herself coming, lying back completely on the table and folding her legs down onto her body.

"*Fuck*, you're so flexible." He maintained his rhythm, slamming into her until she was screaming his name, her walls clenching around him. After a few seconds, he wrapped a hand around the back of her neck, pulling her to kiss him as he came, his thrusts getting more erratic until he leaned over her, fully inside of her and panting.

They lay there for a couple of minutes, trying to catch their breath. Once again, she was struck by how intimate it had felt. She'd expected him to come, pull out, and she'd leave. She had *not* expected him to kiss her as he came or hold her so tightly when he was done.

She didn't let herself dwell on it. Keala knew neither of them wanted more.

When Landon finally helped her clean up, she got dressed. On shaky legs, she moved to the front door.

"Wait, I can make us some food."

Keala looked away. "That's okay."

"Are you sure? I know the guys were going to go out tonight, but I wouldn't mind making some good food and staying in." Something warm squeezed in her chest, begging her to stay.

But the offer was pushing things into dangerous territory. Her eyes met his again. "I took over my colleague's shift this evening, so I should go."

He frowned. "But don't you work tomorrow morning?"

"Yeah." She fidgeted with the string of her sweatpants.

"So you're going to work twenty-four hours straight?"

Keala shrugged like it was nothing. "She needs the help, and I've done it a few times. I'll sleep in on Tuesday." Initially, she'd agreed to it with pleasure because she'd needed a distraction from his offer.

Obviously, that was moot now.

Landon looked like he wanted to say something else, his hands in the pockets of his sweatpants, lips tilted down. She was so used to seeing him cocky and smirking that she hated to leave him like this.

Even still, she opened the door and walked back to Ikaika's apartment.

A few hours later, she grabbed a protein shake for her shift when she saw two containers.

Didn't have much but wanted to make sure you had something to eat. Thanks for the religious experience (imagine I'm winking at you cheekily).

She smiled, ignoring the thrill that shot through her.

It was nice knowing he was still thinking about her, because she sure as hell was still thinking about him.

Chapter Twenty-Four

Landon

> **ESPN notification –** Sabertooths fall in week nine but are still the top seed in their conference. What do head coach Mark Turner and quarterback Colton Beaumont need to fix to keep it that way?

> **ESPN notification –** Looking ahead to week ten: Will Myles Young, Landon Beaumont, and the Sentinels come out of their bye week as strong as they went into it?

Right as Landon tossed on his apron to prep for dinner, there was a knock on his door. Checking the peephole, he found Keala looking gorgeous despite the dark crescents below her eyes, her hair in a messy ponytail with pieces that fell around her face. Landon opened the door, and her jaw dropped when she noticed what he wore, cheeks turning pink.

He grinned. His apron read *My meat is 100% going into your mouth today*. "You like it? It's one of my favorites."

She laughed before her eyes met his, not saying a word.

He'd desperately hoped to see her again, and the urge to bend down and kiss her was strong. Instead, he said, "Ikaika told me you had an event with the girls after your shift tonight."

"I did. Left before it was over so I could turn in early. But I think Ikaika's trying to get back at me for last night because he's hooking up with someone *very* loudly."

Landon chuckled. "Yeah, he met her when we went out last night." He paused. "Have you eaten? I was about to make a quick dinner, but I can order some groceries to make something more."

"It's after nine thirty. Why are you just eating dinner?" He looked at her expectantly, and she ducked her head with a sheepish smile. "Okay, no, I also haven't eaten since lunch. But don't order groceries. Tell me what you need and I'll go across the street."

He frowned. "I'm not sending you out into the night to get my groceries."

"It's the least I can do when you're constantly making me food."

Landon thought for a moment, then went to his bedroom. He took off the apron and pulled on a sweatshirt, grabbing one for her. When he came back up to the main floor, she still stood in the foyer.

"Come here," he murmured. She tilted her head as she stepped toward him, puzzled. Landon held the sweatshirt up for her, and she grew more confused, eyebrows nearly touching.

"What's happening?"

"Arms up, Keeks."

She obliged hesitantly, and he pulled the hoodie over her. His hand brushed her soft cheek as he fixed the hood so it sat on her head properly.

"What are you doing?"

Landon smiled softly. "I know you're going to be upset tomorrow if you're plastered everywhere in connection with me. And I'm not going to let you go across the street to get the groceries on your own. I'm coming with you."

She was already shaking her head. "No. No! That's a horrible idea. I don't want to be seen with you."

"Ouch." He forced his smile wider, pretending the words didn't sting.

Keala crossed her arms. "Landon."

"Look, it's late and we're going across the street." He pulled up his hood and rolled down his sleeves so they covered his tattoos. "Nobody will notice us. I rarely get photographed—"

"You're literally *always* photographed."

"You didn't let me finish. I rarely get photographed unless I want to be. People here aren't our biggest fans anyway since we can barely keep a playoff run in the cards once every three or four years."

Keala squinted at him for a few seconds before she relented. "Fine. But walk a little ahead of me."

"Deal."

They were at the grocery store a few short minutes later, a small basket on Keala's arm. She looked around, worry creasing her brow, but there were only three other people there.

Landon put his hands on Keala's shoulders, forcing her to look up at him. He smoothed the crease between her eyebrows, whispering, "Breathe. It's okay. There's nobody here. And give me the basket."

She obliged without argument, eyes still bouncing around. "Do you think they think we're going to rob the store?"

Landon huffed a laugh as he walked ahead of her. "If so, we'd better hurry."

He heard the squeak of her running shoes as she followed him. Landon had visited this grocery store so many times, whether making meals for himself or for her, that he could grab all the ingredients for dinner in under five minutes.

Keala followed him through the vegetable section, and as they began toward the meats, she said, "I feel like I'm not helping much. It was my idea to come here, so give me half the list and I can go grab the rest of what we need."

Something snapped inside him at the word "we," but he just shook his head. "You're not going to get out of hanging with me that easily. Plus, I like grocery shopping with company. You don't need to help. Just talk to me."

Landon picked up a pack of chicken thighs and added it to the basket after wrapping it in a plastic bag.

"This feels oddly domestic," Keala whispered, pulling his sweatshirt tight over her body.

"I like it." The words slipped out as he looked longingly toward the wine aisle. Cooking for Keala made him want to buy a bottle of wine he'd never drink except when she was around.

He had spent all of last night thinking about her and the hottest sex of his life. It had been so intimate that, for the first time maybe ever, he'd been overwhelmed by emotions as they'd come together. It was a tough pill to swallow knowing he wanted something more than the physical with her and she didn't feel the same. Suddenly he was on the other side of a situation he'd been in countless times before. It had always been him wondering why women couldn't do casual, and now he was wondering why *he* didn't want casual.

He was convinced his parents' relationship had ruined his chances. Every time his mother had challenged his father, whether by asking for more time with her family or suggesting he and Colton spend more time on schoolwork and less on the field, it had spiraled into heated arguments that rattled the house, especially when his father slammed doors. The house had always gotten eerily quiet afterward, as if everyone had been holding their breath, too afraid to break the silence for fear that they would be yelled at next.

Relationships meant emotions, and emotions always had a way of ending in conflict. That's why he'd become a wall of granite with a cocky, charming exterior.

At least that's what Dr. Esposito said.

If Keala cut him open, saw his innermost thoughts, his shortcomings and all the ways he'd disappointed his mother, his father, his siblings, and everyone else in his life, would she stay? Would she still want him in any capacity?

Landon cleared his throat, hoping to fix his wording, reiterate that company in the grocery store was always appreciated, but Keala beat him. "Okay, Mr. Doesn't Fall in Love."

She picked up a box of cashews and slyly added it to the basket.

"How do you know I don't fall in love? Maybe I have so much love to give that I don't know what to do with it all." Keala looked at him incredulously. He shrugged. Turning attention away from himself, he asked, "Do you fall in love?"

"I think...it's so hard to say. My parents are very happy and in love. They dance in the kitchen and cuddle on the couch. I grew up knowing two things: I needed to go to medical school, and I desperately wanted to find somebody who could love me, and who I could love, as much as my parents love each other. But both of those things have been a wash."

She looked down the snack aisle eagerly, so he guided her into it as she continued talking. "I want it so badly that I become someone that I'm...not. I conform to whatever my partner wants me to be and I bend and I bend and I bend until I break. Until I'm not me anymore, not really. I do that with everyone to a certain extent but more so in relationships. I cling to the hope that *this one* will end with the happiness my parents share—once, it got to the point that I would have given up cheer if not for Ikaika talking me out of it."

Landon stopped short. He thought she was her authentic self with him, thought that was what Ikaika had hinted at, but he had to be sure. "You're not like that with me, are you? You don't...morph into someone when you talk to me, right?"

Keala laughed, patting his arm as she grabbed a small bag of sea salt and vinegar chips and added it to the basket. "No, you unfortunately just get boring old me. The first night, I wanted so badly to shed that part of me, hoping it would be the last time I saw you. I thought that since I wasn't going to interact with you again, I didn't need to be what you wanted. But then I couldn't stop thinking about what you would like when I'd promised myself not to be like that—"

"And that's why you were so in your head."

She nodded. "But then I was so upset, mostly with myself, for not being able to do it. For blurting all that stuff out. And for thinking I could avoid seeing you. That anger allowed me to push aside the urge to be what I thought you wanted, I guess." She waved her hands over her body. "So again, boring old me."

"Stop saying that. I don't need you to be anyone else." Landon caught the smile on her face before she could hide it, hating that it made him want to always be around to remind her of that fact. He guided her into the next aisle, picking up the ingredients he'd memorized.

Keala seemed more at ease as they neared the end of the last aisle, seeing no one around them.

She sent him a sidelong glance, the corners of her lips still raised. "So, Mr. *Always* Falls in Love?"

Landon laughed. "Not quite."

"Have you ever been in love?" When he didn't respond, she asked, "Why?"

"Your parents have a good relationship. Mine did not. Didn't seem like a good idea for me."

"Ah." She nodded knowingly but didn't press him.

"You're not going to ask me to explain?"

"I assume you will if you want to. If you're willing to talk about it, I'm happy to listen. I just don't make a habit of pushing people with things like this."

"'Things like this?'"

Her lips thinned as she thought through her next words. Landon grabbed the final item on the list and guided them to self-checkout.

"How often do you let people in? Like, do you talk to people about your past and your feelings?"

"God no."

"Right. So I figure I'm no different." She took items out of the basket and scanned them.

But she *was* different. Sharing didn't feel scary when it was with her. It felt *right*.

She continued when he stayed silent. "Just so you know, I'm happy to listen if that ever changes."

"I was never anyone's favorite," he blurted. His lips twisted to the side. "My dad favored Colton, obviously, and Mom and Maya were always closer. My mom tried hard to give me the attention I needed, but I spent most of my childhood on the field with my dad. And when he didn't give me the validation I wanted, I got emotional. I was a kid, you know?"

Keala nodded. She'd stopped what she'd been doing, staring at him. Needing a second, he finished scanning their items, paid, and grabbed their bags. Still, she remained quiet, waiting.

Walking with his head down, he began again. "I would cry if something didn't go my way, or express sadness or frustration over small things, like wanting him to coach me more. Any time I expressed any kind of emotion, he would berate me or call me a disappointment. Mom would step in and help, but then she'd get stuck in the crossfire and I'd feel worse."

Talking to Keala over the last few months, paired with seeing Dr. Esposito, had forced Landon to confront this part of his past. It was only fitting he let his guard down and tell Keala what he'd learned about himself.

"So instead of continuing that cycle, I figured I'd get the approval I was searching for elsewhere. Fell in with the wrong crowd and started doing dumb things. I realized it got me attention from my parents, even if it wasn't the good kind. Mom tried harder to be what I needed, but then she got sick and the little bit of good attention I was getting was gone. I didn't know how to handle the fact that she was dying, so I got worse. Drinking, partying, doing drugs, missing school. She was dying, and I was fucking around and…"

Landon sighed. "She needed me, and I was too stupid to be there for her. I disappointed her 'til the very end, and I knew that's all I would ever be. So I became what I am. Enjoyed doing it. I enjoyed the media's attention and the attention of women. It was all I'd ever wanted. And I promised myself relationships were off the table. I never wanted someone to rely on me. To expect something of me and…" He trailed off.

They'd made it back into their elevator, and Keala stepped closer to him. "You don't want to be in a situation where someone wants something from you that you can't give them."

He nodded once, wanting to look away or make a dumb joke. Instead, he kept his eyes locked on hers. "Failing people is easy when you do it on purpose. It's a different story when you try and *still* fail."

She pushed onto her toes and kissed him softly. "I'm sorry," she whispered. Landon smiled at her gratefully.

Keala had listened to one of his darkest secrets, and instead of running, she'd broken one of her rules.

Suddenly, his shoulders felt lighter and breathing came easier.

Chapter Twenty-Five

Keala

Annie ambled into the room as Keala finished rinsing out the container she'd brought lunch in. "You've been eating real lunch instead of snacks recently." Annie smiled. "Good for you. Some days, I can put together something quick, and other days"—she shook her head—"not so much."

Unsurprisingly, the lunch she'd eaten was thanks to Landon. He'd left a note under this batch that read *Thank you for letting me open up the best way I know how.*

Short and sweet and another example of a version of him she never would have imagined before getting to know him. Keala had noticed the way his shoulders had dropped at the grocery store a few days ago, losing tension as he'd told her about his childhood.

"I'm the same way. Most of the time, I'm too tired," Keala responded.

She tucked the container and spoon into her purse before getting back to work.

The moment she stepped out on the floor, the frenzy began again and she fell into the routine of it all. One room, then the next, then the next. She moved through the chaos, eyes scanning rooms as she juggled patient histories, lab results, and the usual ebb and flow of emergencies. One moment, she was suturing a deep laceration on a fourteen-year-old's leg, and the next, she was interpreting an ECG for a suspected heart attack.

It was two and a half hours before she was able to check her phone again, and when she did, her stomach dropped.

Two missed calls from her mother could mean one of two things: someone in the family was gravely injured or dead, or she had forgotten Keala's schedule again, which wasn't uncommon.

Keala ducked into a supply closet and called her back.

"Hi, sweetie."

"Mom? Is everything okay?"

"Everything is more than okay! You'll never guess what we just found out."

Keala couldn't think of anything, but she attempted a joke. "I hope I'm not about to have another sibling."

Her mom laughed, as Keala had hoped she would. Her mother was the first person she'd always wanted to please, after all.

"Nothing like that, no." She chuckled again. "The next time Akoni is in town, we're going to be celebrating big because he was accepted into his first program! More are going to come in, of course, but it's the start of something very exciting for your brother..."

Her mother continued talking, but Keala's throat had closed. She slammed a hand against the closet wall to steady herself as the floor flew out from under her.

Keala had spent almost every moment of her life trying to outrun Akoni or, at the very least, keep pace with him despite him being younger. And finally, the moment she'd been dreading was upon her.

Not only had he caught up, he'd done the thing she hadn't been able to do.

"Sweetie? Can you hear me? You're so quiet."

Keala swallowed over the sandpaper in her throat. "No, that's so great. I'm so happy for him. We knew it was coming."

And a part of her *had* always known it. Healthcare for her had been the way to prove to her parents she was worthy of their love. It had never been a passion. But Akoni? He had been made for brain surgery, and her whole family had known it the moment he'd asked for a model of the human brain for his sixth birthday.

It shouldn't have come as such a surprise to Keala. And yet, here she stood, trying to hold in the beginnings of a panic attack in a closet in the emergency department, where she was *just* a nurse practitioner, according to her family.

Not a doctor.

Her hand still rested against the wall, uncertain that she could manage her weight without it. The feeling of failure that had shoved its way down her throat five years ago when she'd found out she hadn't gotten into any programs—a feeling which had grown dormant and had been assumed gone because of it—was now alive and well. And the only thing it told her was that her years in healthcare, no matter how hard they had been, no matter who she'd helped, no matter that she'd treated patients in almost every way that an MD could have, none of it made a difference.

She was back to being the sibling her parents were mildly proud of but not as much so as their prodigy. She was the girl who had lied about her intelligence and abilities, buried herself in a mountain of debt to pretend things were okay, and who still wasn't good enough.

And it hurt so much to know that she would never be able to rectify it because there was no way in hell she was going to force her way through medical school now.

Which meant her only avenue to stay within shooting distance of her brother was to push herself harder at work, treat more patients, prove as valuable as she could now before he was doing his residency and moved on to bigger and better things. Keala needed to finish paying off her debt, work hard to find an NP job that paid more, and prove to everyone that she *was* capable. That there was a reason they kept her around.

Keala would salvage every last drop of pride her parents had ever shown her for a little longer.

"Yes, we did, but still, wish him well so he knows you're thinking of him. And the next time you come home, we can all do a video call."

"That sounds great."

Keala shoved down the bitterness, the jealousy, the hurt. Every horrible emotion she had never let herself feel because of how it brought others down. She would smile and applaud her brother, she would text him how proud of him she was, and she would throw herself back into her work to prove she was, at the very least, half the child he was.

"And how's work?" her mother asked, as if it were an afterthought. Though Keala knew she didn't mean anything by it, the question still carried that subtle undercurrent of disappointment that Keala had *chosen* not to go to medical school.

Or maybe it was all in her head.

"It's good. Busy."

"And it's never too late to go to medical school. You got in once, you could do it again. You have so much training now. You could do derm and never be on call. It would be a better life."

Now would have been the time to come clean. Tell her mother she hadn't chosen this life over medical school. Tell her she hadn't gotten into a single program, even with her extracurriculars, time spent in the field, and test scores. That careening down the path of NP had come out of necessity because she wasn't as smart or perfect as Akoni.

But all that honesty would do was prove to her parents she was the failure she'd been trying so hard not to be.

Better to lie. "Okay, Mom. I'll look into derm." After a beat, likely because of how overwhelmed she felt, she whispered, "I don't want to disappoint you…I don't want to be anything like Nohea."

Her mother was so silent, Keala thought she'd hung up. She'd broken the Lōkahi-Prices' cardinal rule: never talk about her older brother.

"What…what do you mean?"

Aaliyah knocked and stuck her head into the closet. "There's a cardiologist here to consult for the patient in room fifteen."

"On it. Thank you, Aaliyah." The nurse nodded and left. "Mom, I have to go. I'll talk to you later."

"Okay, sweetheart. Will you be coming over to watch the game on Sunday?"

"Probably not. I promised I'd watch with the girls, but I can come over before."

"Great. Love you."

"Love you too," Keala answered quietly before clicking her phone off and letting out a sigh. She texted her brother quickly, then threw herself into the rest of her shift, trying to distract herself from feelings she thought she had laid to rest.

Later that evening, after dance practice at Zoe's, the girls had convinced Keala to come out for weekly drinks. She'd missed a lot of bonding time with them because of work, and with her newfound promise to focus more on her job, this could be her last opportunity for a while. It helped that going out meant not seeing the guys, especially Landon.

Keala liked what she and Landon had right now. They'd hooked up once since the first time Sunday, and though she'd given small pieces of herself to him, she wasn't ready to talk about the feelings her conversation with her mother had brought up. Landon would have been able to read it in her face in a second, and she couldn't stomach explaining it to him. Didn't want to see his face when she told him the full spectrum of her inadequacies.

She would get back after they were asleep, then tomorrow they would be on a plane to Florida for their game, giving her a few days.

And it was Friday. Did she need any other reason to go out?

"And then he came in my hair when I *specifically* told him not to," Kennedy said so loudly, three separate groups of guys at the bar turned to look at her. Keala and Zoe leaned into each other, giggling, three margaritas in.

"Wait, believe it or not, that happened to me too," Carol chimed in. "Two hours before call time for a game."

As one, the girls groaned in understanding.

"Exactly! I couldn't wash it, so I had to go in and clean it up manually. Brooklyn found me double-checking that it was all gone in the bathroom and helped."

Nova, a third year, sat up taller on her stool. "Did you guys hear Brooklyn's looking at other teams?"

There were gasps around the table. Keala wasn't all that surprised, considering Brooklyn hardly paid attention during choreography sessions, but she was a sweetheart. The team would certainly miss her.

"Do you think Cora and Angelica know?" Jamie asked.

Nova scoffed. "There's no way. Angelica would have skinned her alive by now."

"Graphic," Zoe muttered, slipping her hand into Keala's and setting her head on Keala's shoulder.

"But true," Keala responded quietly.

Their waitress brought out a tray of shots. Aurelia, one of the captains, set her drink down and clapped a couple of times. "Ladies, I think we all know what time it is. Nova just got engaged, and that means—"

"Shots!" most of the girls yelled.

Zoe laughed when Keala jumped. "Zo, there's no way I can take shots. I have work tomorrow and I'll be lucky to wake up on time as it is."

"Don't worry." She nodded toward the shots, then tapped Keala's empty margarita glass. "It's clear liquor. Dump it in here when we knock them back and pretend the ice is melting."

"You're a genius."

"I know!"

The girls each took a shot, and when they tossed them back, Keala poured hers into her glass.

Mackenzie chimed in. "Now we each have to tell a story of our favorite Nova moment. Zoe first!"

"But I have so many." Zoe pouted, thinking. "Okay, okay. Two years ago when she got drunk, climbed onto the roof of her ex's house, and took a selfie on top of Rudolph."

Nova pointed at Zoe, nodding. "Yes! One of my better moments. I'm so glad you guys were there to save me when I slipped off the gutter."

"Love you Nova girl!" Zoe yelled.

Mackenzie faced Keala. "KayKay, your turn!"

Keala thought about her more recent interactions with Nova, but because they weren't in the same group, they hadn't had many. "Tryouts this year. I was nervous because everyone knew each other and had formed friend groups and I didn't think there was a place for me. But Nova hugged me like she'd known me her whole life, and when she saw my first solo, she told me she would give up her spot if I didn't make it. It was the sweetest thing to say, even if Angelica would have spit on the idea, and it made me feel like I'd found my people. Like my last year in a new place didn't have to be lonely."

A chorus of awws went around the table.

Nova, who was all the way across the long table from Keala, got up and drunkenly ran to her, throwing her arms around Keala's shoulders. "You aren't supposed to make me cry!"

"I mean it," Keala responded quietly, patting her arms. "I was so intimidated by you guys, and you made me feel like I belonged."

"Love you," Nova whispered.

"Love you more, and so happy for you."

Nova returned to her seat, and each of the rest of the girls who'd come out gave their favorite stories about her. When everyone had either made Nova laugh so hard that she almost fell out of her seat or shed a few tears, conversation turned to other topics. During Jamie's graphic explanation of a dog neutering surgery gone wrong, Keala's phone vibrated under her leg.

She had seven messages from Landon: five from over an hour ago, one from half an hour ago, and one just now.

Landon

> Smash isn't the same without you.

He'd sent a photo of him and Ikaika playing the video game.

Landon

> Bet you thought I was talking about sex.
> I must be rubbing off on you.

> Hah, that one was sexual too.

> You should come over after you're done with practice. I can promise two earth-shattering orgasms. At least.

> You doing okay? Let me know when you're on the way. I'll wait up.

> Keeks?

Regret and longing twisted in her chest, even as something fluttered in her stomach. She so badly wanted to respond, but she'd also spent a lot of her week focusing on him and how giddy he made her feel. Did she have time to continue what they were doing? Keala didn't think so.

"KayKay! Who's got you blushing?" Jordy asked from a couple of seats down. Keala clicked her phone off, putting it back under her leg.

"Is it the guy from Halloween? Did you end up going out with him?"

Keala laughed nervously, checking if Zoe had seen anything. If so, her friend seemed very nonchalant. "I went out with him once, but no." Trying to come up with a way to spin this, she continued, "I've been hooking up with...a guy from work. It's not exactly allowed, but I'm not sure it's going to continue anyway."

"Why not?" Jordy asked. The table quieted.

"I...He's not a relationship guy, and it seems like a bad idea to keep going when it isn't permitted."

"Show us a picture!" someone yelled at the same time Mackenzie asked, "Do you like him?"

"I don't have any pictures. I like hanging out with him and we're compatible, but I'm so busy with work that even if he were a relationship guy, I'm not sure it would work out."

A few of the girls nodded thoughtfully.

"Is he hot?" Jordy asked.

"Insanely."

Nova slapped the table. "Does he make sure you finish?"

Keala nodded slyly. That was an understatement.

"Then fuck it," Mackenzie said. "And keep fucking him."

The girls laughed, a few murmuring their assent. Keala wasn't sure they'd feel that way if they knew the truth of who he was. Plus, she still wasn't ready to face his well-meaning scrutiny after the call with her mother.

Keala shoved Landon from her mind, enjoying the rest of the evening with her girls. She hoped the Sentinels kept winning so she could have more times like these.

After this season, nothing would be the same.

Chapter Twenty-Six

Landon

ESPN notification – Colton Beaumont's Sabertooths are unstoppable. Week ten highlights and more...

ESPN notification – Jacksonville fans stunned silent by Sentinels tight end Landon Beaumont on three separate occasions. Could he be the difference between a no-playoff season and a championship run?

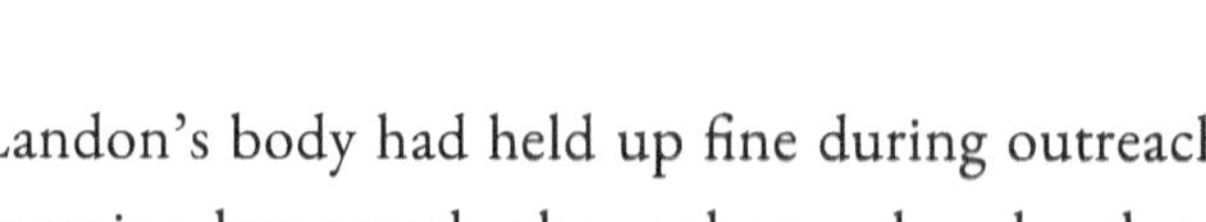

Landon's body had held up fine during outreach Monday morning, but now that he was home, the aches that came with being slammed down by defensive backs made themselves known.

As if that wasn't bad enough, he was growing suspicious that Keala was avoiding him. Again. Was it because of what he'd admitted in the grocery store? It didn't make sense, seeing as they'd slept together two days later, but he couldn't explain away the ignored texts. Maybe it had been too much to handle.

Needing something comforting, he grabbed a hoodie and walked toward the elevator. He would have asked Ikaika to join, but Landon was pretty sure he was occupied with the woman he'd been seeing.

The elevator opened, and out stepped Keala in her scrubs, dark semicircles below her eyes and her hair in a ponytail. It had grown since they'd met, and he had to stop the mental image of how he'd used it to pull her head back the last time they'd hooked up.

"Keeks, hey."

Her eyes widened, and by the time he'd blinked, she was behind him.

"Hi!"

"I'm going to the store. Do you want to come? I can make you dinner." He hadn't been alone with her in a week, and he wanted to apologize for talking about himself so much. Ask her if they could go back to how things had been before because he missed hearing about her long days. "Plus, I think Ikaika has someone over again."

"Oh, that's okay, but thank you. I've got dance soon, and then I took an extra shift tomorrow morning." She turned and practically ran down the hall, refusing to meet his eyes as she entered the apartment and shut the door behind her.

Landon stuck his hand into the elevator as it began to close, jumping in and pressing the button for the first floor. He didn't want to go to the store, knowing it wouldn't put a dent in his wallet to have groceries delivered, but a part of him knew the more he left the apartment, the more chances he'd have to see her again.

Except now it was clear she *was* avoiding him. While, yes, she often practiced at one of her teammates' places, she *always* went straight after her shift.

His heart sank, and he dialed the first person who came to mind.

"Hello?" his sister answered sleepily. He was glad she'd picked up. If she hadn't, he would have called Savannah, who was on tour and unlikely to be of help since she was as emotionally stunted as he was.

"Mai, hey. I'm sorry, did I wake you?" He checked the time, noting it was after ten for her.

"No, no. It's just been a long day. I'm still at the courts. What's up?"

He walked out onto the first floor, smiling at Richard behind the desk as he left the building and trudged around the block.

"My friend has a problem." He hadn't thought through what he would say, but he wasn't off to a good start.

"Okay...?"

He cleared his throat. "So, basically, he slept with this girl. Wait, let me back up. Originally, back in August, they almost had a one-night stand, but she was in her head, and when he offered to take her home, she blurted out some personal things. Then, they both realized they'd be living on the same floor and have since gotten to know each other."

Sounding more awake, Maya said, "Right. Gotcha. Yes, so your friend slept with her?"

"She'd been tense and in need of something, so he offered to help, and after a couple of days, she took him up on the offer. It's casual, right?"

"Right."

"So then they hung out a couple of times after, sometimes with another person—let's say her cousin."

"You're friends with her—I mean, your friend is close with the girl's cousin?"

"Yes. Anyway, they hung out a few times, and one of the times they were alone, he confessed some things about himself. They hung out with the cousin a few times after and hooked up one more time, but now she seems to be avoiding him. What would you tell my friend?"

"I'd ask what your friend confessed to her." She paused, then blurted, "And if it has to do with anything criminal, I don't want to know because I don't want to have to serve as a witness against you."

Landon rolled his eyes. "Please. You know it'll never come to that. And it's not about me."

"Good. So, what did he tell her?"

"He...sort of expressed why he's scared of relationships. And she responded well, but now..."

"Now she's avoiding him."

"Yeah. And this isn't new. She avoids him any time things change between them."

"Based on the very limited information I'm working off here, it sounds like something happened in her personal life. If she's been normal with you—him, sorry, after he confessed those feelings, and then is avoiding him a few days later, maybe something happened in her life that made her need some time away."

Landon looked at the grocery store, but he was no longer hungry. "Like what exactly?"

"I can't say without knowing her. How long has this avoiding been going on?"

"Since Friday."

"So it hasn't been that long. Tell him to give her another day or so and wait until she's ready to talk about it before trying."

"And if she never wants to talk to him again?"

"What makes you say that?"

Landon was silent for a minute as he continued walking around the apartment building. If there was anyone else in his life he'd been honest with or who, at the very least, understood the way he acted with others, it was Maya. "I think he's worried that he was too honest with her and it scared her away."

It was his sister's turn to remain silent. Then, "Landon, I know it's scary to let your guard down with people, but if she's stuck around with all your teasing and has you this in your head, I have to imagine she's not that kind of person. Give her time to tell you what's going on. You opened up, now give her the space and capacity to do the same." She paused. "Have you ever felt this way about someone before?"

"My friend. This is about my friend. And, no, he hasn't."

"Right, sorry. Then tell your friend to let her work it out. If things are meant to be, they will be. And also tell him I love him and that if he needs to talk to someone about what's going on with him, his sister is here for him."

Landon cracked a smile. "He really likes this woman. And he's terrified."

"Well, I'm proud of him for recognizing something good and wanting to hold on to it."

"Yeah." Quietly, he added, "I, uh...I started therapy. It...I think it's helping." He chuckled. "If I'd had a session before calling you, I wouldn't be such a mess right now, I think."

Maya laughed along with him. "Landon, that's amazing. I'm so glad it's helping. If you ever want to compare childhood trauma notes, I'm just a call away." She laughed again. "And I'm glad we're finally done playing the 'my friend' game."

"I appreciate that. And thank you for going along with it."

"Anytime. Let me know how everything goes, and don't forget to talk to Colton."

Landon groaned. "Maya, please. Can't you see I'm dealing with something here?"

"Yes, yes. I can see that. But I'm giving you a deadline to make things right. You guys have been up and down over the years and I'm tired of gatherings being tense. Whenever we have Mom's celebration of life this year, which *is* going to happen, by the way, I will sit you both down and make you talk if you don't figure it out before then."

"I texted that I was free last week. This time, it's Colton's fault." They liked to have their mom's celebration of life the week of her birthday whenever they could, but with so many busy people trying to make it work, it had been moved all over the season the last few years. This year, it'd been more of a struggle with both their seasons, Maya's charity, and Colton's daughter.

"Landon, I swear to—"

"Alright, alright. You mentioned that one week in December. I can do that if it's on the West Coast. I have a game that week; Colton doesn't." It was a little less than a month away, which gave him plenty of time to procrastinate. The last thing he wanted to think about right now was burying the hatchet with Colton. He and Dr. Esposito had barely scratched the surface of his issues with his brother, and he'd probably need months of unpacking before he was ready.

"Great. We'll do it with Nana and Nani in Los Angeles," she said, referring to their mom's father and mother. "I'll text in the group about it."

"Can't wait," he responded, only mildly sarcastically.

Though the conversation had turned, his thoughts remained on Keala. He hoped she'd be willing to talk to him soon because not having her in his life was driving him insane.

And *that* terrified him.

Chapter Twenty-Seven

Keala

To say Keala was tired would have been an understate-ment. In the interest of throwing herself into her work even harder to prove herself—and okay, yes, avoiding Lan-don—she had offered to take an extra shift yesterday, which hadn't been her brightest move. She'd made it to Tuesday practice approximately thirty seconds before eight, and An-gelica, who had cooled down on her marginally, hadn't been happy.

At least she hadn't seemed to spend much of her attention on Keala today other than to remind her that she needed to get her "face energy" up. As the choreography session after practice drew to a close, Cora walked up to Keala, who lay on her back on the practice field, trying to catch her breath.

"Keala."

She sat up. "Yes, hi. Do you need me to do something?"

"Yes. I need you to sleep."

"Sorry?"

"You look like you haven't slept in three days."

That wasn't very nice, as true as it may have been. Her inability to fall asleep, and then to stay asleep, had been flaring up. "I slept in this morning." Until eight, when her internal alarm had told her to get her ass up and get to work on something. Anything.

"You might not be a captain, but as a senior member with years of experience under your belt, you are a team leader. I need you to take care of yourself and set a better example for the women who look up to you."

It wasn't as if she hadn't been *trying* to sleep. Every time she closed her eyes, she imagined Akoni in his white coat, and her eyes flew back open. Then, when she pushed the insecurities that image brought up out of her head, her mind turned to Landon and all the things she wanted him to do to her. It had been a week since they'd last hooked up, and her body was betraying her, aching for more of him.

She was trying so hard not to give in, too afraid that he'd see the failure written across her face and she'd have to tell him about it.

"I'll do better," she promised before Cora went to talk to Jordy.

Zoe helped her up. They packed their things and walked to the lot together. "Are you doing okay? You seem more tired than usual."

"Just family stuff. Trying to pick up more shifts at the hospital." Zoe was her closest friend in the city besides Ikaika, but the thought of having to dig through the past, her lies, and all the rest made Keala's skin crawl.

"I'm sorry. Happy to talk it over if you want." Keala nodded with a reassuring smile. They continued toward the lot. "Oh! If you're not doing anything for Thanksgiving, a few of us are getting together for the game since it's away."

Keala had been so busy, she couldn't believe it was already mid-November. Her family didn't celebrate Thanksgiving, so her parents took the week to travel together. "That sounds good. The hospital gets crazy on the holidays, especially Thanksgiving, so I might go in if it gets too hectic, but I'll find a way to be there for the game."

"Great! It'll be fun." When they reached their cars, Zoe must have seen something in Keala's face because she reached out and hugged her. "See you tomorrow?"

"Aye aye, captain!" Keala joked, hoping her friend would stop worrying about her. She gave Zoe one more squeeze before getting into her car.

The drive home flew by. Keala had been so focused on what she would say when she saw Landon next, she barely registered pulling into the parking garage and putting her car in park.

As she stepped out of the elevator, she was faced with the man who'd been on her mind more often than not.

"Oh, hi." He was in a Sentinels sweatsuit, black with red lettering and the mascot emblazoned on both the sweatshirt and sweatpants. Calling him handsome didn't do him justice. Even without his signature smile, he was devastating.

"Hi."

She tried to skirt around him, but he stepped in front of her. "Keala, what's going on? I know you're a busy woman, but it seems like you're avoiding me. It seems like half the time we've known each other has been spent with you brushing me off, and I don't get why."

She faltered for half a second before blurting, "I've been busy. You're the one who said this was nothing more than sex." As soon as the words were out of her mouth, she wished she could shove them back in.

His face dropped, clearly hurt. That look flipped a switch inside of her, and it had nothing to do with her inherent need to please everyone in sight. This was specific to him, and all she wanted to do was hold him and tell him she was sorry.

He moved past her toward the elevator, but she grabbed his arm, tugging him back. "Stop, wait. I'm sorry. Can we talk about this in your apartment?" She realized he was on his way out. "Or are you going somewhere?"

"No, let's talk."

She dropped his arm as they walked in the direction of the apartments, not feeling as though she deserved to touch him. When they got to his apartment, he sat on the couch and motioned for her to do the same.

Keala thought she had figured out what she'd say, but now that she was in front of him, she wanted to sink into the cushions and disappear. She didn't want to see his face when he came to the realization she wasn't as perfectly put together as everyone thought.

"Keeks, it's me. What's up?" he asked earnestly.

He was right. It was him. She'd never had an issue being honest with him. And after she'd told him he could open up to her, it was hypocritical for her to shut him out.

"I told you a bit about my brothers." She sighed, closing her eyes. "What I haven't told you is that I knew if I wanted my parents to see me the same way they see my younger brother, I needed to push myself to get into medical school. It was just a means to an end for me. Only, I put in all this work to find out that I'm not smart enough for it. I didn't get into a single program."

She opened her eyes, looking for a reaction.

"Do you think you didn't get in on purpose? Like a subconscious thing?"

"No? I mean, I spent countless hours around school and dance studying for qualifying exams and getting clinical hours in. I worked so hard on my applications, and it just wasn't enough."

Landon's lips thinned like he had something to say, but he didn't verbalize the thought.

"I always knew the day would come, but for some reason, I haven't thought about it recently. Friday, I found out that Akoni got into medical school. One program sent him an acceptance, and I'm sure there are more to come. And I'm happy for him, I am. It's just..."

Keala put her head in her hands as she admitted the final piece. "I told my parents that I got in too and chose not to go. Because I was so embarrassed they would see that I'm not Akoni. As soon as I knew I didn't make the cut, I applied to a graduate program so I could become an NP. I threw myself into it. I pushed myself so hard because I'd acted like this was the path I wanted. I have to prove it."

She turned to him. "I'm so terrified of being another family screwup. Yeah, a piece of me is always choreographing, always wishing I could be out on the field every second of the day, but this is what I have to do."

"To what end?"

"All this hard work will pay off eventually," Keala said, confused that he wasn't understanding. "As long as I stay the course, I'll be able to pay off my loans and live the lifestyle my parents want for me. They'll be proud of me."

She blinked and saw Nohea stumbling home after being gone for days, haggard and disheveled, acting strangely, bruises and cuts all over his face. Saw the way her parents yelled at him, yelled at each other while they figured out what to do with him. Her mother's random bursts of tears and her father's stoic sadness after Nohea had been kicked out. Sure, she would never reach that level, but since seeing him leave the house for the last time, her life had become a series of pushing herself to be the best, the brightest, the reason for her parents' pride.

Keala wasn't sure her parents could survive another family disappointment.

"And once you have that lifestyle? What, you'll work yourself to the bone until you collapse?"

Keala frowned, crossing her arms across her chest tightly. "If I'm successful in society's eyes, in my parents' eyes, then I'll be happy." Her voice wavered slightly, but she held firm. "I just have to get there first."

Landon didn't answer immediately. He blinked at her, eyes searching her face. It was obvious he wasn't convinced. His jaw tightened, like he was gearing up to argue, but instead, he let the silence stretch out between them.

"What do you think I should do then?" she snapped, the words coming out like a plea despite her defensive tone. "I don't know any other path for myself," she added. Trying to have this conversation with him had been a mistake.

For a moment, she thought Landon would pull back. Instead, his face softened, eyes filled with concern as he reached for her arms, gently pulling them from her chest. "You don't have to prove to anyone that you deserve to take up space, Keala," he said, his voice low but firm. "You don't need to justify your every breath, your every movement, by constantly doing what everyone else wants." His thumb traced over her hand almost absentmindedly, as if trying to soothe her. "I used to think I needed to work to the point of physical pain to make myself worthy of the attention Colton got. I thought, if I got it, I'd finally matter."

Keala opened her mouth to protest, but he continued, "Obviously, things changed when I lost my mom. I did a complete one-eighty, pretending I didn't care what people thought while partying to numb the fact that I still wasn't anything more than Colton's little brother. I won't lie and say I'm over it, but *you've* shown me that's not true. You've proven that I can be imperfect and still be seen. You don't need to sacrifice yourself for someone else's idea of what you should be any more than I need to make a name for myself separate from my brother. You can just *be*. Live your life for yourself."

Landon's hands tightened around hers, his grip warm and reassuring. "If you hate this job as much as it sounds like you do, stop killing yourself trying to make others happy with it. You deserve more than that."

She swallowed hard, tears pricking her eyes. He'd read her like a book. Her life's work was justification after justification of her existence, the need to prove she belonged in every room, the need to be liked by every person around her.

And to know that someone saw that, acknowledged it, knew the way it ate her up inside, sent waves of something unidentifiable through her body.

His other hand cupped her face, and then he lifted her chin so her eyes met his. "I have never seen you happier than when you're dancing or talking about dance. During games, I spend half the time defense is on the field—and sometimes when offense is too—watching you in your element. You're so excited and beautiful, and then you go to work and it's like someone's sapped every last drop of it from you. Stop saying yes to things that rob you of your happiness, Keeks."

Without a thought, she climbed into his lap, legs on either side of his, arms around his neck, face pressed to where his heart beat a steadying rhythm. Zoe had seen that she'd needed comfort, it just hadn't been the right kind. And how could it have been when Keala hadn't been honest with her?

But she had been with Landon, and instead of looking at her like she was an idiot for not getting into medical school, he'd *seen* her. The one person she couldn't keep from seeing the real her—the version of her she barely knew—wasn't put off.

Strong arms clutched her to him tightly, like he needed this as much as she did. Into her hair, he murmured, "Please stop avoiding me. I never know what to do and I hate it. If you still want to use me for stress relief, you can find me when you have the time, but don't run away. I've missed talking to you, and I know Ikaika has too."

"Okay," she whispered back.

Landon kissed her head, her temple, her cheek, her jaw. Keala leaned back, capturing his lips softly and slipping her hands into his hair. After a few moments, she deepened the kiss, needing more. He groaned into her mouth when her body moved against him.

"We don't need to do this tonight. Let me make you food."

"You've made me plenty of food. I want this."

He searched her face, then nodded. "Okay. But I didn't say all that stuff for this. I just missed you."

"I know," she breathed, then kissed him again. All the more reason to want this with him. Her body had missed the feel of his big, calloused hands holding her, and after a long week—long month, long *year*—she deserved to feel good.

Keala continued grinding on him, enjoying the friction and the noises he made until she knew she was ready for more. She reached down, palming him over his sweatpants, and he twitched, laughing a little.

"I'm glad you're...learning to focus on...what you want," he panted between kisses.

"I have a good teacher." Her hand slipped beneath his boxer briefs. She shoved them down, his cock springing free. When she looked at him, he was watching her with that soft, tender look she'd been seeing on his face recently. Keala was so sure that, to him, this was a casual hook up. But moments like this one made her wonder if this was a bad idea, because she was starting to feel something *more*. Maybe she had just been seeing what she wanted to see on his face.

Landon placed a hand on her cheek, guiding her lips back to his. "Get out of your head. What do you want?" he asked against them.

She bit her lip, looking down. "Can I ride you?" She'd never had much of an interest in it, but with the way her body felt from the friction, she was sure it would be good.

"Of course you can." He moved to the drawer in his end table, a hand still holding her close to him as he pulled a condom out. When she raised an eyebrow, he smirked. Landon ripped the wrapper with his teeth and rolled it onto himself, spitting on it. "I like to be prepared. Now let me see how ready you are, baby. Show me how badly you need my cock."

Keala raised up, and when his finger slipped inside her without resistance, they both moaned. He pulled out and held his finger in front of her lips. She took it in her mouth as she positioned herself over him, sinking all the way down. Landon's eyes closed, and when they opened again, she could hardly see the brown of his irises.

She moved up and down slowly, then sped up until her legs ached. Keala felt the tension in her spine building, the friction of the position and him filling her enough to push her to the edge. He mumbled praises against her neck as he kissed her reverently, and when he felt her slowing down, he took over, hands on her hips, slamming into her and kissing her mouth hard until they both shook and cried each other's names.

When it was over, he pressed his head to her chest, breathing heavily with both hands gripping her waist like he wasn't ready to let go.

Chapter Twenty-Eight

Landon

Landon kept his head pressed to her chest as his breathing evened out, feeling an immeasurable sense of peace with her in his arms. He was still riding the high of knowing his words had made her feel a bit better, even if not completely. He wished he could solve it all for her, make it so she never felt insecure about being herself ever again. If only it were as simple as helping her find a choreography job that she loved, that fulfilled her and didn't dim her light. He'd have spent every penny he had to take care of her if he believed she would have let him.

He closed his eyes as that thought flitted by, knowing he was beyond fucked for Keala.

She shifted in his lap. Frantically, he pleaded, "Please don't leave." The other two times, she'd hightailed it out of his apartment. He leaned back, eyes on hers. "Let me take care of you. You spend all week taking care of others and caring about what everyone else wants. Let me do that for you."

Keala searched his face for something. Nodded. Landon pulled her into his bathroom, helping her out of her clothes and into the tub. She gave him a soft smile as he scrubbed soap over her freckled skin. Smiled wider when he gently shampooed and conditioned her hair. She kissed him when he toweled her dry. Again after he got her into a pair of his boxers and a T-shirt. Again, harder, after he fed her a few bites of food from the facility.

When he finally tucked her into his bed, he asked, "Do you want me to sleep upstairs?"

Her voice was so wobbly, and exhaustion was clear in every crevice of her face, every inhale of air, every tremor of her hand, like the last leaf of autumn clinging to a branch in the wind as she responded, "No. Stay with me, please."

Thank god.

Landon got under his comforter with her, and she folded herself against him, soft, damp hair pressed to his chest.

"Will you be at the children's hospital Monday?" she asked quietly.

"I will." Every year, the team set up visits for players to go to children's hospitals around San Jose and sign autographs, take pictures, and just generally boost morale. Every year, Landon offered to go despite how much he hated hospitals. "You're not working?"

"I switched to a Wednesday shift. I'm rarely able to do events, so sometimes I feel bad and move things around." Keala turned, and even in the dark, he could feel how beautiful she was. "I know we can't interact, but I'm glad you'll be there."

"I'm glad you'll be there too," he whispered, pulling her close to himself. "I hate hospitals."

He thought they'd sleep, but she sat up slightly, and though she said nothing, he knew she wanted an explanation.

"I was in the living room with my mom when she collapsed. Dehydration from the chemo, they said. She'd been doing well, so we all thought she'd be back home in no time. Just there for a day or two."

He swallowed, his throat tight with the pain of remembering. "But she'd developed an infection, and her chances of recovery seemed to dwindle by the day. That was the first and only time I ever saw her cry...and I think it was then that I finally realized how serious it all was. And being at that hospital...god." He gritted his teeth, trying not to slip into memories of what the hospital evoked in him. "It felt like walking into a haunted house. I'm sorry, that's a horrible thing to say, but every time I went to see her in the hospital, which was rare since Dad always had me on the field, I hated every second of it.

"I hated seeing her so frail and weak. Maya, my little sister, didn't understand that Mom wasn't coming home after we learned about the infection, so Colton and I tried to shield her from it. We had to act like everything was fine, at Mom's request. And honestly? It was kind of easy to act that way when I spent most of my life playing football. I pretended she was at home, waiting for us to come back, like she had been before she collapsed. I wasn't allowed to cry about it when Dad was around anyway, so Colton and I had to find a way to be okay and hide how we felt. No surprise, he was way better at it than I was."

Keala stroked a finger across Landon's collarbone, then tucked her head under his and hugged him just that much tighter at his words. A show of understanding, of knowing what it was like to grow up and see yourself as lesser when compared to your sibling.

"But the hospital was where I had to face it head-on, and I didn't know how. The walls closed in on me, and I…I hated it, that feeling of grief and hopelessness. And, *god*, of disappointing her. I knew what I was doing wasn't going to make her better, and yet I kept getting caught smoking or skipping class or fighting. I couldn't help her, and I could barely help my sister. I craved Dad's approval, and if not his approval then his attention, so much that I did anything I could to get it. And I hated myself for it."

Sometimes, often, he still hated himself. But he didn't say that out loud.

Keala kissed him softly.

"I don't think she was disappointed in you. I think she understood how hard everything was for you, how tough it was to handle that as a teenager. I think she knew you were being strong for your sister, and even if she didn't get a chance to say it, I know she was and is proud of you. Because there's not a sane person on this planet who could know you like I do and not be," Keala whispered, kissing his shoulder once.

When Landon squeezed her, she continued, "And if on Monday you feel that way, like the walls are closing in on you, look at me. I'll be there, waving my poms and smiling. Even if I'm not looking at you, know that I'm smiling for you, okay?"

"Okay."

Somehow, despite wanting to spend the evening taking care of her, Keala had ended the night doing the same for him because that was who she was. Her words felt like tangible brushes of her fingers against his cheek, comforting him.

Landon was more than fucked, and he knew nothing, not even trying to hit pause on whatever they were doing, would stop it. It was only the first evening he was getting to sleep beside her, but he realized he wanted them all to be like this.

That should have scared him, but he was too tired to deep dive through all the reasons this could end poorly. Reaching toward his phone on the nightstand, he set a quieter alarm for thirty minutes before he would normally wake up so he could hold her for a little longer before football.

Chapter Twenty-Nine

Landon

> **ESPN notification –** With San Jose's Landon Beaumont stepping up the last few games, it's possible we'll get a Beaumont showdown in the championship game. Here's what would have to happen...

Do you feel like you'll be okay going in now?" Dr. Esposito asked him five days later. He sat in his car in the hospital garage, finishing up his session before the event began, growing ever more thankful that she made herself available around his schedule.

The itch he felt all over his body told him the answer to her question was *probably not*. "I know I'll be fine, but I still don't feel good about it."

"And that's completely understandable. I commend you for taking on these events every year. Your willingness to help others in spite of your personal feelings is remarkable."

Landon didn't agree with that sentiment, but he stayed quiet. He'd hoped talking to her would make this event a breeze. Unfortunately, while she'd helped him understand his younger self's actions and reminded him that there was nothing more he could have done for his mother—something he was still struggling with—the itch was present and persistent.

"Our session is coming to an end and I know you have to go in now, so I'll let you go."

"Thank you, Dr. Esposito. I'll have Sebastian schedule my next session."

"I'm glad to hear that. Take care."

After she hung up, Landon looked toward the elevators that would take him to one of his personal hells. He got out, locked his car, and steeled himself in preparation, knowing it was the best he could do.

Landon signed another jersey, smiling at Alice, the small, frail girl in the hospital bed in front of him. When her parents stood to get a picture, he leaned over so his face was closer to hers, plastering on a smile that he hoped didn't look as fake as it felt.

He wanted to help boost morale for these children, who were in dire need of something to lift their spirits, but his skin tingled every time he remembered where he was. Which was, well, almost every moment. He hadn't sat beside any of the kids yet, because he was sure when he did, that tingle would only intensify as he fell back through time to when he'd sat at his mother's bedside hours before she'd died.

"Will you score a touchdown for me on Thursday?" Alice asked so softly that he barely heard her.

Thursday's Thanksgiving game against Seattle would be a battle, but he'd promised himself he would do his best for the rest of the season. Just to see what would happen.

"I am certainly going to try." He smiled down at her once more and then exchanged a pat on the back with Myles, who was rotating into her room next.

As Landon walked out of the room, he saw Keala and her teammates down the hall from him, waving their poms in unison. They weren't dancing, but they stood out as bright as a match struck in the dead of night.

Keala most of all.

Her wavy hair was down, and she wore her red long-sleeve bodysuit. It zipped in the front to mid chest and had a tight red belt that extended to a half skirt across her ass. It was hot as fuck, and with the tall white boots, her legs looked like they went on forever.

After she'd slept over on Wednesday, she'd come over again the next two nights, but he hadn't seen her much since Friday.

Saturday had been walk-through day, and then he and the team had stayed at the hotel before the home game, like they typically did. Landon had seen her dancing during the game yesterday, but she'd fallen asleep on Ikaika's couch by the time they'd gotten back from the stadium. Then she'd been gone for her pre-work workout before he'd gotten up this morning.

Looking at her quieted the uncomfortable feeling that had been chasing him since his conversation with Dr. Esposito over an hour ago, and when she caught his eye and smiled for a split second, it winked out completely. That soft smile was the reassurance she had promised him, and he'd needed it desperately.

Ikaika sidled up to him. "I hate hospitals," he grumbled, shoulders tense, and Landon could only imagine the pain his friend must have been in, knowing what he'd gone through with his sister.

Rather than brush off the feeling, he said, "Me too. I feel like I have bugs crawling all over my body."

"I feel like I'm going to throw up, but that's..." He cleared his throat. "I don't know how Keala does this all the time."

"I know. But I don't think she thinks she has any other option," Landon replied, remembering what she'd shared with him a few days ago.

Ikaika sent Landon a knowing look. "Right."

"What? We talk sometimes."

Ikaika snorted. When Landon exchanged another secretive glance with Keala, one that had her blushing and turning around, Ikaika said, "Don't be a dumbass. I told you I don't care what you guys do as long as things don't end up going poorly. But Angelica"—he pointed his chin in the direction of a woman with sharp features, thin blonde hair, and a face that looked as though she only knew how to frown—"will sniff it out faster than you can blink if you're not careful. Keala's an adult, and if she's willing to risk it with you, that's fine. But I'll sink my fist into your face if you ruin her last year of dance, no matter how much of a pretty motherfucker you might be."

"Aw, you think I'm pretty?"

Ikaika rolled his eyes. "Be more careful. I have no interest in dealing with a police report."

"I got it, man. I'll stop looking at her."

"Oh, and if you make her life any more difficult than it is, or make her think about crying—"

"You'll punch me in my pretty motherfucking face. I got it."

Ikaika shrugged. "I wouldn't say you're the best at following directions, so reiterating seemed like a good idea." He walked off to talk to the running backs coach.

Landon couldn't help but glance over one more time, but Keala was listening to something one of her friends was telling her. He did, however, catch Zoe's eye, who raised an eyebrow as she looked between the two of them. Heart racing, he turned around and almost slammed into Myles coming out of the room he'd been in.

"Hey, bro. Have you seen Avelina yet? The girl with CF? I meant to tell you earlier, she was asking for you when I was in there. Kid might know more about football than I do."

"Which room?"

"215." He pointed to a room right next to Keala's group of cheerleaders.

"Oh, no I haven't been to see her." The last one on his sheet to visit had been Alice. "I'll head over there now."

Landon made a concerted effort not to look at Keala as he walked down the hall toward her group, even as his thoughts stayed on her. His thoughts had been doing that more and more recently, and now that he'd had more time to digest his feelings, it was terrifying.

It was terrifying that he had practically begged her not to avoid him because he'd missed doing mundane things with her—like talking while they played video games or shopped for groceries. It was terrifying that he'd continued pushing her to use him as stress relief because he knew having her physically was better than not having her at all, though he now realized he cared far more about the emotional side of things with her.

And that was the most terrifying of all. Landon was opening himself up to something he had spent his entire life running away from—with good reason. But with Keala, he wanted to line up at the plate of every expectation she had of him and knock it right out of the park. He wanted her to see he was capable of being whatever she needed him to be.

Though she had never asked him to, he'd been trying harder at practice, lifting outside of their daily training—even pushing himself so far that he'd nearly busted his phone when a weight had fallen near it—and he had been more locked in than he had ever remembered being.

She made him feel like he could be something great.

But how long before she decided she'd seen enough and didn't like what made him *him*? And if, somehow, he was lucky enough that she let him in after what she'd admitted about herself in relationships, how long before she expected something out of him that he couldn't provide?

How long until this delusion wore off and he disappointed her, losing the first woman he'd cared about like this in an instant?

The group shook their poms as he walked up beside them. "Hello, ladies," he drawled, smirking.

He made sure not to look at Keala before he turned and opened the door, smiling wide. "I hear *somebody* wants to teach me how to fix my ground game."

Chapter Thirty

Landon

Keala giggled as she pulled away from Landon the next day, her lips swollen and her eyes alight, tipping into the green side of hazel. "I just came over to give your containers back and see if you need me to look you over after that game."

"Yes, please. I'll take off all my clothes and you can look me over." Landon pulled his shirt over his head, and Keala laughed again.

"You played so well that nobody could tackle you. I'm sure you don't have a scratch on you, and if you do, the team trainers probably already helped."

Landon smiled at the praise that came so easily from her lips. "You're the one who said you wanted to look me over, so you'd better double-check." He picked her up and set her on his couch, then put his arms on either side of her. "But *I* need to check something first."

Landon lowered his body so his lips met hers, and he could feel that she was still smiling into the kiss.

"I don't want to be gone for Thanksgiving. I don't like the idea of you being by yourself," he said against her lips.

"I'll be fine. I have a shift tomorrow when you guys leave, and then I'll watch the game with the girls. It'll be fun. And then you can make it up to me when you get back."

"Damn do I like the sound of that." He kissed her again, taking advantage of her giggle to slip his tongue into her mouth. After a few kisses, Keala bit his bottom lip. Landon groaned, and she wrapped her legs around him, pulling his hips so they slotted perfectly against hers.

A knock sounded, and Landon grumbled but didn't move away. Keala pulled back slightly, smiling up at him, and with her hair around her head on the couch, she looked like a princess.

When he still didn't move, she whispered, "It's probably Ikaika getting back from the facility. We have to do better about the three of us hanging out more. I feel like he's missing us."

"He's had you your whole life. I just got you." He leaned down, but as soon as their lips touched, the knock sounded again, more insistent.

"I'm busy," he called out loudly. Through a small laugh, Keala pulled him on top of herself and then rolled them off the couch before Landon realized what was happening. He let out a whoosh of air as he hit the ground, absorbing the impact for the both of them. "Keeks, what the hell?"

"I had to get you up one way or another."

"Trust me, I didn't need you to do anything else to get me up—I was plenty ready."

She rolled her eyes, standing. "Put your shirt on."

"You're paying for that later."

Keala walked to the door, winking at him over her shoulder. "Good."

She was getting so confident around him, and Landon wondered if that meant something. Maybe her other relationships hadn't worked because she'd spent every free minute trying to make them happy, but Landon didn't need anything but her—exactly as she was—to be happy.

Landon chuckled, pulling his shirt on as Keala opened the door.

"Sorry, I was just giving Landon his—oh."

When Landon leaned to see who was in the doorway, he noticed his sister, grinning ear to ear and waggling her eyebrows at him.

"Hi! I didn't mean to interrupt anything, sorry."

Keala cleared her throat. "Oh, no, not at all. Like I was saying, I was returning some containers Landon lent me."

Maya smirked at Landon. "Yes, and I imagine that's why his shirt is on inside out *and* backward."

"Landon," Keala hissed when she noticed, frowning at him. He wanted to kick his sister out immediately for ruining what they'd been about to do.

But he had also missed her dearly, and she was his most favorite family member.

"Hey, Mai. This is Keala. Keala, this is my sister, Maya, who apparently is allowed to roam about the building."

Maya smiled coyly. "I sweet-talked Richard."

Keala's eyes widened as she realized. "Oh! It's so nice to meet you. Landon didn't tell me you were in town or I would've made something."

Landon snorted. When Keala whipped around to glare at him, he made quick work of fixing his shirt.

After Keala and Maya exchanged pleasantries, Keala said, "I can head out. My cousin is probably waiting for me anyway." She pointed across the hall.

"Oh, please don't go! I'd love to talk more."

Keala looked at Landon, and he smiled reassuringly. Hesitantly, she replied, "I can stay for a bit."

"Maya, are you hungry?" he asked, moving into his kitchen.

"I could eat."

Landon pulled ingredients out of his fridge. Normally, they'd have Tuesday completely off, but because of their Thursday game, he'd been at the facility until half an hour ago. He'd left while most of his teammates, Ikaika included, had stayed back for food.

Maya and Keala sat across the large island from him on the barstools his interior designer had found for him earlier this month, when Keala had started spending more time at his apartment.

"Again, I'm sorry to just drop by. Typically, our family gets together to celebrate our mother at the start of November, but we've all been so busy this year that it got pushed to December. And though I always want to come to Landon's games, this season has been busy for me at work. With his game on Thanksgiving, I figured I could stop by for a few hours since I was in LA."

"What do you do?" Keala asked politely, and Landon could see the gears turning in her head, trying to get his sister on her good side. He wished she'd stop doing that and let everyone see the version of her he got to see.

He grabbed a cutting board and knife and began chopping while they talked.

"I run a charity that coaches tennis to underprivileged kids."

"That's so exciting. Is it based out of LA?"

"Originally, yes. But we've since expanded to a ton of cities, and I'm working out of Charleston now."

"I bet that's so much fun."

"Yeah, it's nice. I get to see Colton more often than I used to, and my boyfriend is on the Sabertooths, so it's perfect." Landon tried to focus on chopping the vegetables and not on the sinking feeling in his chest that he couldn't fully comprehend. It lightened when Maya continued. "I wish I could clone myself and be in two places at once though. It stinks missing so many of Landon's games."

Keala looked at him, and rather than sympathy, he saw something akin to an *are you okay?* His heart shoved at its seams. Without having to express to her how he felt, she knew.

"It's crazy that your brother and boyfriend are on the same team. Is that weird?"

"Not really. It's how we met, actually. That's how you both met too, right?"

"Oh, we're not—"

"Yes." Landon smirked at Keala as she blushed. "Ikaika is her cousin. I think you met him once. One of my closest friends. Lives across the hall."

Maya nodded. "Right! Is he home? I have to get back to Charleston tomorrow morning, but we should go out tonight!"

Keala looked at Landon worriedly. He was sure she was apprehensive about someone besides Ikaika knowing about them, but Maya wouldn't tell anyone if he asked her not to.

"We're not allowed to talk, let alone hook up." The words rolled off his tongue oddly. Minimizing what they were doing to "hooking up" felt like a betrayal to the strength of emotions he felt when he was with Keala. He was too scared to see her reaction, so he focused on the food.

"Ah, forbidden relationships. I know something about that." Maya laughed.

Landon tossed her a small smile. "That's because Cooper was Colton's friend first."

Maya's grin widened. "Yes, but he's mine last." Landon wondered if Cooper would finally ask her to marry him now that he and Colton were planning to retire after the season and her charity was fully operational. Cooper had asked Landon over two years ago for his blessing to propose to Maya, so it was about time. Although, knowing his sister, he had probably asked many times and she was waiting for life to be perfect before she said yes.

Maya turned to Keala. "So, tell me about *you*."

They all laughed, and Keala talked about working at the hospital and cheering for the team. His sister was having a grand time getting to know Keala, and Landon listened carefully as he made stuffed bell peppers for them. He needed to make sure Maya didn't say anything that might reveal how deep his feelings for Keala ran.

When the food was finished, he put a portion onto three plates and then stood across from them as they ate.

"Any plans for dining chairs so you don't have to stand while you eat?" Maya asked.

Landon's eyes met Keala's, grinning when he saw her blush. The last time he'd used the table had been with her. He shrugged. "I spend so much time across the hall that I barely need furniture. I certainly don't have enough people over to need dining chairs."

Maya smiled slyly, looking between the two of them. "Oh yeah? Spend a lot of time at her apartment, do ya?"

"Maya, you're making my guest uncomfortable."

Keala covered her mouth and shook her head frantically. "No, no, I'm fine! It's funny. And plus, it's mostly to see Ikaika. I just happen to live there."

"It's not mostly to see Ikaika and you know it, Keeks."

The room quieted as she smiled into her food.

Maya slapped the granite countertop of the island, startling Keala. Landon frowned, not liking the look on his sister's face as she began speaking. "I don't know how serious you two are but—"

"We're n-not—"

"But," his sister continued, cutting Keala's disagreement off, "it would be great to have you at our mother's celebration of life. We're doing it in LA this year at our grandparents' house. You can meet Colton and his wife Lucia, who"—she put a hand up to block Landon's view of her mouth, whispering—"is my favorite sibling. And their baby girl. Cooper will be there. Luckily our dad will *not* be." Maya looked meaningfully at Landon. He still frowned, his eyes flicking to see Keala's reaction.

Keala glanced at him, then back to his sister. "This seems like a family thing, so I think that would be an intrusion, but thank you for the invite."

"Not an intrusion at all. The more the merrier. Our family will love you, and if you're worried about the whole no-fraternization thing, Landon seems to have gotten better at flying under the radar for someone who was plastered all over the news three months ago. It'll be very private at the house."

His sister had been paying attention. Or maybe his lack of media presence was just that obvious. He'd had no reason to look for attention elsewhere when Keala had been treating him like a regular person more than almost anyone else in his life.

"Nothing with Colton or Cooper is ever private," Landon grumbled.

"Cooper will make sure it is," Maya said, and again, he knew there was a greater meaning to it after what they'd endured a couple of years ago.

Keala looked to him, whether for permission or an out, he didn't know. "It's up to you, Keeks."

Maya put her hand up. "Fair warning that I'm very stubborn and will likely badger you until you say yes."

He wanted Keala there, but he also didn't want her to feel pressured, especially since this was a big ask for someone he wasn't dating. And yes, Maya was stubborn, but if Keala agreed to it now and didn't want to go, he would make sure she didn't have to. He hoped she knew that.

"What days?" Keala asked.

"December tenth and eleventh." Maya was beaming like she'd already won, and when Keala checked her calendar and nodded, her smile widened further.

"I can move my shifts around that week."

"Perfect." Maya pulled out her phone. "And let me give you my number while we're at it."

"Maya," Landon warned. "Please stop pestering my..." He trailed off, unable to find the right word. Keala waved him off with a smile.

He'd wanted to call her his girlfriend, which was a first. He wanted her to be *his* in every sense of the word, even if the thought sent adrenaline coursing through his body in panic.

When they'd finished exchanging numbers, Maya excused herself to use the bathroom and Keala stood, heading to the sink to rinse the dishes. Landon set a hand on hers, turning off the water. "Stop. I'll clean up."

"But you cooked."

"And I'll clean." He smiled down at her and whispered, "Don't you know I like cooking for you? It's a privilege, not a burden."

Her smile mirrored his own.

As she began to turn away, he tugged her back, putting his arms around her shoulders. "And if you don't want to come to my mom's celebration, don't feel like you have to. I can make excuses for you. My sister will live."

"Do you want me to come?"

"I don't want you to make a decision based on what I want."

"But it would be very embarrassing if I said yes and you didn't want me to tag along. I don't want to be embarrassed."

"I would never allow that. And if it helps you decide to come"—he tugged her hair gently so she looked into his eyes—"because you genuinely want to, then yes. Of course I want you to come." He wanted to show her the house he'd grown up in, even if it had its share of bad memories. He wanted to show her the field he'd practiced on as a kid and the place he and Maya used to sneak out to eat at, though the food was lacking in many ways.

Landon just wasn't sure how much *she* wanted that.

"Okay. I'll come. But we have to be careful. Maybe take separate flights or something."

His stomach did a victory flip. Or it could have been nerves. "Sure, whatever you want."

They heard Maya's footsteps as she came back toward the kitchen, and he let Keala go when it was clear she wanted to move away.

"I'm sure Ikaika's back by now, so I'm going to get going. Maya, it was so nice to meet you and I'm excited to see you again." She turned to Landon. "I'll see you after the game. Kick Seattle's ass." She hugged Maya before walking out.

"No goodbye kiss for my brother? I don't mind looking away," Maya called after Keala, and Landon shoved her. Luckily, Keala pretended not to hear her, closing the door as she left.

"Would you stop it? She's agreed to a lot by saying she'll come to Mom's thing."

"You're welcome, by the way. I did all the work, and now all you have to do is not fuck it up."

"Who said I wanted her to come?" he asked, knowing it came out entirely devoid of emotion to insinuate the opposite.

Maya rolled her eyes. "Don't be an idiot. It's so obvious. I've literally never seen you like this in my life. I'm glad things are going better than the last time we talked about her."

"I mean, we're still in agreement that it's just physical."

Maya scoffed. "Then you're both in denial. I saw you interact. You're disgustingly into each other, and though she seemed hesitant to tell me too much about herself, I can tell she's good for you. You seem happy."

Landon didn't want to hope that his sister was right. The thought of being able to be with Keala, truly be with her, made his heart soar.

"I am, but I've never done this before. I don't know what's happening or what to say to get her to see I want more, and even if we do get to that point, what if I do something dumb and..." He looked away.

"You have to stop worrying that you're going to disappoint everyone, Landon. You're sure as hell never going to make everyone happy, but you can do your best to make *her* happy—and make yourself happy in the process. Don't do something dumb now with the hope that it'll prevent you from doing something dumb when things are good."

Landon turned around, rinsing the dishes before loading them into the dishwasher. He loved his sister, but he still wasn't at a point where he could talk about this so freely. He couldn't reconcile his own emotions about it all. "God, you're so preachy now that you're in love."

"I know! Isn't it fun?" She plopped back onto the bar stool. "Now you owe me for inviting Keala to Mom's celebration, and I'm cashing in. You're going to have that conversation with Colton."

"I already said I would."

"Good. I don't want to have to get Cooper to kick both of your asses. I don't care if I have to mediate or if you attempt to tear each other's throats out, we're putting it to bed this year. No more family division."

"I knew you didn't come here just to see me."

Maya smiled.

And a pit of dread opened up inside Landon. He didn't know if it was because of his situation with Keala or the impending hell that would be talking to his brother.

Chapter Thirty-One

Keala

Keala's hip twinged as she jumped from the kick line into a split. It took considerable effort not to let her smile fall as she waved her poms at the empty stadium in front of her. Because they'd had a Thanksgiving Thursday game this week, they had switched Wednesday and Thursday practice for a longer, more thorough practice Sunday afternoon. And now, on hour four, she was feeling it.

Luckily, when she stood and began the next number, she could tell her hip was just sore and not torn. Out of the corner of her eye, she took Zoe's cue to twirl, and then the smile wasn't so forced because she had yet to miss a single beat this practice. Angelica hadn't been able to say a word to her because, though she felt that perpetual exhaustion in her bones, she'd been eating more—thanks to Landon—and getting slightly better sleep than usual.

Well, that was on the nights she slept at Landon's.

She, Ikaika, and Landon had spent both Friday and Saturday evening hanging out, and both nights, Landon had texted her to come over after. Sure, the release she got from him each and every time they were together was soul changing, but more surprising was that he asked her to stay over and she managed to sleep through the night every time.

She had woken up this morning after he'd left for the facility, a note on the nightstand that read:

You're so beautiful...especially when your hair is a tangled mess from letting me take you from behind in the middle of the night.

PS you still owe me a favor for pumpkin carving. Care to venture a guess as to what it'll be?

It had all been a change she could admittedly get used to. She knew he wasn't a relationship guy, but things had *seemed* different the last few weeks, and while she'd promised she would no longer try to make something work if it didn't, what she and Landon had felt special. Even if he refused to be anything but cheeky ninety-seven percent of the time.

He took care of her without her asking, he held her when she was sad, and more than that, she felt somehow able to express what she wanted when she was with him. If things did work out and he *was* interested in something more, she wouldn't have to bend to his will until she broke, because that was never the expectation with him. He only ever seemed to want her as she was.

Keala couldn't remember the last time she had felt so *good*.

When Angelica deemed them done for the day, Cora asked Keala and the captains to come talk to her.

"We're going to forgo choreo today because we've been at this for a while. We have three new songs we want to get choreographed, so I'm hoping you can work on a piece before each of the practices this week. It won't be more than thirty seconds to a minute. Zoe and Aurelia, I'll send you what we want done for Tuesday practice. Jordy and Mackenzie, you'll work on a piece we'll learn Wednesday. And Keala, you'll work on a thirty second piece for Thursday. Are all of you okay with that?"

A chorus of yeses from the five of them. Keala smiled wider with excitement. She wouldn't have much time, but the thought of being able to choreograph an entire number for the team made all the physical and mental toll of work and the season worth it. This was exactly what she wanted.

Cora pulled her aside. "You doing okay?"

"I'm doing great!" Keala exclaimed, and for once, she meant it. Cora studied her face, then smiled.

"I'm glad. You looked amazing out there. I know you're one of our busiest Sirens, but I'm proud of you for showing up every practice polished and ready to go. You set a great example." She pointed at Keala's face. "And you look like you're getting sleep."

"I promised I'd do better."

"I know. But I also know the feeling of *not* knowing when to sit down for a second and rest. When to take a moment to breathe and not constantly run around doing something, always keeping yourself busy. So I'm proud of you for doing better in that way too."

Tears pricked Keala's eyes, and on a whim, she threw her arms around Cora. Though Cora had kept relationships with the girls professional, she and Keala had taken to each other so quickly that Cora felt more like a very close mentor than a team choreographer. "Thank you."

Cora hugged her back and smiled when they pulled away. Keala walked to where the girls were stretching, and she plopped down between Len and Zoe to join them, working her sore hip.

"He's so hot." Kennedy giggled with a couple of people from her group. "God, I wish we could fraternize."

"Who?" Jamie piped up, looking over her shoulder at a photo on Kennedy's screen.

"Landon Beaumont. Look at him in a suit. He looks like a god."

"Who's that girl with him?"

For a heartbeat, Keala's entire body stilled and she didn't so much as breathe. Her stomach sank until she realized that if they were questioning who the woman in the picture was, it likely wasn't her. Her secret was safe, at least.

She strained to hear what her teammates said next, ignoring the odd look Zoe threw her way. "Oh, that's the girl from earlier this season, right? I feel like I remember seeing her in a picture with him and Savannah Blake a few months ago."

"Weird that he's at an event with her. I feel like he usually doesn't go to these things with people he's slept with. Do you think they're together?"

"He has been out of the news for a while. Maybe."

"Damn. She's so lucky."

It was too much for Keala. Her stomach was ripping itself to shreds, and the urge to vomit sprang up quickly. She whipped out her water and took a big gulp, pulling out her own phone.

After searching Landon's name, she found a couple of articles from an hour ago, and when she clicked on the top one, her heart flew to her throat, her stomach still churning. In it, he was indeed wearing a suit, his hair a slight mess.

But the thing that stood out was the beautiful woman on his arm. They both smiled for the camera, though his was more of his faintly annoyed smirk. The fact that Keala could identify his emotions just from his expression made her feel even more violently ill. Tears pricked her eyes again, but for an entirely different reason, and she stood.

"I have to use the restroom," she managed to say as she rushed away.

She made it into a stall right before the heaving began. It had been a few hours since she'd eaten, so it was mainly Pedialyte, but the feeling of it wracking her body, tears streaming down her face, made her wish she'd never met Landon.

The bathroom door opened, and Keala tried to calm herself, wiping under her eyes and patting her cheeks.

"Kay?" someone asked uneasily, and it only took a moment to realize Zoe had followed her. "Are you okay?"

Keala saw white boots stop in front of her stall, and when she didn't reach for the lock to let her in, Zoe said, "Don't make me climb under the door. You know I will."

Reluctantly, Keala opened the stall. Zoe's face softened when she saw her on the floor, what was sure to have been a scolding gone in an instant.

"What's wrong?"

"I don't want to talk about it."

"Well, that's not an option. Is this about Landon?"

Keala searched her friend's face, looking for any sign of judgment. Telling anyone about what she'd been doing with Landon could be a mistake, especially anyone from the team. But this was Zoe.

"I saw the way he looked at you, you know. At the club on Halloween, at the children's hospital. Your cousin told him off on Monday for it, but he couldn't keep his eyes off you."

Keala felt another sob coming on, so she dug her nails into the skin of her palms to stop it the way she used to. When her parents had fought about Nohea and she'd been terrified of what was going to happen to her brother and whether her parents were going to get a divorce because of it, this was one of her strategies. She had always been on the verge of tears when she'd heard the yelling, but she'd learned to cope, to find ways to stop the tears from falling when she knew Akoni was looking to her for comfort.

When her parents needed her to be the easy one.

"I—I don't..." Keala sighed. "Please don't be mad at me."

"You know the only reason I'd be mad is because you've been hiding something juicy from me, and I'll give you a pass if it is about Landon because I get it."

So Keala quietly explained it all. The first night when she'd thought she'd been off the team for good. How she'd found out he was moving in across the hall, and the many evenings they'd spent in Ikaika's apartment together until she couldn't deny the tension that culminated on Halloween and had finally let it happen. All the meals he'd cooked for her and the notes he'd left her. The feelings that had been brewing over the last few weeks, and the thought that maybe he was in the same place as her.

"It was so dumb. I'm so embarrassed for thinking he would want something more."

"Oh, sweetie, no." Zoe lowered down with a grimace, trying not to let any part of her practice shorts touch the floor until she gave up and threw herself down unceremoniously. "You're not dumb. If I were in your shoes, I'd think the same thing."

"I just thought he would've told me? Like, let me know that 'hey, I'm hooking up with other people and going out with them publicly.' But then on the other hand, I know he doesn't owe me anything. He is literally known for this. I don't know why I expected that I'd be different. We agreed it was only going to be casual, and it makes sense that he would want to do more with other people. He's so...advanced. And I'm not."

Keala had thought the sex was good, even if it wasn't the only thing she looked forward to with him anymore. He'd seemed to like it. But he had also mentioned kinks that first night, and maybe, since he always made it about what she wanted, he wasn't being completely fulfilled.

Zoe pulled Keala into a side hug, resting her head on top of Keala's. "I'm so sorry, sweetie. And I'm sorry you felt like you had to do this on your own. I know nobody can ever know about what happened between you two, but I'm glad you told me. Even if I did force you to," she joked.

"Oh my god." Keala pulled away, hand gripping the toilet again despite her empty stomach. "What if he had people over while I was across the hall? How often do you think I was going about my day at my apartment while he was hooking up with someone else? Oh my god, he probably did." She knew it was none of her business, but the thought that he'd smuggled someone in without her knowledge while she was *right there*, right across the hall—nausea built in her throat again, hot and angry.

"Do you think he would sleep with other people? I know he's a known ass, but did he give you any indication he would do something like this? Because from the way he was looking at you—"

"I don't see why not," Keala said, cutting her friend off. She didn't want to know how he'd looked at her, because clearly it hadn't meant anything. "If he didn't tell me about this, it's not like he'd tell me about anything else. And that's his right.

He has every right to hook up with whoever he wants because we agreed to one thing: that it was just sex."

Keala slapped a hand over her mouth. This was horrible. Was this what happened when someone allowed themselves to sink into a relationship? Her whole body ached, her face taut from drying tears, and her stomach was in dire need of Pepto-Bismol or a carbonated equivalent.

"But it wasn't for you," Zoe whispered.

"It wasn't for me," Keala agreed. "And I was stupid for hoping."

She whipped out her phone and pulled up their texts.

Keala

I don't think us hooking up is a good idea anymore. For Ikaika's sake, I think we should go back to how things were before.

Zoe looked over her shoulder as she typed, rubbing her arm and nodding. Keala took her agreement as encouragement to send it.

She could be an adult about this. She wouldn't avoid him this time. Sure, her feelings were hurt right now, but that was just the shock of it all. It would wear off. Keala could remove herself from what they'd been doing, put Ikaika first in this friendship, compartmentalize like she'd been doing since she was little, and go back to being Landon's friend.

And if she struggled in the beginning, well, then it was a good thing she was so busy with dance and work.

"I'm sorry, KayKay. I hope you know that we're here for you, even if you don't tell the rest of the girls who it is. You've become family to us over the last few months. We're your sisters, and we will rage with you and hold you up until you can do it on your own again, okay?"

Before Keala could respond, Zoe continued, "And you know what? Screw him. There are so many other people out there who will love every part of you. Who will make it clear that they want *only* you. Who will make you feel like you can be yourself with them. They won't let you wear yourself down to please them because they'll see you, know that's who you are, and want to take care of you instead."

Except that person was Landon. Keala wasn't sure she'd ever find someone who so easily allowed her to be herself with them. Who asked for nothing more and nothing less.

Keala cursed Landon for being so good to her, because all it had done was confuse her. And now she was hopelessly lost and so very sad.

She flipped her phone over so she couldn't see the screen, leaning into Zoe.

Keala just hoped he would be out late so she didn't have to sit through Sunday evening football with him and Ikaika.

Chapter Thirty-Two

Landon

Sebastian rarely came to the facility unless something was wrong, so when Landon saw him standing outside the locker room, he frowned.

"What's up?"

"You didn't respond to my text."

Landon held up his smashed phone, careful not to touch the shattered glass. "Sorry, I dropped a weight on my phone this afternoon. It's not turning on. Probably have to get another one."

"Coach let you bring your phone in during lifts?"

"No, I decided to do a few more reps after everyone left and wanted music. What's up?"

Seb covered his shock well, likely surprised that Landon was doing anything more than the bare minimum. "Savannah's end of tour party and Best Album award celebration is happening right now. We talked about it a couple of weeks ago."

Landon closed his eyes, vaguely remembering the conversation. "Shit. That's today?"

"Yes, and you promised you'd be there. Her agent wants to make sure the party is huge. Talked about it being 'one for the ages' or some shit, I don't know. She kept going on and on about it. You forgot?"

He'd been surprisingly focused on the season, and even more on Keala, that he hadn't thought of much outside of the two. "Yeah. Do you think my gameday suit is good enough? It's all I have here. Or do I have time to go home?"

"You have about five minutes. I have a limo here for you, so go change. You know Savannah will have your head if you're late."

While Sebastian was right that Sav was surprisingly punctual, he was sure she wouldn't notice whether he was there or not, and certainly not what time he arrived. Still, he changed quickly and followed Seb to the car.

"If this party is going to be so big, I don't understand why I can't go home real quick. I'm sure Sav will be so busy that she won't notice." Honestly, he wanted to take a shower and use his own products. He also wanted to see if Keala was back from practice yet and tell her that he'd be gone for a few hours since his phone was useless. Landon wanted another evening with her in his bed, even if she had to leave early for her shift tomorrow.

"Man, I swear you don't read anything I send you. You're picking up Elara," he said referring to Savannah's girlfriend, who he would pretend to be with so that Sav's relationship remained under wraps.

Landon nodded his understanding. "Of course. Sorry." He slid into the car. "Are you coming?"

"God, no. I have so much damn paperwork for your sponsors, but with you not answering, I figured I should come down. Be good. Don't do anything that ruins Savannah's night please. That's the last thing I need to deal with right now."

"I've been on my best behavior the last few months, I think I can make it through an evening." Keala's eyes flashed in his mind at their joke—*Your Favorite Asshole on his Best Behavior*—and he wished he could bring her with him as his date instead.

"Yes, you've finally made my job manageable, thank you." The words came out harsh, but Landon could tell Seb was teasing from the quirk of his lips. "I promised you'd stay for at least a couple of hours, but I'm sure you'll want to be there longer."

Landon shrugged. He'd stay as long as Savannah wanted him there. It was her big night, and she was always there to help him get into trouble when he needed to.

Which he'd needed less and less of as of late.

"I'll have your new phone to you by tomorrow." Seb closed the door before he could respond, and Landon watched him yell into his phone as the driver sped off.

Landon spent the entire night wishing the woman on his arm was Keala.

Later that evening, before going to his own apartment, Landon tried Ikaika's door, opening it when he found it unlocked. "Who's ready to watch New York beat Cincy?" he asked as he stepped inside. Keala and Ikaika were both on the couch, watching the game.

"Nah, Cincinnati's got this in the bag," Ikaika responded.

"Keeks?" Landon asked, wanting her input. Instead, she stiffened almost imperceptibly and shrugged. She wouldn't meet his eyes when he slipped out of his shoes and walked into the room.

"I don't know. Don't care about either team," she answered quietly.

Odd. Landon wondered if something had happened at dance practice earlier.

"Where did you go after practice looking so sharp?" Ikaika wondered.

"I stayed back to lift a little more and then forgot I had to be at a thing for Sav."

"She's back?"

"Yeah. Seemed to have had a very successful tour."

Landon loosened his tie and unbuttoned the top button of his shirt to get more comfortable, his eyes on Keala as he sat a few feet from her on the couch. Ikaika took up the entirety of the other side.

This time, she definitely tensed up.

"How was your practice?" he asked as he rolled up his sleeves and sank into the cushions.

"Good." The word was clipped, and even Ikaika glanced between the two of them with a frown.

Landon crossed his arms, turning to the TV but unable to focus on anything that was going on. Ikaika said something about the game and Keala replied to him. Landon could only focus on the way she tucked her legs underneath her body, angling herself away from him.

Clearly, she was upset with him. What wasn't clear was why. He'd woken up this morning with her still sleeping peacefully in his arms, so what could have caused such a quick turn around? Had the—kind of—joke in his note offended her?

He'd planned to talk to her about becoming more after the event, but now he was doing exactly what they hadn't wanted to do: making things uncomfortable for Ikaika. Their hangouts had never been so quiet. When halftime rolled around, Ikaika jumped up, eyebrows drawn as he made eye contact with Landon. "I'm going to call my family. I'll be back for the second half."

His meaning was clear: fix this now. Make things right.

Or Landon would get a fist to his pretty motherfucking face, he was sure.

"Keeks..."

"Did you not get my text?"

Landon pulled out his phone and set it between them, thankful that an unreturned text was all this was. "Broke my phone at the facility today. Decided to do a lift on my own. Guess that's what I get for trying for once," he joked.

But she didn't smile. She pulled up something on her phone and shoved it toward him. He read the text once, then twice, then once more.

"I don't understand."

She tossed her phone onto the couch, then clenched her fists. "Landon, please don't make me say it."

He dropped to his knees in front of her. "Baby...I'm so confused. What happened?"

"Don't call me that. I saw the photo. All the photos, actually, because they're plastered everywhere."

"The photo?" He'd never sent anything untoward because of how easy hacking seemed to be nowadays, so he didn't know what she could be talking about.

"Of you and the pretty blonde girl. At Savannah Blake's event."

Realization dawned. "Oh," he drew out the syllable. Landon reached for her hands, opening them and trying not to pull her into him when he noticed the half-moon indentations etched into her palms.

Her voice was shaky, eyes wet, but she set her jaw and whispered, "I know you don't owe me anything, but I think I've developed some...thing for you. And I can't keep doing this, because it's going to kill me to see you with other people."

"Kee—"

"And I'm also terrified that I care more for you, who I've been hooking up with for three weeks, than I ever did for my past partners." She ripped her hands away, closing in on herself, wrapping her legs in her arms and angling away from him again. "Please, Landon, just let me pretend I have some dignity and go home. We'll work on the whole 'being friends' thing for Ikaika's sake, but for tonight, while I'm still figuring all of these feelings out, please go."

"Keeks, I don't want to be your friend."

Her façade broke, and a tear fell as she let out a half scoff, half cry. "Well, we have to be or Ikaika's going to kill you."

"We both know neither of us want that," he joked. She held back a small smile but still wouldn't meet his eyes. "Please look at me?"

After a few seconds, she complied.

"I don't want to be your friend, because I want to be more. I want to be with you. Only you." He frowned. "I don't know how to do this, but with you, I want to try."

Keala crossed her arms, glaring at him. "I'm expected to believe that when you were just..." She waved her hand around. "Again, you're allowed to do whatever you want. We agreed it was just sex. But don't think you're going to come back to my bed after being with someone else less than an hour ago."

"Technically, it's *my* bed." At her scowl, he smiled. "Right, sorry, not the right time. I'm working on the 'using humor to subvert emotions' thing. But it's not my place to tell you who she is. I'm protecting a friend."

"Bu—"

"Baby, please," he interrupted, desperate. "The entire time I was there, all I could think about was coming back to you and telling you I want more. I don't want to be your stress relief anymore. I want to be the person you come to when you're happy and sad. I want to be *yours*."

She still didn't look convinced, though she loosened her grip on her legs.

"Have I ever given you a reason not to trust me?"

Keala stared at him, then sighed. "No," she answered softly.

"I know it's not a good look right now, but there's a reason I haven't been hanging out with anybody I've hooked up with before. Because, since the day I met you, I haven't been able to get you off my mind."

"But *she's* someone you've been with before. I saw the pictures of you two from the past. Before we met."

Landon looked at her meaningfully. "I've never done anything with her. Again, it's not my place to tell you specifics, but of all the people I've ever been linked with, she's not one for you to worry about."

"So..."

"So, moving on from that, I'm going to give you my small speech. If that's okay."

She hid a smile. Nodded.

"I know that you're a lover of love but that you're terrified of getting into relationships because you become someone else. But with me, I want *you*. I want the unfiltered, unchanged, exactly as you are, you. You've never given me anything else, and that's all I'll ever ask for." He smirked. "And, if I remember correctly, you still owe me one favor from the pumpkin carving, and I was planning on cashing in with a real first date."

Keala smiled fully, dropping her arms and legs. Landon, still on his knees, slid his hands up the sides of her legs until they rested at the hem of her shorts, his chest against her knees.

She set her hands on his. "We still can't go out in public together. At least not until the season's over. Zoe knows, and I trust her, but I'm not sure about anybody else."

"I know. We'll stay hidden, and if it makes you more comfortable, we can do it at my apartment."

"We've already done that."

Landon's smirk widened. "Did you just make a sex joke?"

"Never."

"You told Zoe about us?"

"Yeah."

"I think she might have known before you said anything."

She nodded as she spoke. "We didn't do a very good job of hiding it on Halloween. And she said you couldn't keep your eyes off me at the hospital. I thought she was making things up." Keala ran her fingers through Landon's hair, and it was the first time that had ever happened outside of sex.

He liked it a lot.

"She's right—I couldn't. Ikaika had to tell me to quit it so I didn't get you in trouble."

Keala giggled. "Well, Zoe doesn't like you right now. She was kind of there when I saw the picture and had to watch me...handle it," she said carefully.

"That's okay. I'm charming as hell. When I finally meet her for real, I'll change her mind."

Keala laughed again, pulling him up so she could kiss him softly. "One date. But if you make *one* joke about the kitchen incident, you're done."

"Fair. Come over after the game?"

She nodded before kissing him again, deeper. After a minute of his hands roaming her body and their tongues dancing, Keala pulled away. "Ikaika is going to be back soon. I don't want to make him uncomfortable."

"Fine." Landon kissed her nose, then sat beside her, finally letting her hand go when Ikaika came back.

"All good?" Keala asked sweetly.

"All good."

Ikaika and Keala exchanged a look, and when Keala nodded, Ikaika nodded back.

"Alright, Cincy. Let's do this thing."

Chapter Thirty-Three

Landon

ESPN notification – Week twelve takeaways: Saber-tooths and Sentinels at the top of their conferences, Beaumonts riding high...

Bay Area News 5 – Landon Beaumont went to Savannah Blake's Best Album Award party with heiress Elara Covington. Who she is and why they could be San Jose's newest "It" Couple.

When the final whistle blew later that night, Landon left Ikaika sleeping on the couch and headed back to his apartment. Keala said bye to him at the door, promising she would be over in a few. True to her word, she knocked twenty-four minutes later, clad in his favorite of her pajamas: his Sentinels shirt and one of her many pairs of black-and-red plaid shorts.

Landon wrapped an arm around her waist, pulling her inside and kissing all over her face. "Missed you," he murmured, shutting the door behind her and walking her to the living room.

Keala laughed. "I saw you less than half an hour ago."

"Mm, and it was too long." He continued peppering her with kisses.

"Landon! You were supposed to change out of these clothes. It's time for bed."

Landon pulled back. "I saw the way you were watching me as I left. Don't pretend you don't love the way I clean up."

She shrugged, looking around until her eye snagged on the dining table. Landon followed her line of sight and cursed.

Keala walked over to the table—which still lacked chairs—and stared at the open calendar.

It was the Sentinels Sirens yearly calendar for the next year.

"You do know it's November and not May of next year, right?"

Landon was slightly embarrassed he hadn't hidden it. In it, Keala wore the small black skirt and tinier long-sleeve black top that tied in a knot right in the middle of her chest. She was smiling wide, a hand on her waist, toned stomach exposed.

"Uh, yeah." He laughed, rubbing the back of his neck. "I saw them at the facility a few days ago and swiped one. I'm surprised you haven't seen it the last few days—I think it's been on the table for a while."

She tapped the photo. "I was shocked they chose me. If it were up to Angelica, I wouldn't have been, but the team voted. It was also probably a diversity thing." Keala smiled coyly, turning and running a finger down his chest. "Can't imagine what you were going to do with this."

"If you mean fuck my hand while I thought about you, you've given me plenty of memories I can use. It's hot, but nothing compared to the video I see when I close my eyes."

"Do you do that? Use our...time together to get off?" Her eyes glazed over, and Landon grabbed the hand that had stilled against his stomach.

He hummed. "Do you like that? Knowing I can't get you out of my head?"

She nodded slowly. "Yes." Keala dropped her eyes to his dress pants, then dragged her gaze up his long-sleeve button down and tie until she landed on his lips. "I suppose it would be a shame to waste this."

Landon pulled her to himself by the hand he held, kissing her hard. She kissed him back just as hungrily, making those pretty little moans he loved so much.

"What happened to bedtime?" he joked as she kissed his jaw.

"Screw bedtime—I sleep better after anyway."

He was confused when she moved away, opening the door to his balcony. It was late November in Northern California, so he flicked on the heater switch. The two on either side of the doorway hummed to life, and Keala smiled gratefully at him.

Grabbing his tie, she pulled him to herself, unbuttoning his shirt and kissing a line down his body to his pants.

"Keeks, what are you doing?"

She looked up at him, her hand resting against the top of his dress pants. "I've known the real me as long as you have. I don't know half the things I love or hate because I've spent so long suppressing them in favor of what others want. You want me to do what I want? Right now, I want you to fuck me out here. And before that, I want to do this." She undid his belt, then the button and zipper until his dick was out of his boxers.

Landon looked around, taking in the city lights twinkling far below them. Otherwise, it was dark, and there were no buildings as tall as theirs for miles. He knew no one would see them. Still, he asked, "Are you su—"

Keala took him in her mouth, and he couldn't remember what he'd been saying. She bobbed her head, licking and sucking and moaning until Landon felt his balls tighten. "Baby, slow down. If you want me to fuck you out here, you have to stop."

She pulled away with a pop and stood, tugging her shirt off and turning so her front pressed against the parapet, which was entirely made of stone and hit her at mid-stomach. Landon stood by the balcony door, shocked by the unexpected twist the night had taken. Keala looked over her shoulder at him expectantly, so he hurried out of his pants and grabbed a condom from inside.

He loved when she took charge.

Landon rolled the condom on, grabbing her throat gently until her back hit his chest. Pushing her hair out of the way, he kissed her neck, his other hand slipping beneath her shorts and lace thong. When he found her soaking, he groaned. "You liked sucking me off, huh? You like knowing what you do to me?" he whispered against her ear, and she shivered. When she didn't respond, he lined himself up, pushing her thong and shorts out of his way. "Tell me what you want, baby."

"You." It was all she said, breathed out into the night quietly, so with one hand around her throat and the other pushing her clothes out of the way, he sank into her.

He felt little resistance, and when she began pushing back, moaning happily, he picked up the pace. Landon moved both his hands to her waist, smiling when she gripped the top of the wall. "You can be as loud as you want out here. That's what you want, right? People to know how good you take me?"

She moaned louder, as if in agreement. Landon wanted to focus on her, making sure she came first, but his balls started to tighten again. He slipped one of his hands back into her shorts, rubbing her until she was practically screaming. "You like knowing someone could be looking at these sexy fucking tits bouncing, baby? Hearing me fuck this pretty cunt? I bet you like that, don't you?"

"Yes, Landon, *please*," she whined. "Make me come, please. I'm so close." Landon leaned over, kissing her smooth back, picking up the pace with his fingers and cock until he felt her tightening around him, her whole body shaking. Keala breathed heavily when she was done, pulling his hand to hold her tit as she bounced on him. "Now I want you to fill me up again."

And that was all it took. Something inside him contracted, then he felt a rush in his chest as he came inside her. Landon hadn't known he was holding his breath until it was over, when he finally released it.

"Damn it," he groaned against her skin. "You are fucking perfect, you know that?" His body shook as he pulled out, spinning her around so he could kiss her, wrapping both arms around her as he did so.

"I've never done that before," she whispered, voice breathy. "Have sex outside, I mean. I know nobody could have seen us, but I...did like the idea that they could hear it."

Landon squeezed her in response, too tired to speak again so soon. He loved that she was discovering things about herself, and that he was lucky enough to be the one to learn what she liked along with her.

Though the last few times they'd had sex, possibly every other time, had felt important in some way, this time was far more significant because it was the first time he was with someone exclusively. Not that he'd been hooking up with anyone else since he'd met her. The thought hadn't crossed his mind.

But now that they'd agreed to be together, it all felt so real. Her bare skin against the sliver of his chest exposed by his open shirt. His cheek pressed against her head, his hands in the divots of her waist. It felt peaceful and it felt right.

"Proud of you for figuring out what you want. And asking for it." He kissed her forehead. "Let's get cleaned up."

Half an hour later, Keala was sitting across Landon's lap in the one chair on his balcony. She stared up at the stars sleepily while he fed her grapes and gave her sips of her Pedialyte. She had been very insistent about the latter.

"The day we met, you joked about your kinks. Do you have many?" She blinked at him, and that ache in his chest intensified. She was so damn beautiful, her freckles just visible, her hair in a messy bun, her eyes half open.

"I don't know what *many* means." It wasn't that he was uncomfortable discussing this. He just had never talked about it with someone he cared about. "But I would say I have some, yes."

"I'm scared you're going to want someone who can provide you with all those things."

Landon squeezed her to himself. "I don't want anyone but you. I don't need all that stuff if you're not comfortable with it. I get off on knowing I'm giving you what you want."

"But I want to make you feel good too. I haven't done anything crazy, but"—she sat up, resting her head against his shoulder—"I'm open to trying things. I liked this, and it was kind of kinky, right?"

Her voice was so small and worried. Landon felt he was ruining this; he didn't know how to express how seriously he meant what he was saying.

"Yeah, Keeks." He kissed her temple. "It was. And it was hot as hell. But don't worry about all that, we'll work you up to it if you're comfortable. I want to go slow with you."

"Okay." She snuggled against his chest. "More Pedialyte please."

He smiled, picking up the cup with a straw for her. He wondered if that ache in his chest and the stone in his throat were what love felt like.

Chapter Thirty-Four

Keala

Thursday evening after practice, Keala lay in Landon's arms, strands of hair twirling around her fingers. It had only been four days since they'd agreed to be together, but she'd spent every night since at his apartment. When they were with Ikaika, they were a group of unlikely friends, but after Ikaika went to sleep, they could finally hold each other.

"Wear my jersey for the Philly game Sunday."

Keala smiled, her lips an inch from his. "What's with men and asking women to wear their jerseys? Or rather, demanding."

"It's hot. Do you know how hot it is to know that someone's proud to be yours?"

"Not really."

"That's because you were with idiotic men. If you had a jersey, I'd wear it all the time."

Keala giggled. "Now I'm picturing you in my cheer top."

"Sexy, right? I could totally pull it off."

She nodded. "You would."

"So you'll wear my jersey?"

"Landon, you know I can't. I'm going to be watching with the girls, and just because Zoe knows doesn't mean I'm looking to tell the rest of them."

"So wear it underneath a sweatshirt. If it peeks out, say it's Ikaika's. I want to know when I get on that field that I have my girl back home wearing my jersey and rooting for me."

"Rooting for you *and* Ikaika."

"Yeah, yeah. But think about how well we're doing this season. We've only lost three. Not only are we likely to get to playoffs, but we could have a shot at a championship. And I'm playing so well. Don't you see the correlation?"

"What's the correlation?"

"You."

Keala scoffed playfully. "That's a lot of pressure to put on me. And correlation is not causation, haven't you heard?"

"Keeks, I went to school so I could play football. I didn't pay attention to anything."

"You're ridiculous. But you're not going to stop until I say yes, are you?"

"Nope."

She sighed. "Fine. I'll wear it. But only if you score a touchdown for me."

"You know I will. God, even the thought of it is sexy. Want to put it on and go again right now?"

"My legs are still shaking from the last two."

Landon leaned in, kissing her neck and then exhaling. "I'm so powerful."

"I'm going to sleep," she joked.

"And making you come is an otherworldly experience. You didn't let me finish!" When she was quiet for a few moments, he continued, softer, "I've never asked anybody to wear my jersey, you know."

Affection burrowed deep inside her at his words, and how vulnerable and small he sounded as he admitted that to her. He still struggled to talk about his feelings, but compared to how evasive he had been when they'd first met, she was incredibly proud of him.

"Thank you for letting me be the first."

"And last?" he asked quietly, pulling back to search her eyes.

Keala thought about her parents dancing together in the kitchen as they put off cleaning dishes. She remembered how her mother would laugh as her father spun her around, how happy they always were when they weren't fighting about their kids. Suddenly, those happy faces morphed so they were Keala and Landon, dancing in the kitchen he spent so much time in.

She ached for it, and while she knew she should be scared after the failures of her past relationships, she couldn't bring herself to be.

"And the last."

He kissed her softly, sweetly, and she felt rewarded, like she'd said the right thing. "Are you sure you're still okay meeting my family next week? We can cancel. We can stay in. Have a sexcation. I could slather you in chocolate sauce and lick every inch of you."

"Mm. I don't think I'll make a very good impression on your family if, in the first two weeks of us being together, you're absent from the one time you all get together each year."

Landon kissed her jaw. "Screw impressions. If I tell them you're spectacular, they'll believe you're spectacular. Hell, I'm sure they already think that since you're the first person to tame me."

"Ew. Don't say 'tame me.'"

"The first to get me to settle down?"

"Better, I guess. But no, I'm excited to meet everyone. I moved my shifts around and everything." She'd been apprehensive about changing her schedule, but it wasn't like she was working less. Just changing *when* she worked.

"You've been doing much better about not making every second of your life about work. I love it."

"You love it because I spend all my free time with you."

"Yes, I want a monopoly on your free time. I would pay you a better salary than you make right now to have you with me all the time."

She rolled her eyes, though the thought of that made her heart skip, hop, and topple over. "As if you're not plenty busy. I'd be sitting around twiddling my thumbs half the time."

"Yeah, but you'd be twiddling your thumbs in my jersey, waiting for me at home."

Keala scoffed again, turning around and pulling his arm around her body so that he spooned her. His large, warm palm dragged under her shirt, settling against her stomach.

"Wake me up before you leave for work tomorrow," he whispered into her hair.

"I'll try, but you sleep like the dead."

"You're one to talk."

Keala smiled, ready to fall into a restful sleep. As she felt it take over, he said, "Now that you're mine, I can tell you a deep, dark secret." He paused. "I totally cheated to win the pumpkin carving contest. I had a step-by-step tutorial on while I carved it. I just wanted to win a favor so I could convince you to go out with me."

"I knew it," she mumbled. "Your pumpkin was too perfect. Ikaika's going to be so mad. Now *you* owe *me* something."

"Anything you want," he whispered against her neck.

***

Keala was squished between Len and Zoe as coverage of the fourth quarter of the Sentinels' week thirteen game continued. Zoe's townhouse was bustling with Sirens, and Keala couldn't help feeling like she was a part of something more. Sure, she always tried to watch away games with the team, but usually she had a million thoughts racing through her head, mainly items on her never-ending to-do list. Now, despite an itch to do something productive, she was genuinely enjoying herself.

And like he'd asked, Landon's jersey was tucked into her jeans and covered by one of the many Sentinels sweatshirts she'd "borrowed" from Ikaika.

Len passed a bowl of chips to Keala, who took a couple and passed it on. "I can't watch," her friend said, turning her head and putting it on Keala's shoulder. "What happens if we lose this one?"

They were only down six, but time was running out.

"It's not ideal, but the season won't be over. An eight-four record isn't the worst," Keala answered reassuringly. They'd have to win a few more to be in a comfortable position for playoffs but nothing to be worried about.

"Better than last year's," Zoe piped up.

"True. The fact that we're eight-three right now is a miracle," Aurelia said from beside Zoe.

"It's because we finally have a real Beaumont." Keala didn't see who'd said that but didn't care to comment.

"I think the new coach may also be a bit of a help, Nova. One player doing better isn't changing everything."

"Yeah, but Landon *and* Myles are playing better in general and together. That's huge."

The conversation continued, but Keala tuned it out. Landon *had* been playing much better, and his extra effort seemed clear to everyone. She didn't care about stats but she'd heard

his were way up this season. He'd mentioned something similar.

She was glad he'd been feeling so much better. Keala had
hardly heard him talk about his brother or father recently,
and he'd stopped answering the latter's texts entirely. Not that
there had been any of substance to warrant a response.

"Should've stopped a long time ago, if I'm honest," he'd told
her a couple of nights ago. "I kept waiting for something good
to come out of his mouth but…"

"But you don't need him to tell you how good you are. You
don't need *anybody* to tell you how good you are. You're a top
tight end, and you always have been. *You* just needed to see
that."

He'd smiled softly at her, pulling her close. He'd been doing
a lot of that lately. Only two-thirds of his smiles were the
cheeky ones, and if they were alone, she could guarantee he
would be touching her in some way.

Keala loved it. She loved it even more that she didn't feel like
she had to be anyone but herself with him. When they were
together, they didn't have to think about disappointing their
families. When she was with him, the fear of being so much
less successful than her brother didn't make her want to die.

Maybe cry. But that was still progress.

The girls quieted, and when Keala looked at the TV, she
realized why. The Sentinels were driving, and it was probably
their last shot to get the game back. A field goal would do them
no good.

Myles called a play in the huddle and clapped before the linemen and receivers lined up. Landon was in, and the moment the center hiked the ball to Myles, Landon got in a quick block, juked left, and then ran right. He hopped into the air to catch Myles' pass, a defensive back closing in on him.

The girls all cheered, Keala probably the loudest. She clutched Zoe's hand as Landon stiff-armed one defensive back, faked out another, and continued running. Everyone stood from the floor and various pieces of furniture as Landon moved farther and farther down the field. Six-five and built, Landon dragged a man with him until he finally went down at the one-yard line.

Pride ballooned in her chest. When he scored the one-yard touchdown with a catch in the back of the end zone, his cleats both just touching inbounds, that balloon exploded with the sounds of the girls screaming so loudly, Zoe would probably get a noise complaint.

Landon had done it. He'd scored a much-needed last-minute touchdown to tie the game. It may not have been a pivotal game, but every win was important on the road to playoffs. She couldn't hold back her smile as he celebrated with his teammates in the end zone, posing like their mascot with an imaginary sword held over Ikaika.

He jogged toward the sideline, his fingers held in the sign of a half heart. The camera focused on him as he did so, commentators speculating who it could have been for.

"Bet I know," Zoe whispered softly enough that no one else could hear, the women around the room still buzzing excitedly.

Keala, hiding a smile, elbowed her friend, and Zoe laughed.

Landon may have gone his whole adult life without someone saying they were proud of him, but she would end that streak. She wasn't going to let him continue thinking he was a disappointment. She hadn't ever seen him in Colton's shadow, and now more than ever, he'd proved that he was capable of great things himself.

Ikaika was her favorite fullback, but Landon was her favorite player, and she would make sure he knew it.

Chapter Thirty-Five

Keala

Pulling Keala into a bathroom in his grandparents' house, Landon yelled a quick, "Washing up!" before he closed the door. He gave her a peck, then set his hands on her shoulders. "Doing okay? I know it's only been a few minutes, but you've met so many people."

From the moment Maya had picked her up from the airport, things had been a whirlwind. Landon had taken a separate car earlier, texting her the whole time. When she'd arrived at the house, Maya and Landon had made introductions to the whole family—their grandparents, a few of their cousins, Colton's little family, and Maya's boyfriend, Cooper.

Keala let out a breath. "I can't promise I'll remember everyone's names, but Maya seems very excited, which makes me feel better."

Landon laughed. "She is. She loves having new people in the family. You should've seen her the day she met Lucia."

"And you?" Keala asked softly. "Are you doing okay?" The exchange during Colton's introduction had been tense enough that Lucia, Colton's wife, had shared a worried look with her.

"A lot to work through. Just glad my dad's not here. Maya won't invite him to anything like this anymore." Keala was glad when she didn't see his guard go up when he mentioned his father. "My therapist says she thinks this will be a good trip for my growth, especially since he won't be coming, so I'm going to keep an open mind."

Keala tried not to react, in case his being in therapy was something that had just slipped out rather than something he'd wanted to let her know. Either way, pride built in her throat. She cleared it. "Still planning on talking to Colton sometime this weekend?"

He nodded. "Yes, but that's a problem for later. For now, I can just enjoy having you with me at a family event when I normally have to be...alone."

"Have to be, or prefer to be?"

"Okay, preferred. Past tense." Landon lifted her chin with a finger so he could kiss her again. "But that was before you."

She smiled at him in appreciation. "Wash your hands. Any longer, and they're going to think something untoward is going on."

He grinned. "You want something untoward to go on?"

"Landon."

"Fine," he muttered, washing his hands with her before they jumped back into the fray.

Maya waved them over, gesturing to the two seats beside her at the dining table. Landon pulled out Keala's chair, and she noted the look between Colton, Lucia, and Maya.

Dinner moved just as fast. Some of the conversation focused on their mother, which made sense. When her birthday came up, November seventh, Keala remembered the tattoo she'd traced on Landon's chest. A blue butterfly with that date scrawled beneath it, right over his heart. When she'd asked about his other tattoos, he'd told her the sparrow and the message "to the moon and back" that covered his hand was for her as well. The remainder of his tattoos were reminders of his journey through life, he'd said.

The rest of the conversation was checking in on each other. Every once in a while, Keala would be brought in, but she preferred listening and observing, learning about each piece of the puzzle of Landon's life, even if many of them were newer. She'd had no idea until this meal that his grandparents had only recently come back into their lives, but it seemed in the two years since then, a lot had changed and the family had grown closer.

"Keala, Landon mentioned that after this season, you'll be leaving the Sirens. Do you still plan to choreograph or dance elsewhere?" Lucia asked, her and Colton's daughter Lyla cooing in her lap.

Keala had been trying to ignore the impending end of her dancing career, knowing the despair that would fill her when it was over. "I'd love to, but I don't have anything lined up. My cousin thinks I should look at coaching some local college dance teams but..." But she didn't want to get her hopes up. She needed to prove to her bosses that she was their best NP so she could keep getting raises and pay off her debt. She wasn't sure how dance would fit into that picture. Cora had made an offhand comment about Brooklyn rarely being around a few practices ago, but there were so many more talented choreographers that even if Brooklyn did leave, Keala wasn't sure she would be their pick.

Realizing the table was waiting for her to finish her thought, Keala continued, "But dance will always be with me. Even if I'm not teaching a group, I'll always be dancing and thinking up choreography when I feel inspired." She smiled, and a few people around the table nodded.

The conversation moved on to Landon's cousin's new job, and when it had comfortably lulled, all three of their cousins hugged everyone goodbye and left.

The rest of them were staying the night at their grandparents' house. Keala and Landon would leave tomorrow evening since they had a home game on Monday, and Landon's siblings were staying longer since the Sabertooths were in their bye week.

After they finished getting ready for bed, Keala lay on her side with her back against Landon's chest. She traced patterns against the tattoo on the hand wrapped around her. "What are we doing tomorrow?" she asked.

"I want to show you the house I grew up in. Also my schools and the fields I used to kick ass on. All while in disguise, obviously."

"Obviously."

Keala had switched some of her shifts to be here, namely her Friday and Saturday ones for Tuesday and Wednesday. It'd felt weird and a little wrong to ask for the change, but she'd wanted to be here for Landon. Like he'd said, she had been working so hard, they couldn't be upset with her for taking some time to herself, right?

She knew she would get that uncomfortable feeling tomorrow, like she needed to be doing something, but she would do her best to be present with him. Keala was excited to see where Landon had come from.

"Why do you stay here instead of at the house you grew up in if your dad still owns it?"

"Long story, and not mine to tell, but Maya doesn't feel comfortable there anymore. And I think my grandparents like having us all here, especially since they spent so many years absent from our lives. We're so busy that this time when we all come together is sacred for them."

Keala's body warmed at knowing she'd been allowed into something so significant. "Thank you for bringing me. I love seeing where you came from. And meeting your family."

"Thank *you* for coming. I never knew what I was missing when they brought Cooper and Lucia, but now I get it." He squeezed her, setting his chin on her shoulder.

Keala smiled, holding both his hands as she fell into a blissful sleep, dreaming of a man who'd once been so opposed to emotions but who could now tell her how much he wanted her in his future.

Keala woke before their alarm. When she checked her phone, she found it was after nine. Shockingly, her internal clock hadn't woken her, which was becoming increasingly common when she was with Landon. She knew he wanted to sleep in today, so she wiggled out of his heavy arm as carefully as she could, grabbing her toothbrush and going to the bathroom across the hall.

Right as she finished her morning routine, her phone rang. She frowned. It was odd that Annie would call, especially knowing Keala wasn't working her usual week.

"Hello?" Keala asked quietly, assuming everyone else was sleeping in on their day off.

"Keala, I'm freaking out. Oh my god. I'm—" Keala heard retching on the other end and her heart sank into her stomach.

"Annie, what happened?"

More retching.

"Do you need me to call someone?"

"A woman came in yesterday around five. Third trimester with spiked blood pressure and decreased fetal movement. It looked like preeclampsia, so I stepped in and called for an OB to do an emergency C-section." Annie's voice was frantic, cut off with choked sobs. "Deirdre agreed calling for an OB was the right move, and we followed protocol but—" It sounded like Annie was trying not to vomit again. Keala collapsed against the door, her vision blackening around the edges. She slid down, her whole body tingling, static between her ears.

"It wasn't preeclampsia, Kay. They realized it was a placental abruption they didn't catch because the baby was over the cervix, and I-I—"

The prick of a million needles dug into Keala's skin, and she had the good sense to mumble a quick, "Annie, I'm so sorry, I have to go. I'll call you back," before she hung up and allowed the panic to take over.

Keala didn't need Annie to confirm the woman had died; it was clear. Malia had died the same way. Rushed to the hospital, emergency C-section, only to find out that she'd had a placental abruption.

Anguish pressed hard against her chest. She brought in oxygen in short bursts, panting. A few seconds—or maybe minutes—later, Keala couldn't feel her body. All she could think about was that if she had been there, she could've saved that woman. If she'd been there, she would've seen the signs. She would've asked the right questions—was there any bleeding?

Any extreme abdominal cramping? She would have recognized that it wasn't preeclampsia because Keala had become hyper focused on preventing any mistakes like the one that had taken Malia.

And now *she* was the reason that mistake had occurred. All because she'd wanted to believe she was worthy of a fairy-tale kind of love. So naïve. The one time she switched her shifts for a relationship and this happened? That had to be a sign.

It had been foolish of her to think she had time to devote to someone else.

Keala struggled to swallow as her thoughts circled the thing she'd been desperately trying to avoid.

Ikaika had been *destroyed* after his sister's death. When he'd come to Virginia after Malia had died, the light in his eyes had been completely gone. All joy seemed to have left the world. Another family just lost their light, their joy, and Keala should have been there to prevent it.

How would she face Ikaika? She had taken personal time and someone had died because of it. Keala didn't know when she'd be able to look him in the eye again. He'd see right through her, and then she'd have to tell him what had happened. It would tear him apart all over again.

Keala's stomach turned as she thought about the baby. She'd too hastily hung up, and now she didn't know if the woman's family had some hope in the form of that baby the way Ikaika's family had. It had undoubtedly been hard work, but Malia's daughter was six now. Was this woman's child so lucky? And if the baby *had* been born, would they have a family?

If she had been there, she would have called Genevieve on her cell to make sure she got down to the emergency department immediately. Annie and Deirdre had done all they could, she was sure, putting a STAT order into the system, but Keala had been building relationships with other physicians for this exact purpose. She had been monitoring signs on all pregnant patients that came in *for this exact purpose*.

She would have known it wasn't preeclampsia.

If she hadn't been so consumed by her desire to be loved, a woman wouldn't have just bled out.

It was Keala's turn to be sick.

By the time she'd emptied the limited contents of her stomach, she had made a decision.

Chapter Thirty-Six

Landon

Bleary-eyed, Landon searched the room for Keala when he didn't feel her in his arms. She was sitting at the foot of the bed, her duffel packed and on her lap.

"Keeks?"

She looked at him, clearly holding back tears. He sat up, reaching for her, but she shook her head, setting her jaw resolutely.

"I can't do this anymore."

He cocked his head. "Oh, is it too many people? We can leave early, that's no problem. I'll say something came up."

Keala shook her head again. "No, Landon." She gestured between them. "This."

"This." He repeated blankly. "Us?"

She nodded.

"I'm confused. We were all good last night. What happened?" He was trying to cover the shaking of his voice. The one emotion Landon could identify well, anger, was coming to the surface, and he was doing everything he could to keep it at bay.

"Something happened at the hospital. I need to go."

"But you're off. You don't work until tomorrow." He knew she'd switched her Monday shift for Sunday to make it to the game.

"I need to go," she repeated. "And I think it would be best if we steer clear of each other for a while. I'll stay at my parents' house."

"Keala, I don't think this is healthy. We can change our flights, but I don't understand why this has any bearing on *us*. We'll get you to the hospital."

"I should never have agreed to allow anything between us. It's taken too much of my focus from work. I'm too busy for anything like this right now."

The anger he'd allowed to simmer flared. "Are you too busy, or are you afraid of finally being selfish for once? Of telling people no? You hate working at the hospital. So quit and do what *you* want. Find somewhere you can dance. I know you don't want to stop choreographing, so don't. Choose yourself for *once*."

Something snapped in her. He saw it happen right before she stood and said, "I knew you wouldn't understand. I can't! Okay, Landon? I can't do that. I can't choose you and I can't choose dance. My brother just got into medical school, and I'm a washed up twenty-seven-year-old with debt from a degree I wish I'd never wasted my time or tears on and two parents who won't possibly accept that what I want to do, what I've *always* wanted to do, is dance. Dance doesn't pay, does it?"

Keala shouldered her bag, then continued, "Nobody in my parents' circles will understand, and then what? Then I become Nohea. I become the outcast, the disappointment, the kid they expected so much from but who couldn't take the pressure. I'm not doing that. I've worked too fucking hard for too long to make sure I don't become the child my parents refuse to talk about."

Landon wanted to get on his knees and beg her to stay, but he knew she wouldn't. For the first time in his life, after promising he never would, he'd opened up to someone, and like he'd expected, she was leaving.

So when she whispered an "I'm sorry. Goodbye," and ran from the room, he didn't so much as look in her direction.

Landon pretended he was fine through brunch and all through their time at the temple. He knew it was something Maya liked for them to do together, so he'd lied and said something had come up at work for Keala. That things were all good. He ignored the incredulous looks he kept getting.

When they got back to the house, he threw on a pair of sweatpants and went for a run around the neighborhood, enjoying the pain of the freezing cold on his bare chest. It bit at him, taking his mind off the fact that he'd been vulnerable with her in the hopes that *someone* would finally care. He couldn't say he was surprised to learn no one did.

Landon finished his run, sweaty and angry, and threw himself onto Nana and Nani's front lawn. He would go inside when his mind quieted and continue to pretend everything was okay, but for now, he needed a few moments alone with his thoughts.

The front door opened, and to his dismay, Colton came and sat beside him. When Landon sat up and glanced back, Maya gave him a concerned yet reassuring smile before she shut the door.

"I'm not in the mood to talk right now. I know Maya wants us to get this over with, but if it could wait a few more hours..." Landon said roughly. He was surprised that, the moment Colton had come out, a swarm of paparazzi hadn't rushed to take photos of him.

"One thing having an almost two-year-old daughter has taught me is patience, so take the time you need, and I'll talk."

Landon sighed but didn't respond.

"I don't know what's going on with Keala and you, but it's clearly bothering you. Maya practically ripped out her hair stressing about it this morning. You're lucky Cooper's been holding her back, because based on the amount of information she gave me, it seems like she'd have a lot to say to you."

"Nothing is going on, I—"

"Maya and Cooper were in the room next door and heard your fight, so you can stop lying."

Landon swore, lying down so he didn't have to look his brother in the eye.

"If it helps, Lucia and I had some bumps in the road before we got together."

"Really? You, the man who can do no wrong, had issues with your wife? How did that turn out for you? Oh, wait." He didn't know why, but talking to Colton made him regress to a childlike state.

"Look at the chip on that shoulder, man."

"Fuck off."

Landon could practically hear Colton roll his eyes. "All I'm saying is it sounds like she's scared. Obviously, something happened with her job, but based on what Maya told me, it seems like she's spent her entire life trying to be what everyone else wants, and for some reason, you were different for her. I imagine you infuriated the shit out of her—"

"Thanks."

"But that's not the point. The point is, Maya thinks she's been pushing the limits to see how much it'll take for you to prove that she's right. That eventually the people who know the real her will leave."

Landon groaned. "I'm tired of you sick-in-love Beaumonts preaching to me about relationships."

"Can you shut the fuck up for two seconds and listen to me?"

"No, because you're wrong. I didn't leave her. She left me. I was honest with her about my feelings. I told her shit I've never told anyone, things I now know I shouldn't have told her, but I did. And now she's gone."

Colton sighed. "Look, I get it. I get being scared to be vulnerable. But that's not what happened. Something spooked her, and she's retreating. It doesn't have anything to do with you sharing your feelings. If it did, she wouldn't have come here to meet your entire family. Ultimately, it's going to be up to her to choose you and tell you what's going on, but she needs to know you're still there for her to get to that point."

"So, what? I go back and act like everything is all good?"

"I don't know. Maybe iron out the specifics with Lucia and Maya, but do whatever showing up for her looks like, I guess. Let her know that you'll be there when she changes her mind."

"*If* she changes her mind."

"According to Lucia, she was 'radiating love' for you yesterday. Nobody thinks this break is permanent. You can give her the space she needs while not giving up on her. We saw you interact over the course of one meal and could tell how much you care about each other. So don't give up on her."

Landon sat back up, finally shifting so he faced Colton. "What's with the brotherly advice all of a sudden?"

"That's not fair. I've tried, Landon. I've made every effort in the last few years to rectify our issues."

That was true. Landon had spent so much of his life resenting his brother, he had never thought of the efforts as sincere. But that was probably his own issue.

"Okay, yeah. But I don't think you understand how hard it is to be your younger brother. I have spent every moment of my life in your shadow. Nothing I did was ever good enough for Dad, and when we got older, it wasn't enough for anybody else either. In high school, if I made an impossible catch, somehow you would get the credit because it was a good throw. Why did it always have to be you over me? Why couldn't they have seen that we were good as a team?"

Colton nodded. "I know. I've thought a lot about it, and I'm sorry you had to grow up like that. And if it makes you feel better, nothing I do is ever enough for Dad either."

"It doesn't make me feel better. He might still say shit to you, but at least you know he cares about you. He shows up for you. He comes to your games. Everyone comes to your games."

"You can't blame me for geography. Maya is there because of Cooper."

"I can when Dad moved across the country—even though Maya was still in high school and I was still in college—because you got drafted."

"Do you know how much of a living hell that was? To have him come to every game and nitpick my every move? Have you ever thought that maybe I worked so hard because I *wanted* to take the brunt of his attention away from you? Sometimes,

Landon, no attention was better than his full attention, I promise you that."

Landon was about to retort, but he bit his tongue. "You did that?"

"I didn't know in the beginning that it's what I was doing, but I figured it out a couple of years ago. I knew that if I could keep his focus on me, he would leave you alone."

Landon thought about all the times his dad had insulted him for having emotions, even after their mom had gotten sick and passed. He thought about the few times his dad had watched his games. Landon had always thought what *he* did wasn't enough, but if he'd worked harder and his father had come to all of his games, even when he was at his best, would it have been enough for him?

Probably not.

Colton rubbed his chin. "I hate to break it to you, but the way Dad treated you wasn't my fault. I know I was the easier scapegoat, but he just has issues. I'm sorry if I ever did anything to make you feel like you weren't as good as me, because if I did, that was on me. But the way Dad acts has nothing to do with me. I don't ask him to treat you that way."

"Fine. But that doesn't change that the media and journalists won't shut up about my brother and his three championship wins. It's not a good feeling when I have zero, and I'm tired of hearing about it."

Colton scoffed. "Then get your ass up and work for it, man. You think that came easily for me? Hell no. I worked my ass off. If you applied yourself the way I do, you could be as good as any league great. It has never been about you versus me. It's you versus yourself. Choosing to cry about the fact that I've put my whole life into this and consequently have something to show for it isn't doing you any favors. Yeah, you're going to disappoint people sometimes, but you will never be great if you don't *try*."

He hated that Colton was right. "I have been trying. I've been working my ass off this season."

"And look at the Sentinels' record. It'll be the same as ours if you get a win Monday. Obviously there are more pieces at play here, but this is proof that you putting in the work can change so much. It's week fourteen. Stop bitching and start working."

"Alright, man. Stop insulting me. I got it."

Colton stretched his legs out in front of himself. "Do you care about all that stuff? About championship wins and the Hall of Fame and shit?"

Landon thought hard. "Not like you, no. I don't need as many as you, and I don't care if I don't go down as some great player. It would just be nice to know I *can* do it."

"Then stop listening to the noise. Stop listening to Dad and stop listening to the media. Focus on what you can control."

"You don't think I should try to talk to Dad?" As he asked the question, he knew the answer.

Colton shook his head. "I've tried. It doesn't do anything. He's delusional as hell. At this point, it's better to just ignore him. Recognize that we all had traumatic childhoods because of him and that he's a lost cause. He's still going to be around because I can't bring myself to cut him off since, to a certain extent, he did help me get to this point. But I stopped listening to him a long time ago. He has no say in any of my life choices."

"He say anything about you retiring?"

"He said lots of things about me retiring, but like I said, I stopped caring. Lucia and I want at least one more kid and we want to travel. I've done all I need to in the football world. It's time to be present for my wife and kids. Let Luc be the breadwinner in her hot-ass pantsuits."

Landon opened his mouth, but Colton cut him off. "Don't say anything about my wife being hot."

Landon laughed. "Wasn't going to." He paused for a moment, hating how emotional he was allowing himself to be in front of someone he'd thought he would always resent. "And I'm sorry. For being kind of a bitch and blaming you for so much. Thank you for trying to take the heat off me."

"That's what big brothers are for." Colton looked at him meaningfully. "Something you said about Mom yesterday stuck with me. You have to stop blaming yourself for how you handled her death. I know how you feel. But Dad kept us busy. We were kids. We couldn't have done anything."

"I could have tried to be more present. You did such a good job of listening to her, and I just...couldn't cope."

"I pushed the hurt way down to make sure you and Maya were okay, but I was struggling too. I didn't handle it any better than you, just differently. You were a kid and you needed attention. Sure, you didn't go about it the best way, but you can't blame yourself for shit that happened over a decade ago before your brain was even fully developed."

Landon allowed that to settle in his chest. The pair sat on the lawn for a few minutes before Colton finally broke the comfortable silence. "Maya was right. All it took was one conversation we could've had years ago to let bygones be bygones."

"I wouldn't have been ready for it. Not mature enough or in the right headspace for it before now."

"Keala?"

"Yeah. And therapy." Both had helped him see things from more than his own perspective.

Colton nodded. "Good. That's great. I've been going since I found out Lucia was pregnant with Lyla. I don't want to pass on any of my childhood trauma to her."

"It's been helpful, I think. Started pretty recently though, and obviously"—he gestured between the two of them—"I have a lot of work left, but...yeah, I'm glad I started."

Colton chuckled, looking down as a car passed by. "And you love Keala?"

"How do I know? I've never even been in a relationship." But he knew. He knew it from the way his chest had been cleaved in two when she'd walked away, the first tears he'd had in years welling in his eyes. He knew it from the way he'd felt as they had fallen asleep yesterday, him wrapped around her, breathing in her vanilla shampoo. He knew it from the feeling he got when he saw her sad, and how badly he ached to take care of her and show her that she could be anything she wanted—screw what society or her parents thought.

"You'd know it. And I think you do."

"Yeah."

Landon sat there long after Colton went back inside. He sat there as Maya settled in beside him, her head on his shoulder.

And the only thing he kept coming back to was that he was going to push himself out of his comfort zone, keep putting himself out there and being vulnerable for Keala. If she wasn't ready to leap for them, he would.

He could wait as long as she needed.

Chapter Thirty-Seven

Keala

Y ou've been avoiding me," Ikaika said through his teeth as he smiled at the camera, Keala tucked into his side with a similar grin on her face.

It was family day for the Sirens, and since Keala had agreed to do social media, she was the one handling all the pre-game content on the field. Her teammates were teaching their parents choreography for videos that would go up this week, as well as photos of all the girls and their families.

Keala's parents were late, but Ikaika had stepped in. The Sentinels loved any photo opportunity with them together anyway.

Before she could respond, someone yelled, "Get Ikaika a football. KayKay, shake your poms!"

Someone tossed a football to him, and Keala picked her poms up, shaking them for the photo.

"Keeks."

She looked at him, not ready for this conversation. He must have read it in her face because he yelled, "We're going to need a few minutes. Does anybody else want to jump in?"

Ikaika walked to the sideline. Before she followed him, she yelled to Nova, "Can you take over? Just keep filming everyone learning choreo—that'll help me a ton."

Nova gave her a thumbs up. Angelica glared at her.

When Keala stopped in front of Ikaika, his arms were crossed and it was clear she wasn't going to get away from this conversation like she'd hoped.

Ikaika was right, she'd been avoiding him. She had been staying at her parents' house all week, keeping busy by taking on two extra shifts and practicing with the girls or at the facility every night.

"I don't know if now is a good time to talk about this," she finally said.

Ikaika looked around, then dropped his voice. "Is this about Landon? Did he do something? I know you were excited about going to visit his family, but if things were weird…"

Keala shook her head, trying not to picture him. Something she'd actively focused on all week—anything but him.

"Are you sure? Because he's been in a horrible mood, moping and shit."

She closed her eyes, feeling them burn. "No, he didn't do anything. I'm the one who ended things."

"Why?"

"I needed space."

"Space from what? If it's from Landon, then I'll tell him to stay out of the apartment. You don't have to stop coming home because of that."

Keala tucked her hands under her armpits, hoping it would stop her fidgeting. She looked everywhere except at him.

She'd planned to go home soon, get back to how things were before, but she'd needed some time to cool down and keep her head above the ocean of guilt that tried to drown her.

Six years, and Ikaika still struggled with Malia's passing. Of course he did. But after the accident, it was clear he was still easily triggered, and the last thing she wanted to be was a trigger for him. Telling him what had been eating her alive...she didn't know how he would handle it. That's why she'd been working through the guilt on her own.

Taking her silence as an answer, he murmured, "So it's not from him then." Ikaika sighed. "Keala, what the hell is going on?"

"I...I fucked up. I switched shifts to go to LA...and if I'd been at the hospital, things would have been different."

"Things...What things? Why are you talking in riddles?"

Keala took a deep breath. Hoping to keep her explanation vague, she said, "There was a pregnant patient. She came in with concerning symptoms. They operated under an assumption, but if I'd been there..." Maybe it would have gone differently, even if no one else agreed with her.

She waited for his expression to turn dark, to take on that hollowed, intensely sad look. For his light to dim.

Nothing. He just frowned. "And what you took from that was…that it was your fault for doing something for you for once?"

"I—what? Did you hear what I said? It was just like…"

"Malia, yes." He swallowed. "Keeks, you have the biggest heart of anyone I know, but even you can't save everyone. I'm so sorry that happened to another family, and I'm not questioning your abilities, but who's to say things *would* have been different?"

"*Me*. If my patient is pregnant, I'm always on the lookout for those symptoms. To make *certain* I don't let something like that happen to anyone else." Quieter, she said, "To make sure no one else goes through what you did."

Ikaika put a hand on each of her biceps, squeezing softly. "Did you talk to someone at the hospital about this?"

She nodded.

"And?"

"They said there was nothing I could have done if I'd been there. The obstetrician got down there right away and asked all the questions she could, then operated without realizing what the woman's condition was."

He was quiet, staring at *her* with concern. Keala shifted back and forth on her feet, looking away. Gently, he asked, "Then why are you blaming yourself?"

"Because I've spent years making sure to keep watch. I never wanted anybody to go through what you have," she reiterated. "I was terrified that if I came home and tried to keep it from you, you'd see the guilt pulling me under, and then I'd have to explain. You're still dealing with Malia's loss. I—I—" Keala stared up at the sky, willing her tears away. Her makeup was nearly done and she wouldn't have time to fix it later if it smeared.

"Keala. Look at me." She listened. "I am begging you to stop living your life for other people. Everyone has made it clear that even if you hadn't changed shifts, even if you'd been there, the outcome would have been the same. You can't keep putting your life on hold for something you hate. Something that's slowly killing you."

Her brain moved like molasses, still deciphering how Ikaika was taking this so well. She'd expected him to go quiet, decide not to suit up for the game, take some time for himself. Hell, the thought he might ask her to move out had entered her head before she'd recognized he wasn't like that. Instead, his words were similar to Landon's when he'd pleaded with her to stay.

"Keeks, have you been eating? Sleeping?"

No. She'd barely slept in the week since she'd returned to San Jose. And like nothing had changed, the couple of times Keala had needed to stop by to grab something at the apartment—when she'd known Ikaika wouldn't be there—there had been food left in the fridge for her, sans a note.

It made her heart hurt just to think about it. At the start of the week, she'd been able to eat a little, but as Sunday had approached and she'd known she'd have to see Landon again, nothing had been staying down. Not the food he'd made her, not her carrots, not even her Pedialyte or protein shakes. Anxiety had slammed through her every time she'd tried, and then she'd ended up throwing it all up again.

It had been a tough few days, especially with how much energy she'd expended at the hospital and dance.

"I'm okay," she lied.

He recognized it immediately, raising an eyebrow. "Come home, please. If, even after recognizing that you couldn't have changed anything, you don't want to be with Landon, that's fine. I'll make sure he stays out of your way. But come home. I've missed you. And I'm convinced you won't take care of yourself unless someone else forces you to."

Keala blinked, still reconciling. Someone called her name from across the field, but she hardly registered it.

If even Ikaika was okay with this...maybe she could find a way to forgive herself too. And maybe, instead of using her guilt to drown out the ache of missing Landon, it was finally time to think through her options when it came to him.

But she didn't have that time now.

"I'll be back after the game," she promised.

He pulled her into a hug. "Good. I love you. Do you need me for anything else?"

Keala saw Nova waving at her over Ikaika's shoulder and pulled away. "Unless you want to get roped into dancing before your warm-up, I'd head back to the locker room." She gave him a reassuring smile when he shot her another concerned look. "I'm good, I promise. I love you. Go kick ass."

He nodded and jogged off the field.

The rest of her social media work and their practice flew by. When it was time to line up in the tunnel for the pregame dance, Keala felt fatigue settling in her bones. She put on a smile anyway.

The sound of cleats on concrete made her turn. Instant regret.

Seeing Landon on the field during last week's game had been brutal. Seeing him now in this confined space, so close and yet so far, was excruciating.

Her eyes were drawn to him like magnets. His helmet was off, hair in complete disarray, and when he finally looked at her, she saw an almost hollow quality to his cheeks and under his eyes. Her first thought was to run to him, jump into his arms, and kiss him. Tell him how proud of him she was after the way he'd played last week. Tell him how much she missed him and how she couldn't stand to be away from him.

But she remembered where they were and why she'd ended things in the first place, even if she was rethinking it all.

He looked haggard beyond belief, and when their eyes locked, she realized how shattered he seemed. She thought he was about to walk over, eyebrows drawn like he couldn't fathom doing anything but touching her, making sure it was truly her.

He seemed heartbroken and looked as horrible as she felt.

She would have looked like that too if she hadn't slathered a disgusting amount of makeup onto her face. She *had* looked like that all week; she was sure of it because her mother hadn't made a single comment about her job. If she had, Keala would have broken down, something she'd been trying hard *not* to do.

His coach yelled something that echoed through the tunnel. Landon looked at her one last time before running out onto the field for a short practice, his hand barely grazing hers as he went by. He'd been so good about giving her space, keeping his distance, only communicating with the food he left for her.

This was the first time they had touched in eight days, and heat shot through her body at the contact. Like every individual cell was calling out for him to come back.

Zoe, who'd gotten a call about the situation the night Keala had flown back to San Jose, shot her a worried look, stepping closer as if to protect her. Keala was lucky Angelica was at the front of the line, talking to Jordy. She didn't miss the look Cora sent her though, and her stomach turned as she hooked pinkies with Zoe and focused on her breathing.

She couldn't think about him anymore. It was going to be a long, grueling day, and she couldn't start it off feeling even more shit than she already did.

After the team came back, she and the Sirens went out and performed their pregame dance. Keala felt shaky the whole time, but she attributed it to her heart still picking up the pieces of her own mistakes.

She couldn't think about eating the lunch provided to them, her stomach in knots.

Game time came quickly, and before she knew it, she was back on the field, shaking her poms, throwing her hair around, and smiling like it was what she'd been born to do. Baltimore came out strong, but the Sentinels pushed back hard.

Right around the end of the first quarter, Keala's vision began to blur. Breathing became difficult. She was dizzy but put all her energy into each movement, watching Zoe for her cues.

Arms extended up, then dropped down. Left pom to her waist, right elbow to her side. Shake poms as arms move to low V, jazz walk to the next formation.

One, two, three, four, five, six, seven, eight, she counted in her head as she hit each beat. Something still felt wrong, but she powered through, terrified that if she made the smallest misstep, she would lose the last good thing in her life weeks before she was supposed to.

During the break between the first and second quarter, their group met up with Jordy's in the end zone to do one of their four pieces. It was the one Keala had choreographed, so she smiled a little brighter, knowing the cheers of the crowd were because she'd done a good job.

She nailed a high kick, then took Zoe's cue to spin, cueing Carol to her left. Right as she began dance-running toward their next formation, her blurred vision went dark.

The sound of thousands of gasps was the last thing she heard before she blacked out.

Chapter Thirty-Eight

Landon

A collective gasp rippled through the stadium, pulling Landon's attention away from the timeout huddle with the other receivers and coaches. He turned toward the end zone to see what was happening and noticed half of the Sirens surrounding someone on the ground.

He saw Zoe, which meant Keala was at that end zone, but he couldn't find her anywhere. Looking up at the big screen didn't help at all either.

He walked toward them. Ikaika must have had the same feeling because he fell into step beside Landon. The coaches were yelling at them. One medic and then another rushed from their sideline, and dread washed over him. Scanning the group, he still couldn't find Keala, and when the group parted to let the medics in, Landon realized why.

It was her on the ground. He didn't think, just ran as fast as he could. When he reached her, he saw her normally golden skin was pale, especially in contrast to the colors of her cheer uniform. Her eyes, which had seemed tired in the tunnel earlier, were completely shut.

"What happened?" he asked, looking at all the cheerleaders who still lingered around her, then at the medic beside her. "What's wrong?" he asked more forcefully. His voice sounded shaky to his own ears, and he was still panting from his sprint down the field.

"We were doing a routine and she collapsed. She seemed kind of out of it in the locker room and in practice, but I just thought it was because..." Zoe's voice drifted off as Landon locked eyes with her, and he understood what she wasn't saying. She'd thought things had been off because Keala was struggling with their time apart, like he was. "She didn't eat anything for lunch though, and I haven't seen her drink anything either."

The second medic, the one who wasn't on his knees at her side assessing her, put a hand on Landon's chest. "We're going to need everyone to give us some space to work. Now." He used his other hand to gesture to her teammates, who listened.

"Keala!" Landon yelled, trying to get away from the medic. Hoping she'd sit up, reassure him that she was okay.

"I got him," someone murmured, and before Landon knew it, Ikaika was the one in front of him, nudging him back.

"Ik, she's okay, right? She..."

"We need to listen to the medics. They're here to help," his friend said. When Landon took a few steps back, eyes never leaving her, Ikaika let go but kept a hand firmly placed on Landon's chest.

The first medic used a stethoscope, talking quietly with the other. Landon couldn't hear them, and it was driving him wild. Their faces gave away nothing. "What are they saying?" He moved toward them again, but Ikaika pushed him back. "Ik, she has to be okay."

"Let them work. You've seen them. You know they know what they're doing. They'll help her."

A third medic ran up, handing something off to the first, and after speaking to them quietly, took off toward the sideline again.

Why isn't she waking up? Get up, baby. Get up.

They pricked her finger. Nodded to each other. Placed a small, metallic device against two of her fingers, turning their attention to a tablet screen. Landon ran a hand through his hair, hopelessly trying to make out what they were saying.

The third medic came back with a small, reddish-orange, rectangular box. Ikaika turned to watch too. The woman took out a vial of white powder, uncapped it, then pushed liquid from a syringe inside. She shook the vial, then used the syringe to pull out the liquid.

As she got ready to inject it into Keala's leg, Landon cringed. "What are they doing? What is that?"

"I'm not sure."

After putting the syringe back into the case, the second medic pressed on her leg, and then they pushed Keala onto her side. Panic rose in Landon's chest when he noticed a cart coming toward them. She wasn't going to be able to get up and walk? That couldn't be right.

"No, no. She's—she's fine. She's going to—she's fine." He got louder with each word. He'd just seen Keala before the game. She had looked sad, sure, but she'd given no indication that she hadn't been physically okay.

Ikaika looked back at Landon, concern etched into every one of his features. Ikaika, who was so strong, who had been through so much, looked concerned. That broke something inside of Landon. His eyes welled with tears and his throat closed up, scratchy like sandpaper.

The image of his mother collapsing in the living room flashed in his mind. The feel of shock shutting his whole body down, of struggling to breathe while Colton yelled for help to get her in the car. Of doctors poking her, prodding her, buzzing around her in her final moments. Suddenly, it wasn't Keala on the field but his mom, frail from the chemo, dehydrated and tired beyond belief. So many things he hadn't gotten to say to her.

So many things he hadn't gotten to say to Keala either.

Landon inhaled sharply, so desperate to hold her. So desperate for her to wake up and stand, like nothing had happened. *Why* wasn't she waking up?

"I need her to be okay. She has to be."

Ikaika moved his hand from Landon's chest to his shoulder reassuringly, but that only made him feel worse.

He hadn't even gotten to tell her how he felt about her. He had been waiting so patiently, continuing to make her food so that when she finally realized whatever had happened at work hadn't been her fault, she would know she could come back. That he wasn't upset. That he wanted her in his life.

And now he didn't know if she would be okay.

He'd watched his mom slip from his grasp, too young, too hopeless to know what to do, but he wouldn't let that happen again.

Keala's teammates murmured among themselves, and as the cart got to her, Landon saw her stir, her eyes opening. She still wasn't sitting up though, and that panic from before practically choked him.

The three medics loaded her onto a stretcher, then put her on the cart. Landon moved in their direction, but again, Ikaika held him back.

"Landon." Ikaika nodded to where the Sirens stood, most with their hands over their mouths, eyes wide, mixes of concern, fear, and confusion on their faces. Beside them was Keala's boss, Angelica. Landon had seen her a few times, always with a frown, and now she looked even more severe. She glared after the cart like Keala was gum on the sole of her boot. Heat spread through Landon's body, crawling up his neck and prickling against his skin in a way that tightened his chest.

His friend continued, "It's going to be okay. They're going to take her to the hospital. I have a friend on the medic team who'll let me know which. But you need to calm down before we cause any more of a scene. And we need to talk to Coach."

Landon clenched his teeth but mumbled his agreement. His mind had been so singularly focused on Keala that he hadn't noticed the thunderous applause ringing out now that she was on the cart, heading toward what he hoped was safety. None of the coaches looked happy with them, but Ikaika said something to their head coach, Ray, and he nodded for them to go.

Landon ran alongside Ikaika to the locker room, where they ripped off their pads, tossed on T-shirts, and grabbed their phones. By the time they got to Ikaika's car, he knew which hospital Keala was going to, texting her parents to meet them there.

The entire ride to the hospital, Landon had his head in his hands, going over what Zoe had said.

If she hadn't been eating or drinking, she was probably dehydrated. That had to be it. She just needed fluids. She was working herself too hard. It was finally catching up with her, and not even his meals had helped.

If she'd even been eating them.

When they made it to the hospital, they rushed inside the emergency room. Ikaika asked about her, and after Ikaika verified who he was, they were directed to a room right behind them.

A nurse leaving the room smiled. "Hi, is one of you a family member?"

"I'm her cousin, and her parents are on the way."

"Great, you can follow me in and I'll let you know her condition."

Ikaika turned to Landon. "You'll be okay?" Landon nodded once. "I'll be right back."

In the brief moment Landon saw her, he noted the IV in her arm. Her eyes were closed again, and he didn't know if she was sleeping or unconscious.

Time ticked down. The wait, though only a few minutes, was agony. Ikaika reemerged, a small smile on his face as the nurse said she'd be back in a few minutes.

"What's wrong? Is she going to be alright?" Landon asked, words strung together in his rush to get them out.

"She had a hypoglycemic episode, which I guess means she had low enough blood sugar that she crashed. They're giving her fluids and are going to run a couple of tests, but assuming all is well, they'll discharge her tonight. She's napping now."

Relief crashed through Landon like a wave on the shore, and he breathed a sigh, staggering back so his spine hit the wall. "Thank god. That's..." He nodded, gulping down air. "That's great news."

"Yeah. Her parents are close, but I think you can come in if you want."

Landon thought about how unhinged, how out of his mind with worry he'd been on the field when he'd realized it was her. There was no way his feelings for her hadn't been clear, which meant he'd potentially outed their relationship not only to Angelica, but to the world. He was sure there was already speculation online about what was going on.

The last thing Keala needed when she woke up was to find out she'd lost her greatest passion. Despite leaving midway through the game, he thought he might have a good shot at swaying the Sentinels franchise to keep her on.

"There's something I need to do first."

Ikaika nodded his understanding, handing Landon his keys so he could get back to the stadium.

He didn't care what he lost, as long as she woke up knowing the thing she loved the most was still hers.

Landon didn't realize he hadn't felt that familiar hospital itch until he was halfway to the stadium.

Chapter Thirty-Nine

Keala

Pulling herself from the soft clutches of sleep, Keala opened her eyes. The sound of monitors beeping was familiar to her, though the IV in her arm was not. She'd been in and out since being lifted onto the cart, but everything since then felt hazy; it was unclear what had been a dream and what had been real. Based on how dark it was outside, it'd been at least a few hours since she'd been carted off the field.

A bouquet of balloons floated near the door, and the chairs where Ikaika and her parents had been were vacant. Cora stood, looking out the window.

"Cora?" Keala's voice came out raspy.

Cora turned and rushed to her bedside. "Slowly," she warned as Keala tried to sit up. "Your family went to get some food and I offered to stay. I hope that's okay."

"Of course." Keala's eyes fixated on the balloons, wondering, hoping...

"Some of the girls came by right after the game to make sure you were alright." Keala ignored the way her heart sank a touch, thankful that her teammates had gone to such trouble. "Zoe brought your phone and a couple of changes of clothes you left in the locker room. She has the rest she can get to you whenever you need."

"That's so sweet." Cora looked at her, arms crossed over her chest. "Guess I did need my Pedialyte," she joked.

"Keala."

Keala looked at her hands resting in her lap. "I'm sorry."

"Do you even know what you're sorry for?" Keala stayed silent. "I begged you at the beginning of the season to take care of yourself. Focus on your health, on eating right, getting enough fluids and sleep, especially with two demanding jobs. You worked *five* shifts in a row. Nobody in your family has seen you for more than a few minutes in *days*."

"It was a hard week?" It came out more as a question than a statement.

"And yet I was not surprised to learn from your family that this is how you've always been." Cora sighed. "Just because you're good at playing this role for your family doesn't mean it's your job."

Keala looked away, too struck by the words to respond.

Cora continued, "I knew this girl once. She listened to what everyone said she should do with her life. Let their thoughts on her future rock her like a wave back and forth, rock her so hard, she didn't think about her own wishes or wants. All she worked for was what others wanted. Making other people happy. She grew up and hated the job she chose. She wished for a better life, thinking it would come when she got money. She worked and worked and worked herself to the bone, made the woman inside her writhe in pain at not being released. She rarely spent time with her family or friends, and she never felt fulfilled. If you were friends with someone like that, what would you say to them?"

Keala recognized what Cora was doing, but there was only one clear answer. "I would tell her to quit and find what she loves."

"So why can't you take that advice too? Why are you different from everyone else? Why must you suffer—work yourself to the point of literal collapse—when you see that others shouldn't?" Cora clasped Keala's hand. "Who are you working so hard for?"

Who *was* she working so hard for? It wasn't herself. The first answer that popped into her head was her parents, but her parents had never asked her to work like this. Sure, her mom made comments about her choice to be an NP over being a doctor, but that conversation always began because she hadn't been completely honest with them in the first place.

She'd never once told them dance was her biggest passion. Keala had spent her whole life pushing and pushing to be what she thought her parents wanted, to be like Akoni, that she hadn't stopped to wonder if that was the life they wanted for her too. Maybe they thought medicine was her passion. After all, she'd always lied about loving her job.

But now Keala was forced to see that she was burnt out, tired beyond belief, and so ruinously unhappy.

So who was she doing this for?

"Is that a hypothetical or…?"

"I made lots of money as a lawyer, but things didn't get better for me. I thought if I kept putting in the hours, I would have enough money to make sure I was happy no matter what, but it never happened. So, finally, on a whim, I quit my job and chose to chase my passion: dance. Haven't looked back since. It's how I met my husband, and it's enriched my life more than money ever could."

"I—I don't even know where I'd start."

Cora shrugged. "Maybe it's time to take a risk. You're a professional dancer with ties to two professional teams. Any team—professional, college, or otherwise—would be lucky to have you. You're one of the strongest technical dancers I've seen in my fifteen years with the Sirens, if not the strongest. I know it's scary to put everything on the line and potentially fail, but think about how much happier you'll be doing what *you* want."

"But what about money?" Keala thought about her debt, which still sat in the five-figure range. "And do you have to deal with people treating you differently because you're not in a traditional field?"

"We'll find you a position that pays well. And if you have to work a couple of part-time choreography gigs for a few years, that's fine. As for the way people treat me? I stopped caring. I stopped needing to prove to everyone that I could fit in their boxes and decided to make myself happy. It's a hard mindset to kick, and I still have to work on it sometimes, but it was a deliberate effort to take back control. And I finally did."

Could Keala stop caring? She'd tried the night she'd met Landon, but that hadn't worked out.

Landon.

"Did you say Zoe brought my phone?" Keala asked. Cora grimaced but nodded. Frowning, Keala wondered, "What happened?"

"I was going to talk to you about it after the game when I noticed it in the tunnel, but then you went and gave everyone a heart attack on live television. The poor boy couldn't help himself. The moment he realized it was you, he was sprinting to you and calling your name."

Static played between Keala's ears, sharp and painful as she realized what she was about to lose. What she'd already lost. "I'm off the team?"

"Not quite." Cora grabbed Keala's phone from one of the chairs, handing it to her. "Search his name."

Keala listened and was met with results from dozens of news sites from mere hours ago. She clicked on the first one, seeing a photo of a frantic Landon held back from running to her limp body by Ikaika. Then, below it was a video of Landon speaking directly to the camera.

She played it, confused when it panned from the game to him coming out of the tunnel in his postgame sweatsuit. "He didn't finish the game?"

Cora shook her head but didn't answer.

Keala bit her lip, watching the broadcaster ask where he'd been.

"I had to make sure she was okay."

"And is she?"

Landon nodded, relief clear in his face. Her stomach lurched at the sight of him. She'd missed him so much. "She's resting now."

He'd come to the hospital to check on her? He *hated* hospitals.

"And what's the nature of your relationship? You seemed very worried about her."

"I know you all may know me as the sarcastic, fun-loving guy who doesn't take things too seriously. The guy who hangs out with a new girl every weekend." He swallowed. He'd probably been horrified having to share his feelings on live television. "Maybe you've noticed things have been different for me lately. *I've* been different. I'm playing better, and I'm more focused on getting this team to the level I know it can be. That's because of her. I love her more than anyone or anything in this world, and I'm so thankful she's alright." His voice wavered on the last word, but he covered it with a smile. A genuine one.

Keala's lips tipped up, glancing at Cora. "Oh, wow," Keala whispered, wiping under her eyes. "I—I..."

"Feel the same way, I know. I could tell the minute I saw you two interact in the tunnel that he was part of the reason you were so miserable. He's a genius, you know. Angelica and the Sentinels can't do anything about the no-fraternization rule now."

"Why?"

"That video has gone viral on every platform you can possibly imagine. If the Sentinels tried to fire you, it would be a PR nightmare. Millions of people are talking about the star-crossed Sentinels couple."

He'd saved her. Landon had saved her last month of dance, and he'd done so by letting his guard down for millions of people.

"You should've seen him when the girls and I were leaving. He was pacing in the tunnel, talking to his agent about the agreement with the team. I've never seen anyon—"

"Wait, wait. What agreement?"

"Oh, right. Angelica knew she couldn't fire you after the confession. But just to be sure, Landon let the GM and owner know that if you got cut, he would walk."

"Wha—why would he do that? He can't throw away the season he's worked so hard for. If they won today, they're almost guaranteed a playoff spot."

"Don't worry, you're both safe. The franchise is spinning it now and is probably going to have you both taking tons of promo pictures to prove that all's well."

Keala blew out a sigh. She needed to talk to Landon, prove to him how much he meant to her and how sorry she was. She needed to apologize, and not just to him.

She needed to let Josie know she was sorry for not calling more and only texting when *she* needed advice. Keala hadn't been a good friend to her, to her teammates, or to Ikaika.

And she needed to apologize to Akoni for not being more supportive.

She'd put a job she barely liked above her health and her closest relationships.

A knock sounded, and then Keala's mom poked her head in. "Is she up? Oh, sweetie, hi! How are you?" Keala's father came in after her.

"I'm okay." *Just in a deep state of questioning every decision I've ever made.* Cora gave her a stern look, the kind that had the truth spilling from Keala's lips. "Actually, I'm not."

Cora excused herself, saying a quick goodbye to Keala's parents.

"Do you need water? I can grab you some food," her mother said, concerned.

"I didn't get into medical school," Keala breathed. *I guess that's where we'll start.* Their faces were shocked, her mother's hand over her chest. "I'm so sorry I lied to you. I was embarrassed."

If she could've gone the rest of her life never telling them, she would have, but maybe this was the first step in the direction of taking control.

"I...don't understand." Keala read the hurt in her mother's expression. "You've been holding on to this for over five years? You didn't think you could tell us?"

"I'm sorry. I know it was wrong to keep it from you, but I was worried you wouldn't love me as much if you found out I wasn't as smart as Akoni. And I was so embarrassed, I went for the closest thing I could, hoping you would still be proud of me. But now I'm lost and I'm just so sorry." She put her head in her hands, her shoulders drooping in defeat.

Her mother pulled Keala's hands from her face. "Sweetheart, we *are* proud of you. There's never been a competition for our love. We love all of our kids equally, and we're sorry if we didn't make that clear. And that you didn't feel"—her voice broke, but she looked up for a second before continuing—"that you could tell us about medical school. You always worked so hard toward medicine that I thought it was what you were passionate about."

Her father's face pinched slightly, his nose scrunched up like it did when he got overwhelmed by emotion.

"But you kicked Nohea out after he messed up in school. I thought, since Dad was a doctor and you'd always talked about us all becoming doctors, that if I didn't go down that path, you'd be upset with me. Cast me aside like Nohea."

Her parents looked at each other, lost in a silent conversation before they nodded and turned back to Keala. "We asked Nohea to leave after he put you and Akoni in danger by bringing drugs and violence into the home one too many times. We *never* stopped loving him." Her mother's voice shook, and Keala saw her other hand slip into her father's, watching as they held each other quietly.

Just like her and Landon.

"Oh. I didn't know that." All she remembered was her brother getting yelled at, her parents shouting at each other, and bringing Akoni, who had only been a toddler, into her room to play games so they didn't have to listen to it all.

Her father patted her shin. "Of course you didn't, Keeks. We didn't want you to think of your brother like that, but now I see it was worse being dishonest."

Keala's entire life had shifted because of what she'd perceived as Nohea losing their love for disappointing them in some way. And maybe he had, but kicking him out had more to do with keeping her and Akoni safe than not loving him.

It was a blow to the carefully curated image of her family she'd held onto for so long, shattering it into tiny pieces she would cut her hands on trying to put back together.

Her father took a breath. "We kept in touch with him often. Kept paying for his phone so we could talk to him a few times a week. But after a while, I think Nohea felt betrayed that we forced him out, so he cut us off. We haven't heard from him s-since." He stuttered on the last word, wrapping an arm around Keala's mom. "We looked for him for a long time, kept our phone numbers the same, even hired PIs, but we haven't found him. We like to believe he has a family now that loves him as much as we do." His shoulders dipped forward, and Keala's mom leaned against him.

"I'm so sorry. I really...I had no idea." They smiled at her. Nodded. But she could still see the hurt underneath it. "And I'm sorry I was dishonest, too. There were so many times I wanted to tell you, but the longer I waited, the harder it became, and then when you kept asking me to try again...I just worried if you found out that I *had* tried, hard, to become that person, and I failed, you would stop..." *Loving me.* "I didn't want you to see me as a failure when you so clearly wanted a life in medicine for me."

Her mother wiped Keala's cheeks and took her face in her hands. "I only brought it up because I thought you loved medicine and wanted you to have the life I know you deserve."

"I don't. I don't like working in medicine, in any capacity. And I know that because I've handled so many types of cases and not one of them appealed to me. I don't want to be a dermatologist or a surgeon or anything like that. I want to choreograph. I want to *dance*. I don't want to come home from a job that forces me to confront so many of society's wrongs with lead-filled limbs and a brain that won't stop running even after I've showered and gotten into bed, no matter how tired I am."

She breathed, about to deal the final blow. "I've tried to be the person I thought you wanted me to be—someone who could keep up with Akoni—but this isn't the life I would want for my friends or family. If I knew anyone I loved felt this way about their job, I would tell them to quit. So I'm taking that advice, and I'm...going to pursue choreography."

Her mom bent down, setting her forehead on Keala's. She smoothed Keala's hair, a tear slipping down her face and mixing with ones Keala hadn't noticed she'd been crying. When her mother pulled back, she said, "The only person I want you to be is Keala. Whatever that means for you. We don't need another Akoni, honey. We need *you*, happy and healthy. And if dance and choreography are what make you happy, then we'll do anything we can to get you on that path. I'm so sorry we made you feel otherwise."

"And I'm sorry we didn't make it clearer that we love all of you as you are," her father chimed in quietly. "Your mother and I will support you no matter what you choose to do. Watching you dance is one of my greatest joys, Keeks. I can't wait to see you light up the world with your choreography."

Relief bubbled up, and breathing came easier as she smiled at her parents. She could see they were still hurt, knew there would still be lots to talk about, but she'd taken a step toward the life she wanted. The life she deserved.

A step toward a future that filled her with hope and excitement instead of dread and sadness. One where she could coach a group of talented women like her teammates and see them flourish on the field, smiling as she watched her work come to life in front of millions.

One where she could come home at a normal time, feeling nothing but happy and grateful, and hug the man she loved before he danced her into the kitchen to make them food.

Keala would have to take a few more steps to get there, but it was a path she was finally ready to walk.

Chapter Forty

Landon

> **ESPN notification –** San Jose pulled off a win in week fifteen, which puts them in prime playoff position. Could this year finally be the one for Myles Young, Landon Beaumont, and the rest of the Sentinels? Here's why we think a championship is on the table...

> **Bay Area News 5 –** Who is Keala Lōkahi-Price? The woman who is taking the internet by storm...Savannah Blake and Ikaika Lōkahi among celebrities speaking on behalf of changed playboy Landon Beaumont.

A couple of days after Keala's collapse and his subsequent virality, Landon was trying to enjoy his Tuesday off when the shrill scream of a fire alarm startled him. He was pretty sure Ikaika was at the facility, and Keala had been recovering at her parents' house since being discharged a day and a half ago, so unless Chowder had suddenly become a chef, something was wrong.

He tossed on a pair of sweatpants and hurried across the hall, noting the door was unlocked like it always was. When he finally made it into the kitchen, no one was around. Mixing bowls and utensils were strewn all over the counters beside casserole dishes full of baked and not-yet-baked food. Sticky notes were stuck to the counter in front of each dish, though nothing was written on them yet. He looked toward the balcony doors and found Keala with her hair in a ponytail using one of the doors to fan the room. With the cool December air pouring in, the fire alarm stopped in no time.

She turned, and he took in the pink tinge to her cheeks. There were no dark crescents below her eyes, and she looked surprisingly healthy considering where she'd been less than forty-eight hours ago. His gaze dropped to the apron she wore, which read *Don't make me poison you.*

Landon grinned at her, enjoying the way her cheeks turned an even darker shade of pink under his scrutiny. "I thought we agreed you aren't allowed to cook."

Keala groaned. "Damn fire alarm. I wanted to surprise you with a bunch of food on your day off but..."

"But you decided it would be more fun to tempt fate. Again."

"I think I'm actually getting *worse* at this if I'm being honest."

They stared at each other, smiles fading. "I'm glad you're feeling better," he murmured gently. "I'm sorry I wasn't at the hospital when you woke up, but with everything going on in the news and me outing us, I didn't know if you'd want me there."

"I would have come to see you sooner if my parents weren't so insistent that I rest and recover yesterday." Keala walked up to him, grabbing his shirt, and pulled him down to her level. "And don't you dare apologize to me for caring. For doing everything you did to fix it. I can't believe you would have given up football for me." And then her lips were on his and his hand was buried in her ponytail. Landon picked her up and set her on the counter, keeping his mouth pressed to hers.

He'd missed her so fucking much.

He pulled away, about to vocalize as much, but she cut him off. "I want to say something in case what you said on TV was because you were trying to save my job and not because you meant it." She set her hands on his shoulders. "I'm sorry that I ran. I found out when we were in LA that a pregnant woman died the same way Ikaika's sister did. During a shift I switched from. I blamed myself for not being there and recognizing the signs, but...the obstetrician told me there was nothing I could've done differently. Still, to me, it was proof that my focus was being pulled from work, and running was easier than facing the fact that..."

She looked away from him. "The fact that I was working a job I hated for people who had never asked me to do so. I took on two extra shifts to make myself feel better and not have to think about how much I missed you. I told myself it was because showing up to work and proving I was there and willing to take on anything meant they'd think of me for promotions and raises, but it's clearly...Well, that thinking is going to get me killed. I see that now. So, I quit."

Landon took a step back. "Wait, what? You quit your job at the hospital?"

Keala nodded. "I quit. I told them this wasn't what I wanted to do, and they understood. Healthcare is tough on anyone, but especially those who aren't in it for the right reasons." She bit her lip, wringing her hands before saying, "I'm not running anymore. I choose dance. I choose you. I love you so much, and I'm sorry it took a major health scare to come to that realization. You make me so happy, and I love you more than anyone or anything," she said, repeating his confession back to him. "I will never let something as trivial as a job come between us again."

Happiness burst in his chest at the words, and he stepped toward her, kissing every inch of her face until she was giggling and trying to kiss him back.

"You're not mad at me?" he asked.

"Of course not. You literally put everything on the line on national television for me. When I met you, you couldn't express when you were slightly upset, and for me, you told the world how much you care about me. How could I ever be upset with you for that? I was so worried *you'd* be mad at *me* after how I left. I came up with a plan to use the favor you owe me for cheating at pumpkin carving to beg for another chance."

He chuckled. "Keep your favor—I could never be mad at you." He remembered what she'd said at the start of her speech. "And I meant every word, Keeks. I've never lived outside of an apartment since leaving home. It was college apartments to penthouses to here. But since you"—he scratched the back of his neck—"I've been thinking about getting a house." He paused for a beat, watching tears form in her eyes. "I was so terrified of disappointing you that I couldn't tell you until I had to, on live TV apparently, but I want to try for us. I know there's a chance that I fuck it up, but you make me want to put in the work despite knowing there's a long way to fall."

Keala put a hand on either side of his face, setting her forehead against his and smiling. "You could never disappoint me. And I won't let you fall. Not without me."

He kissed her again, sweet soft kisses for what felt like forever. All the fines in the world for leaving the game couldn't take this feeling away from him. All the yelling and tense conversations with the franchise were well worth it if it meant he got to keep her in his arms like this. It had taken the team all of a few minutes to realize what an asset he'd been, this season especially, and they had put the conversation to bed.

Sure, he hadn't made any friends with the higher-ups with the stunt he'd pulled, but they wouldn't be getting rid of him for a while yet. And with all the positive press he and Keala were getting, he wasn't too worried about their future.

Still smelling something burning, he asked, "Is there something in the oven?"

She shook her head, pointing at the sink. "Not anymore."

"Now that this has happened twice, I think we can agree that it'll be my job to cook."

Keala rolled her eyes. "Fine, yes. I won't cook ever again. You can't take baking from me though."

"Wouldn't dream of it. Those red velvet cupcakes were so moist."

She laughed. "Ew, don't say moist." After a moment of smiling at each other, she said, "I'm sorry I didn't do something more, but you've taken all the grand gestures from me, what with declaring your feelings publicly to save my job and everything. Plus, I don't know if you've been outside"—she laughed, likely recognizing the impossibility of him *not* having seen the zoo of reporters outside—"but there are an *awful* lot of people out there, and I didn't want them to be a part of my big thing. It was hard enough sneaking out of my parents' house."

"You snuck out of your parents' house?"

"They are being *very* supportive of my life choices but are treating me like I'm twelve and can't take care of my health right now, so yes."

"Wow, my bad behavior is rubbing off on you." He smirked. "I like it."

Keala's phone went off across the kitchen. "Damn alarm didn't do me much good, did it?" she muttered as she jumped off the counter and walked over to it. "Oh," she said when she picked it up, brows furrowed.

"What happened?"

"Cora's been on the lookout for choreo jobs for me. Mainly local but putting out feelers with all her contacts." She answered the phone, and after a few mm-hmms, she turned to Landon, a bright smile lighting up her face. "That sounds amazing. Thank you so much, Cora."

Landon braced himself to find out she was moving across the country, doing the math on his contract. When Keala set her phone down, she whispered, "Brooklyn got a head choreographer job at Houston. The Sentinels assistant choreographer job will be open at the end of the season." She paused, disbelief between her brows. "Cora gets to choose her assistant and...I'm the only candidate she's considering."

"You're going to stay a Sentinels Siren?"

She smiled wider, if possible, and threw herself into his outstretched arms. "I'm going to stay a Sentinels Siren."

Keala

THREE AND A HALF YEARS LATER

The moment Keala slipped into their house, muscled arms scooped her up and spun her around, the smell of her vanilla shampoo heavy in the air. Landon liked to use it when she was gone for too long and he missed her.

She giggled, wrapping her arms around his shoulders. "Hi," she murmured, leaning down to kiss him.

He pulled away. "'Hi?' I haven't seen you in weeks, and all I get is a 'hi?'" Landon set her down, using a finger under her chin to kiss her.

After a season working as both the assistant choreographer for the Sirens and the head coach at San Jose State University, her public social media account dedicated to choreography had gone viral. Keala had been asked to travel during the off-season to choreograph and teach pieces to teams all over the country, which paid more than both of her jobs combined, so she'd stepped back from her work with SJSU.

She now had three seasons of assistant choreography with the Sirens under her belt plus the many teams she'd choreographed for on her tours over the last couple of years. The only problem with said tours was that Landon's training camp started during them, so they were apart for a few weeks before she came back in June for Sirens tryouts.

"Hello, my most handsome husband. I've missed you so much, and I'm glad to be home," she responded when they finally pulled away for air.

"Mm, much better." He kissed down her jaw, then her neck. Her body flushed at the contact she'd been missing. "Mark my words: this is the year I retire so I can go on tour with you every offseason."

"You'd better win another championship if you don't want your brother's record hanging over your head forever," she joked. Landon had two championship wins and records of his own now. It had taken some time to get used to their new relationship, but now that the brothers were on good terms, it was a running joke that Colton still had one more than him.

Landon had stopped caring a long time ago. He and Colton had a broadcast channel offering them more money than he'd know what to do with to be commentators together when Landon retired. Even though he wouldn't admit it, Keala knew he was excited to get into broadcasting.

"I could not possibly care less about that if it means I get to do this every night," he whispered, his voice gravelly. Landon flipped her so her chest was pressed to their front door, a hand drifting from her stomach down until his finger found her center over her yoga pants. "If we didn't have dinner reservations, these would already be off."

"That's never stopped you before."

He groaned. "Unfortunately, it will today."

Keala frowned. "Why?" She faced him. "What's different about today?"

Landon looked away. "Nothing. Just don't want to miss our celebratory dinner."

"You're a horrible liar. What did you do?"

"I can't be excited to celebrate the fact that my wife is about to be head choreographer for the same team I'm playing for?" Keala's eyes narrowed. "Alright, alright, fine. But you have to pretend you're surprised."

"What?"

"I bought out Bella Stagione for the night," he said, referring to their favorite restaurant. "Your family, my family, and some of the girls are going to be there. It was supposed to be a surprise, but..."

Keala smiled, slipping a hand into Landon's hair and kissing him softly. Against his lips, she murmured, "But you can't keep a secret from me to save your life."

"Exactly."

"I do need to shower and get changed before we go..."

Landon bounded up the stairs to their bedroom before she finished the thought. "I'll get the water running!"

Keala laughed, slipping her shoes off and following him. By the time she made it to their bathroom, he was waiting for her in the shower. Almost nothing had changed about his body—still muscled beyond belief, maybe more so now that he'd been putting in the work at practice, and Keala couldn't take her eyes off him. Especially not when she saw the little K on the inside of his Adonis belt, still red.

"I told you I missed you. And I'd been wanting to get it for a while."

His smirk was so familiar, so missed, that she ripped her clothes off and joined him. He pulled her into his body, his wedding ring warm against her cool skin.

A year and a half ago, after a hard-fought win, he'd made sure the Sirens created problem after problem so Keala couldn't go home until everyone in the stadium had left. Cora had asked her to grab something she'd forgotten from the field, and that was when Landon had shown up behind her, down on one knee with a sticky note that read *Will you marry your favorite asshole on his best behavior?*

A month later, they'd gotten married at the courthouse with Ikaika as their witness because Landon couldn't wait for her to be his wife. The engagement sticky note had been added to the rest of them on a piece of cardstock paper framed in their bedroom.

"I'm gonna take a nap right here. Hold me up," she murmured. Her flight from New York had felt like it had taken an eternity.

Landon chuckled. "No, you're not. But close your eyes and I'll get you cleaned up."

She listened, enjoying the feel of his fingers massaging shampoo into her hair and soap into her skin. When he finished, he helped her dry off, then took his own shower while she blow dried her hair. Keala smiled when she saw the sticky note on the bathroom counter.

I love you. And I'm so proud of you.

Emotion built in her throat, but she knew it would be a long night if she couldn't get it in check. Everyone she loved would be at the restaurant to show their support of her, including her parents, which meant there would be *lots* of emotions to get through tonight.

"I love you more!" she called as she moved to her walk-in closet.

Keala finished her hair and makeup, then threw on a burgundy midi dress and white heels. She was adding her favorite gold earrings when Landon emerged from his closet in a suit.

He put a hand on his chest, his eyes drifting over her. "I know this is inappropriate right now, but I'm already thinking about taking that off you tonight."

She laughed. "That's not very best behavior of you."

He nodded. "You're right. But let's get going anyway because the earlier we get there, the faster we can leave and I can get you on your back on the dining table." Like the thought of it was getting to him, he shook his head, holding a hand out for her. Keala grabbed her clutch and took it.

When they got to the restaurant, Landon turned to her. "Remember. Act surprised. You thought it was dinner with just me."

"I will." She leaned over the center console, kissing him. "I'm grateful you did this, but so you know, I would have loved dinner with just you." Jokingly, she added, "You are *so* getting laid tonight."

Landon pumped his fist, then ran to her side of the car to help her out. "Let me see your surprised face." Keala complied. Landon sighed. "Well, nothing we can do about it now."

They entered the restaurant, Landon's hand on her lower back. When they reached the back room, the lights flicked on, and the smiling faces of almost everyone she loved met her.

"Surprise!"

Keala tried her best to look surprised, sure she wasn't doing a good job, but she was quickly swept into hug after hug. First, her parents, each whispering about how proud of her they were after years of showing up for every game they could to watch her choreography in action. Landon's grandparents, who'd taken her in like one of their own in the last few years. Colton and Lucia, with five-year-old Lyla. The little girl handed her a card with a drawing of Keala, Lyla, and Lyla's little brother, two-year-old Liam.

Next were Cooper and Maya, who she'd grown especially close with over the years. Their twin two-year-old boys, Wells and Lucas, each held one of their hands. Keala noticed the small bump Maya tried to hide in a loose dress, and when she hugged her sister-in-law, she whispered, "Congratulations."

Maya pulled back, apologetic. "I was trying so hard to keep it hidden. I really didn't want to steal any of your thunder. I'm so happy for you." Maya squeezed Keala's hands.

"Take my thunder, I couldn't care less. I'm just glad you're here." Keala nodded to her bump. "Are you finally getting the girl you always wanted?" Maya's eyes filled with tears as she nodded. Keala pulled her in for another hug. "I'm so happy for *you*."

Seeing her nieces and nephews was one of her favorite parts about the whole family coming together. She and Landon had agreed they didn't want children, especially after all she'd seen working in the emergency department, so getting to pick them up, twirl them around, listen to them giggle, made her happy. Keala loved being the fun aunt.

"KayKay!" After Maya was Zoe, Eleanor, Aurelia, Jordy, Nova, and Kennedy. They all hugged her, Zoe the tightest, and Keala promised to circle back so they could catch each other up. They often got drinks together, but with Keala on tour the last couple of months, she hadn't talked to them as much.

Next was Cora, and when they pulled apart, both had tears streaming down their faces. "It's been an honor working with you, Keala. I'm so proud of the choreographer you've become, and I can't wait to get my season tickets every year knowing you're going to carry on the Siren legacy for me. You've made retiring an easy choice."

"Thank you for believing in me from the beginning." Keala dabbed at her face, laughing at them. "I know I'm going to see you all the time—I don't know why I feel like this is goodbye."

Cora waved her hand dismissively. "You know if you ever need me, I'll be there. Plus, with Angelica leaving and no director selected yet, well, you may be seeing me at tryouts in a couple of weeks."

"Are you serious? Have they been talking to you about it?"

Cora nodded. "They have. It's a big move and I'm not sure how many years I can give, but it would be fun."

"I would love that."

"We'll see what happens. I'll call if I hear anything else in the next few days."

Then there was Akoni, who'd flown in for the evening. They'd been getting together every couple of months for dinner and drinks, and, especially after she'd left medicine to do what she loved, their relationship had grown significantly. Now he was the one complaining about medical school, though it was obvious how much he loved it.

Finally, when she'd made it around the room, she got to Ikaika. Ikaika, who had been her best friend for most of her life, and who had, in a way, given her the husband she loved so much. Keala threw her arms around his shoulders, holding on tight.

"I'm so proud of you, Keeks. More than you could ever know. It's everything you've worked so hard for, and it's so deserved."

"Thank you," she whispered. "I didn't think I'd see you until later."

"I can't stay for long, but I had to be here." They shared a meaningful look. A lot had happened in Ikaika's life the last few years, and Keala was glad she'd been allowed to be a part of it.

When Keala made it back to Landon, he gave her that charming smile, pulling her against his side. Almost every important person in her life stood in front of her, conversing.

As if reading her mind, Landon said, "I didn't let Josie know early enough, but she'll be here in a couple of days. She was hoping to stay with us. I figured that would be okay."

Keala turned to him, smiling as she slid her arms up over his shoulders. "I'm surprised. Does that mean you only have two days to do all the things you've been texting me you want to? I'm not sure there's enough time for that."

"If I never let you out of the bedroom, we just might make it work."

"There are children at this function," Colton said from beside them, and Landon and Keala laughed, reluctantly moving away from each other.

Landon pulled out her chair, then motioned for everyone to sit around the large table. Before long, they were all talking, some about Landon's final year and his and Colton's potential future as commentators together, some about dance, and some about other things entirely. Keala listened to it all, sitting back and sipping her water as she watched.

Landon, likely noting her quiet observance, leaned over with a cocky smirk and whispered, "Aren't you glad you fell head over ass for me?"

Keala rolled her eyes but couldn't hold back her smile. He was right, after all. Five years ago, she never would have imagined such a fulfilling life could be hers. But it was.

And it had all started because she'd gone tumbling over her tight end.

Acknowledgements

I've been told (by myself) that I need to keep this shorter than the last two, so I'm going to try.

Thank you to my alphas—Marja, Miah, Lisa, Heather, and Giuliana—for finding the big picture things that weren't working in my draft and helping me rework them until they were. Giuliana, thank you for all of your medical knowledge. This book would have been concerningly inaccurate without your help. Thank you to my betas—Rachel, Miranda, Hannah, Sarah, Georgia, Kie, and Casey—for helping me fine tune Keala and Landon's story. Sarah, your knowledge of all things dance was invaluable and I appreciate you so much.

Thank you to Rachel for being the best editor, champion, and general sounding board for my silliness. As always, very sorry for the million stress messages followed closely by a million messages of how I already figured out the problem and solution. I cannot imagine having to do this without you.

Thank you to Chelsey and Laura for finding the little things I missed. Your attention to detail is always so appreciated.

Thank you to my family for championing me. To my bestie gals Marja and Miah, who I would simply be lost without. Thank you for lending an ear throughout my many stages of this book, this series, this process in general. Indie publishing would be near impossible without you. I love you endlessly.

Thank you to Ethan for supporting me in everything I do and for being my biggest fan forever. Writing about love is easier with you by my side.

And finally, thank *you* for picking up this book and finishing this series with me. Whether you've been with me for ages or this is your first time reading a book I wrote, thank you so much for your support. I hope you enjoyed reading about Keala and Landon as much as I loved writing about them.

ALSO BY VAI DENTON

The Beaumont Legacy series
Gridlocked on the Gridiron – Colton's book
Love on the Line – Maya's book

The Off Court series
Drop Shot
Cross Court
Kick Serve

About the Author

Vai Denton is an American author, romance enthusiast—especially if sports are involved—and book lover. She has spent much of her life struggling to find her identity between her two cultures, using books as a sanctuary. Her hope is that her stories provide readers with the escape she once sought. In each of her books, you can expect swoony, healthy relationships that will have you kicking your feet.

If she's not reading or writing about love, you'll find her playing tennis, watching football, Pride and Prejudice (2005), or any number of her favorite romcoms with her two cats and fiancé.

If you'd like to contact Vai, find her on instagram @vaidentonauthor or via email at vaidentonauthor@gmail.com